ALSO BY CHARLIE N. HOLMBERG

The Paper Magician Series

The Paper Magician
The Glass Magician
The Master Magician

Other Novels

The Fifth Doll
Magic Bitter, Magic Sweet
Followed by Frost

THE PLASTIC MAGICIAN

CHARLIE N. HOLMBERG

47NORTH

Text copyright © 2018 by Charlie N. Holmberg
All rights reserved.

Published by 47North, Seattle

www.apub.com

Amazon, the Amazon logo, and 47North are trademarks of Amazon.com, Inc., or its affiliates.

ISBN-13: 9781503951778 (hardcover)
ISBN-10: 1503951774 (hardcover)
ISBN-13: 9781542047913 (paperback)
ISBN-10: 1542047919 (paperback)

Cover design by M.S. Corley

Printed in the United States of America

First edition

To Tess, a strong woman who went through quite the ordeal, and who ultimately inspired this story.

CHAPTER 1

WHILE ALVIE WAS RATHER excited to be receiving her diploma, she could not stop staring at Mg. Jefferson's mustache. He hadn't sported a mustache the last time she'd seen him, and that had been only two months ago. What made a man, especially a man of Mg. Jefferson's age, decide to up and start a mustache?

It was a thick and dark mustache, well groomed. A good German mustache, her papa would say. Which left Alvie wondering if Mg. Jefferson had German heritage, too. Was it odd for her to ask after his lineage during an exit interview?

Two months. The mustache had to be at least a centimeter long. Ten millimeters. At roughly sixty days of growth, presuming the length of the hairs had not been trimmed . . . that was a growth rate of 167 micrometers per day—

Mg. Jefferson cleared his throat rather violently, the noise of which broke apart all the numbers piling up in Alvie's head. She blinked, coming back to herself, and lifted her gaze from Mg. Jefferson's mustache to his eyes.

"Are you listening, Miss Brechenmacher?" he asked.

She stiffened in her seat, back straight, and quickly swept a piece of too-wavy chestnut hair behind the thick rim of her glasses. "Yes, sir. I mean, mostly." *Focus, Alvie.* The class of 1905 had been the largest yet, which meant Mg. Jefferson's schedule was chock-full of meetings with graduates, and Alvie should not take up more of his time than was absolutely necessary. She was about to find out the details of her apprenticeship—where she'd be spending the next two to six years of her life and, more importantly, with whom.

Mg. Jefferson breathed deeply through his nose and wove his fingers together on the desk in front of him. "As I was saying, I'm intrigued to see you listed Polymaking as your first choice of magic disciplines. Any reason plastic has caught your eye?"

Alvie smiled. "It's a new and exciting venture, isn't it?" Very new—the newest of the seven known man-made materials that could be used as a medium for magic, six of which were actually legal. Polymaking, or the magical discipline of plastic, had only been discovered thirty years ago. That was the point of the last two years of vigorous study at the Jefferson School of Material Mechanics: Alvie hoped to win an apprenticeship under a magician and, after two to six years, become a magician herself—a Polymaker. The Jefferson School set a rigorous schedule and was expensive to boot. If students couldn't learn all they needed to in order to become responsible, ethical, and well-rounded apprentices within three years, they were cut from the program altogether.

"There's so much to discover, and so much to learn," she continued. "I want to know the secrets of Polymaking."

Her next choice was Siping, or rubber-based magic. It had been a Siper who first discovered plastic, after all. A sensible second pick.

Mg. Jefferson nodded, looking over some papers on his desk—her grades, perhaps? "You certainly have the mind for it. An emphasis in math and science in secondary school, and very good grades in your measurements for magic and fiscal-responsibility classes here. I'd expect nothing less from the daughter of Gunter Brechenmacher."

Gunter Brechenmacher, inventor, cocreator of the light bulb. That little confection of filament and glass was the reason Alvie's family had been able to afford the steep tuition at the Jefferson School. The bulk of the praise—and the money—had gone to Mr. Edison, of course, but her father had been granted a large sum for agreeing to let his more experienced partner file the patent.

Mg. Jefferson turned a paper over, then lifted a finger to stroke his mustache. Alvie forced herself not to look at it. "I am required to tell you of the advantages of Folding."

Folding, or paper-based magic. The least popular discipline. So much so that Alvie could almost count the number of active Folders on her hands. She'd heard that across the pond in England, they actually *forced* students to study it.

She shuddered at the thought. Folding was number five on her list, second to last, just before Pyring, or fire-based magic. Throwing fire was far too basic—and terrifying—for her.

"I'd rather not." Alvie adjusted her glasses, which had begun to slide down her nose. She absently rubbed the top of one of her ears. Her frames were so terribly heavy; they always made her ears ache by midday.

"No surprise there," Mg. Jefferson agreed with the hint of a smile. He was a Smelter, or a magician of metal alloys. Number three on Alvie's list. "Well, I'm happy to inform you that your application was reviewed by the board and accepted. You mentioned your willingness to study abroad . . ."

Needles of eagerness pricked Alvie's torso. Abroad? Were they actually sending her abroad? "I . . . y-yes, sir."

"The good news continues. You know of our sister school in England, the Tagis Praff School for the Magically Inclined, yes?"

Alvie nodded, making her glasses slide down her nose again.

"It just so happens that the nephew of its founder had his last apprentice recently move on. He's agreed to tutor you. His name is Magician Marion Praff."

Alvie's jaw went slack. "*The* Magician Marion Praff? The creator of the Imagidome?"

"The very one."

Alvie could barely sit still in her chair. So much excitement flashed through her she was surprised it didn't spill from her like water. Mg. Marion Praff was one of the most prestigious and esteemed Polymakers in the world. He was constantly featured in *Superior Technology* and *Magicians Today*, both magazines to which her father subscribed.

"Miss Brechenmacher?"

She shook herself. "That's . . . fantastic. Wonderful. I couldn't . . . I couldn't have asked for better."

He smiled. "Excellent. Everything has been scheduled for you." He reached under his papers and pulled out a thick envelope with Alvie's name scrawled across it. She took it in shaky fingers. Her diploma, lists of what she would need to acquire for her apprenticeship, and a reservation for mirror-transport to Dover, Delaware.

"Dover?" she asked.

"If the itinerary is agreeable, we'll go forward with the purchase." Mg. Jefferson clasped his hands before him on the desk. "Departure is in three days. From Dover you will mirror-transport to Hamburg, Germany, and then take a ship to England, followed by a train to London. I apologize for the indirectness of it all, but you know how the United Kingdom is with magicked public transport, and France requires a special passport. Even if you applied for it now, we'd be lucky to get you settled in by Christmas."

Alvie nodded. Transportation laws in the United Kingdom were notoriously strict. Only Gaffers, or glass magicians, could travel via mirrors. Alvie understood the laws, of course—a magician could get trapped

4

indefinitely inside a scratched or broken mirror. But if Americans hadn't taken such risks, the West never would have been settled.

At least this way she would get to see Germany, if only for a short time. She hadn't been to her parents' homeland since she was seventeen, three years ago.

Clutching the envelope in her hands, she said, "Thank you, Magician Jefferson. Truly. This is a dream come true."

His mustache smiled. "I'm very glad to hear it." He extended his hand across the desk, and Alvie shook it firmly, as her papa had taught her. "Send a telegram when you arrive so we know you're safe and sound. We'll be checking up on you, Miss Brechenmacher. Do us proud."

"Mama!" Alvie called as she burst through the front door of her family's modest home. "Mama, I got it!"

Her mother, dark curls pinned up atop her head, popped out of the kitchen. "The Polymaking?" Her thick German accent weighed down her words, yet somehow refined them, too. Alvie could mimic the accent perfectly—she'd grown up around it, after all—but she'd been born in Ohio, and all her years of public schooling had made her sound like any other midwestern American.

Alvie tripped over her feet, trying to get her shoes off. She ran to her mama and grasped her elbows. "With Magician Marion Praff!"

"Who?"

Alvie pulled back and pushed up her glasses. "He invented the Imagidome! Nephew of Tagis Praff?"

Her mama's smile faded. "*Du gehst nach* England?" she asked, speaking German. *You're going to England?*

Alvie grinned. "Be happy for me, Mama. I'm going to pass through Hamburg on my way there. And I'm sure I'll be let loose for Christmas. We'll get you a new chatting mirror, and we'll talk every week."

Her mama sighed, but the smile managed to return. "I knew you would make it, Alvie. We moved here to achieve our aspirations. Your papa will be home soon. He'll be happy to hear the news."

Grinning, and feeling like electricity fueled her limbs, Alvie bounded upstairs to her room. Two large bookshelves were crammed into one corner, and a clock she and her papa had rebuilt hung over the bed, its face replaced with glass to show the working of the gears beneath. Her wardrobe was small and worn, an antique that had come across the ocean with her mother some twenty-two years past. A round woven rug took up the floor, and her simple bed had a down mattress she had received two Christmases ago. Despite the sunlight streaming through the gossamer curtains, she flipped a switch on the wall, sending electricity to the four bulbs hanging from the ceiling, a reminder of her papa's greatest achievement. She, too, would achieve great things, in her apprenticeship and beyond.

Alvie popped the button on the waistband of her skirt and yanked it off as she went to the wardrobe, letting the fabric pool onto the rug. She loathed skirts, how they tangled up between her knees, or let dust or cold air puff up her legs. A person could only sit in so many positions wearing a skirt, and Alvie couldn't tolerate being inhibited. Unfortunately, important people tended to prefer women in skirts. Actually, most people preferred women in skirts.

She pulled a pair of slacks from the drawer at the base of her wardrobe and tugged them on, sighing in relief. Slacks were becoming more popular—if seeing one other woman wearing them in the last year counted as "more popular." This was Ohio, though. Perhaps on the coast they were more common. Slacks for women were hard to come by in stores—her mama had sewn these for her, giving them a little extra body in a weak imitation of a skirt. Alvie only owned two skirts, and they were both in pristine condition from lack of being worn.

Alvie turned around, eager to read the contents of the envelope Mg. Jefferson had given her, and noticed a parcel at the foot of her bed. She grabbed her pocketknife off her nightstand and cut open the package, eyes bugging when she pulled free the red apron and black top hat that would mark her as an apprentice magician. She had assumed Mg. Praff would give her the uniform when she arrived in London, but she would happily don the clothing now.

She tried it on, pulling the strings of the apron tight, fitting the top hat over her frizzy hair. She glanced in the small mirror on her wall. The hat made her look a bit clownish, her hair sticking out like old broom bristles beneath its brim. She took off her glasses—the room blurring into mottled colors as she did so—and wiped the thick lenses on the corner of the apron. Slipped them back on. Yes, better without the hat. Fortunately, she'd only have to wear it for formal occasions. Still, the hat and apron were the mark of an apprentice in material magics—a uniform recognized worldwide. Alvie admired the mark of her achievement a little longer before removing the hat and untying the knots of the apron, which she reverently folded and set at the foot of her bed. A *Polymaker*. Her. It was really happening, wasn't it?

Pulling her gaze from the apron, Alvie turned and studied her room. So little time to prepare, to pack. She should visit Abigail and Lucy, her closest friends, tomorrow and let them know the news. They lived nearby, so a magicked mail bird wasn't necessary. Would her mama want to mirror-communicate with her *Oma*? Alvie would be in England by the time any posted letter reached Germany.

Worrying her lips, she retrieved her suitcases from the topmost shelf of her wardrobe. What to bring, what to bring? She built a list of items in her mind, then started calculating the weight for each. When one carried two suitcases, it was best to pack them so they weighed evenly. It didn't make sense to do otherwise.

The front door shut downstairs, and Alvie heard the heavy steps of her papa followed by his asking what was for dinner. Alvie dropped her suitcases and fled from her room to tell him the good news, leaving the electric bulbs buzzing in her absence.

———————

Alvie and her parents stood in the wallpapered foyer of the Columbus Mirror-Transit Station, terminal four, waiting for the conducting Gaffer to call her name. He was likely a Gaffing apprentice who had failed his magician's test, or perhaps dropped out before the conclusion of his apprenticeship, since no one would spend up to nine years training to be a glass magician only to use that education shuffling people in and out of mirrors. Gaffing was one of the only magical disciplines that offered work for those without a magician's license. As far as Alvie knew, Polymaking did not, nor did Folding, though many firefighters were bonded to flame. She watched the conductor, wondering. He wasn't terribly old, maybe six or seven years her senior. How long had he worked this job? Was he happy?

Alvie twisted the toe of her shoe against the tiled floor. What would happen to her if she didn't make it? She couldn't think of any jobs available for flunked Polymakers. Taking a deep breath, Alvie set her jaw. *Doesn't matter,* she told herself. *I'm going to pass.*

It was hard to fail at something you loved. At least, she was fairly certain she would love it. She'd studied theory for all six standard disciplines at the preparatory school, and Polymaking had been vastly more interesting than the others.

"It's not too late to request something closer to home," her papa murmured under his breath beside her. His large hand clasped her shoulder.

Alvie leaned in to him. "I think the closest availability is in Maryland, anyway. That's far enough that it might as well be in England." Her mind spun. The Atlantic Ocean was about 3,700 miles

THE PLASTIC MAGICIAN

across, if she remembered her geography right. It was 535 miles from here to New York City—that was the path the family had taken for their last trip to Germany. Assuming London was, oh, maybe a hundred miles in from England's west coast, that would put London roughly 4,335 miles away, which was about eight times farther than Maryland.

She opened her mouth to tell her papa of her error, but she closed it again as the numbers settled. Eight times farther than Maryland? She certainly was going far away from home. How much of that distance could magic and technology fill for her?

Alvie's heart began to ache, and she hadn't even left the station yet. *But the adventure of it all,* she reminded herself. She couldn't even fathom the journey that awaited her on the other side of that mirror.

"Alvie Bre—" the conductor called, and he stared at the clipboard in his hand. "Breckenmatcher?"

Unless she married someone with a simple last name, Alvie expected she'd be hearing her surname butchered for the rest of her life.

She turned to her parents, embraced both of them, and blinked rapidly to shore up her tears. She'd be home before she knew it, and she didn't want wet eyelashes smearing her lenses. "Love you," she whispered.

"Gute Reise," her mama whispered. Her papa kissed the top of her head.

Alvie drew in a deep breath, straightened her shoulders, and smoothed her apprentice's apron. She didn't *have* to wear it yet, but it lent her courage, and reminded her of her goals. Smiling at her parents, she picked up her suitcases and called, "Here!"

"Come along, come along," the conductor urged her, waving her toward the large coppery frame that housed a flawless silver mirror. If it was made of the same glass as the mirror in her room, it would have to weigh—

Alvie shook the equation from her head. It didn't matter, did it?

The conductor touched his hand to the mirror, and Alvie's reflection swirled into a vortex of silver. Alvie handed him her ticket, which he marked with a pen before passing it back.

"To Dover. Step quickly now." The conductor gestured her forward.

Alvie glanced back at her parents one more time, waved as best she could while holding two suitcases, and stepped through the mirror to her future.

CHAPTER 2

ALVIE HAD MIRROR-TRANSPORTED DOZENS of times in her life, but the coldness of the magic still shocked her. It was as though she passed through chilled mercury, and no part of her was safe from its icy bite. It seeped through her clothes and whispered through her hair, sending long lines of gooseflesh down her back and arms.

New light hit her eyes; the pale-orange glow of glass-encased Pyre lights and the white blast of electric bulbs. The sounds of too many bodies and conversations rushed around her, mingled with the distant honking and roaring of automobiles and the bell of a trolley beyond the walls of the station. Alvie blinked, the gooseflesh slow to leave her skin. She'd never been to Dover before. Its mirror-transporting station was larger than the one in Columbus, and far busier.

"Move along, make room," called another conductor, this one much older, his hair and beard nearly white. He gestured impatiently. Gripping the handles of her two suitcases, Alvie picked up her feet and hurried from the mirror, trying to find an open bench to set her things down so she could orient herself. Every sitting place she saw was occupied: a couple with a baby, a group of men all speaking what sounded like French, a school class all dressed in plaid uniforms. A few eyes lingered on her as she walked past—or, more so, on her red apprentice's apron. Perhaps her slacks, but she saw one other woman wearing something similar, so she wasn't a complete anomaly in that sense.

She nervously scoured the terminals—so many mirrors!—and did the math in her head. Point-zero-one percent of the women here wore slacks. Alvie usually wore a skirt when she needed to impress, but she hated traveling in them, and Mg. Praff had already agreed to the apprenticeship, hadn't he? Besides, this was her nicest pair of slacks.

Near the center of the station grew a large tree—the architects must have decided to build around the behemoth rather than tear it down. A hexagon of benches surrounded its trunk, and Alvie spotted a free space. She hurried over, set down her suitcases, and pulled out her envelope of papers to have a look at her ticket.

She was set to depart from terminal 13B at 9:00 a.m. It was already eight thirty, so she needed to find her terminal quickly.

Tucking her ticket and passport away, Alvie grabbed her suitcases and wove through the bustling crowds—spotting another red apron on her way—until she found the correct terminal. She stood in the long line and set down her luggage so she could wipe cold perspiration from her palms. She'd never traveled so far by herself before. Adventure, indeed.

Someone came by to check her ticket and stamp her passport. "You'll have six stops: Nova Scotia, Newfoundland, Greenland, Iceland, Norway, Germany. You've traveled cross-Atlantic before?"

Alvie nodded. Even the largest mirrors enchanted by the most powerful Gaffers couldn't transport someone across the ocean all in one go.

The employee handed her a blue sash, which she slipped around her neck and shoulder. Everyone in line before her wore a matching sash, meaning they all shared her destination. It was a measure to ensure none of them ended up in Prague rather than Hamburg.

The line moved forward. Alvie grabbed her luggage and, focusing hard on the blue-sashed traveler in front of her, passed through the cold embrace of an enchanted mirror, again and again and again.

———————

Though Alvie had slept a bit on the ferry, she was exhausted by the time she reached the shores of England. That fatigue made it hard to get excited about the place she would soon be calling home. She boarded a bus to the train station with several other passengers. Fortunately, the train arrived just minutes after she got on the platform, and she was soon within one of its long cars.

She spied around for seats and found an empty one across from a man who was perhaps in his forties. He had dark hair and a strong receding hairline. A slender mustache sat atop his lip, not at all as impressive as the one Mg. Jefferson had grown. He was busy with a newspaper. Alvie hefted her luggage forward, sat across from him, and set the suitcases next to her, turning her knees so she wouldn't bother the stranger.

Rubbing her eyes under her glasses, Alvie took a deep breath. She looked out the window at the twilit landscape. There were a few lights on distant hills, but Alvie didn't see much more before a tunnel swallowed the car. She frowned. Tomorrow would bring a better view of England, surely. She was tempted to lean her head back and snooze, but she feared missing her stop, and she had a tendency to drool, besides. When the train emerged from the tunnel, she stared out the window for a good while, though there wasn't much to see without daylight.

A short time later, she reached into her bag and retrieved her tickets to recheck her stop. She needed to be alert.

"Apprentice?"

She turned to see the man looking over the top of his paper at her red apron. She smiled. "Yes, but just barely. I haven't even bonded yet."

"Is that so? And all the way from the United States."

She blinked in surprise.

"Your accent, my dear."

"Oh yes. Left this morning."

"This morning?" he repeated, a thick eyebrow raised. "Oh yes, that ghastly mirror-transport."

"It's much faster than a ship."

"Very dangerous. But then again, that's what Americans are known for, isn't it?"

"We're not the only ones who travel with—"

"You're in luck," he interrupted, folding his paper and setting it on his lap. "I'm a magician myself."

She perked up. "Really? What sort?"

"A Polymaker. Coming back from Paris from a rather important conference, actually."

"A Polymaker!" she repeated, and he seemed pleased with her enthusiasm. "Why, that's my discipline as well! Or it's going to be."

"Ah well, it's a very difficult medium to work with." He looked her up and down, his dark eyes scrutinizing. "Especially for a woman."

Alvie's excitement fizzled out. "What do you mean, 'especially for a woman'?" Goodness, she hadn't gotten a remark like that one since her acceptance to Jefferson.

He shook his head and waved his hand, brushing her question away. "Never mind, never mind. I don't have an apprentice myself, too busy, too busy. There's so much to do as an accomplished Polymaker. Do you read the news?"

"Yes, sir."

"Good. Perhaps you've heard of me. I'm Magician Ezzell."

She racked her brain, but the name rang unfamiliar. "I'm sorry, I haven't."

He frowned. "Where in the States are you from?"

"Ohio."

"That must be it." He folded his arms and nodded to himself. "If it was New York, surely you'd have heard of me. But where are my manners? You've just arrived. Been to England before?"

"No, sir."

"And who are you studying under?"

Her smile returned. "Magician Marion Praff."

Mg. Ezzell's expression didn't change except for his eyes. The skin around them tightened in a peculiar way, like he'd just eaten something bad but didn't want to offend the cook. "Is that so?" His voice was a little tight, too. She wondered why. She didn't smell anything foul . . .

"I think he has a driver waiting for me at the station." She glanced out the window. "Oh dear, I hope I didn't miss my stop." She hadn't been listening to the announcer.

"Here, let me see." He leaned forward and plucked her ticket from her hand. Took a moment to read it. "Ah, you're in luck. It's the next stop."

"Oh, thank you!" she said, accepting the ticket back and stowing it in her bag. "I'm eager to get to the house and meet him."

The train began to slow. A few passengers rose from their seats and inched toward the door. Mg. Ezzell only said, "I fear you may be disappointed."

She blinked a few times. "Huh?"

He tipped his head toward the exit. "Off you go."

"But—" she began, but the train came to a stop. No more time for chitchat. Alvie quickly thanked the man and grabbed her suitcases, funneling out of the train behind the other passengers. The chaos of it all pulled her question about being "disappointed" right out of her brain.

The train had traveled with remarkable speed thanks to its Smelter-spelled rails. She would have loved to study the tracks, to see where the magic started and the technology ended, but her curiosity proved less powerful than the fear of finding her nose between the ties when another train sped in. At least finding a bench was much easier this time, and she checked her itinerary. Mg. Praff's chauffeur was to pick her up, but where was she supposed to meet him?

She searched for a clock, finding one on the far wall. Eight o'clock. Already? Goodness, her brain was set to afternoon. She'd eaten a little on the ferry, but certainly wouldn't mind a bratwurst or the like.

She observed the people around her as they chatted or filed onto the train. Everyone spoke so roundedly here, so proper, like their tongues were too low in their mouths. It sounded rather pretty and only slightly confusing.

Taking her suitcases in hand, Alvie walked from the platform into the station, looking around for . . . she wasn't sure. There were plenty of people waiting with signs for disembarking passengers, but none of those signs read "Alvie," "Brechenmacher," or "Lost Apprentice."

She walked back to the platform, her hair stirring as a train whizzed past without so much as slowing, bound for a different destination. People began to gather together, murmuring, idling, waiting for their ride. No one here appeared to be looking for her. Alvie checked her itinerary again, hoping to see something she'd missed. The information remained unchanged, of course—it said the chauffeur was to pick her up. Her pulse sped a bit, which made her palms sweat. She shuffled back into the station and found an employee, then another, to ask, but none of them had heard anything about a Brechenmacher from America or a Mg. Praff.

Nine o'clock now. Trying not to let her arms shake with worry and from the weight of her bags, Alvie walked toward a map of greater London on the wall. It depicted three stations in London—at least on this rail. Was she at the wrong one? But the man on the train had seemed so certain. Would she have to buy a new ticket? She hadn't exchanged any of her American money yet . . .

Alvie stepped closer to the map. When did the trains stop running? They went late in the States, but the English were so backward with their transport . . . what if she had to spend the night in the station? What if Mg. Praff marked her as a no-show? What if—

Something soft and sparkly collided into her left side, sending Alvie sprawling. Her suitcases flew from her hands, and she landed hard on her elbow. Pain cracked up her arm and into her collarbone. The force jerked her glasses from her face, and she looked up just in time to see a very large and very purple blur hustling past her in a race toward one of the platforms. The woman continued in her headlong rush, the sound of her clacking heels filling the air without pause. Alvie clenched her teeth to keep from crying. Was catching a train so important that the woman couldn't even pause to apologize?

Alvie reached for her glasses, but her fingers swept only dusty floor. She pushed herself up onto her knees and swept out the other hand. Still nothing. Her own hand was peachy fuzz against a muted background. She gritted her teeth even harder. Inching forward, she swept her hands out. Found the handle of one of her suitcases.

Another set of footsteps reached her ears, these heavier and quieter, drawing near. "Are you all right?" asked a male voice. Alvie looked up to see a blur of a man. She could make out his dark slacks and white shirt, as well as hair bright as sunshine atop his head. The features of his face were lost to her poor vision.

"Um." Her tongue stuck to her teeth. She swallowed and blathered, "I lost my glasses. Can't . . . see a thing without them." She swept her hand out and, as though the universe wanted to punctuate that declaration, smacked her head on a bench.

"Oh dear. What do they look like?" he asked, and the sunshine-topped blur dropped down to her level.

"Um." Her thoughts were all a jumble, clotting inside her head like old cream. "Black frames. Big, bug-eyed things, really. Should be hard to miss."

"I saw that woman crash into you," he said as she pressed an ear to the floor to sweep her hand under the bench. She cringed when she felt something sticky. "Awfully rude of her. We're not all like that."

Alvie lifted her head and squinted, trying to see the man better. She could make out the shadows of his eyes and mouth when she did that. "We?"

"The English . . . by your accent, I take it you're not from around here. Ah, I think I see them!" He stood and walked several feet away before bending over and scooping up something. Alvie stood and brushed off her knees. Blinked. It was so disorienting, staying in this blurry version of the world for this long.

She sighed in relief when her savior placed the familiar weight of her glasses across her outstretched palm. Thank goodness the lenses were Gaffer glass and hadn't broken. Ignoring the ache in her elbow, she turned the glasses about and pushed them onto her face. "Thank you—"

Her throat constricted as she finally took in her companion. He was young, only a couple years older than herself, she guessed, and only a few inches taller. His eyes were dark brown, his bright hair straight and cropped. Despite the radiant paleness of his tresses, he somehow had darker eyelashes. And a perfect nose.

Alvie felt herself blush, and she was not a woman prone to blushing. "I, uh, thank you for finding them." She knew she looked silly with the things on, magnifying her eyes like they were wont to do, but it was better to be capable than pretty, even when standing in the scrutiny of a handsome man.

"I'm Bennet, by the way," he said, extending a hand. Alvie tried to sneakily wipe her own hand off on the back of her slacks before shaking it. "Bennet Cooper." He released her hand and glanced to the map. "Are you lost?"

All the air rushed out of her at once. "Desperately."

He smiled. His teeth were particularly straight. She resisted the strange urge to count them. "All right. Where are you supposed to be?"

She shuffled through her pockets and handed him her ticket. "London . . ."

"Well, you made it that far." He looked over the ticket.

"I-I'm Alvie," she said dumbly. "Alvie Brechenmacher."

Bennet looked up from the ticket. "An American German in London. No wonder you're lost."

She managed a nervous smile.

"Ah," Bennet said, handing the ticket back to her. "You want Fenchurch Street—this is the Euston station."

Alvie stared at her ticket. "But I thought . . ." Had the magician purposefully *lied* to her? No, certainly not. He must have made a mistake.

"It's easy." He offered her a bright smile, which melted the worry from her bones. "Just head back onto that platform"—he pointed—"and wait for the next eastbound train. Here." He bent and picked up one of the toppled suitcases, then reached for the one by her legs.

"Um. I can carry it," she assured him, scooping up the luggage. "But thank you. So much. You must think it's absurd that I got the stations switched."

"We've all done it." He started for the platform, and Alvie followed. "What discipline are you going to study?"

"Hm?"

He gestured to her red apprentice's apron.

"Oh. Uh, Polymaking."

"Really?" He turned about, nearly smacking the suitcase he was carrying into the one Alvie was lugging. His face brightened, and Alvie couldn't help but think it pretty—in a boyish sort of way. Bennet continued. "I wanted to go into Polymaking. Fascinating stuff."

"You wanted to be a Polymaker?" she asked as they stepped on the platform. She looked him up and down. "Are you a magician?"

"Hopefully soon," he said, setting her luggage down beside a bench. He gestured for her to sit, so she did, awkwardly hitting her suitcase against her knees. She gritted her teeth to hide the pain that shot up her leg. "Still need to take the test. Folding."

"Were you forced into it?" Alvie asked, then clamped a hand over her mouth. She dropped it. "I'm sorry, that was an awkward thing to say."

Bennet shrugged and sat beside her. "Don't worry about it. I was, actually. But I'm glad, in the end. I quite like it now."

"In the US, there's a law that says a student can't be forced to study a discipline against his or her will."

He offered a slight smile. "I'm glad you've got where you want to be."

Alvie frowned. "I'm sorry. I'm being impolite. Again."

"Not at all."

She eyed him, his sunshine hair and brown eyes. A train rumbled into the station, so Alvie stood, but Bennet halted her. "That's the west train. You want the east."

"Oh." She sat back down. "Thank you." She let out a breath of relief that Bennet was willing to wait with her. She glanced to him. "You don't have any bags. Are you from here?"

"I live just outside London with my tutor. Just visiting my sister."

"Is she a magician, too?"

"Ah, no. She's in the local hospital."

"Oh. I'm sorry." Alvie rubbed her hands together. Pushed her glasses up. "Is she ill?"

"Something like that."

Alvie reserved herself to smaller, more polite topics of conversation until the train arrived. Bennet helped her up into the car, chatting a little bit about his tutor, a Mg. Bailey. He seemed impressed when Alvie mentioned Mg. Praff, which was a relief after Mg. Ezzell's strange response. When they stepped off the train, she found a rather weary-looking man holding a sign with her name on it. Relief filled her like the cool touch of an enchanted mirror.

"There he is! Thank you so much." She took her suitcase from Bennet. "I would've slept in that station if not for you."

Bennet smiled. "I'm sure you'd have been fine. Good night, Alvie."

Alvie watched the Folding apprentice go. Rejuvenated, she grabbed her bags and hurried over to the man whose sign bore her name. "That's me!" she called. "I'm Alvie! I'm terribly sorry. I got lost and—"

"Thank goodness," the chauffeur said, lowering his sign as his eyes rolled back in relief. "I thought I had missed you and would be out of the job. Here we are." He scooped up both of Alvie's suitcases, casting a quick, confused look at her slacks. "The buggy's right this way, miss."

"The what?"

"The automobile."

"Oh. Thank you."

The chauffeur marched with quick strides that Alvie was more than happy to match, eager to put the mess of trains behind her and see her new home for the first time. The chauffeur wasn't a man of many words, but he was efficient, tying up her luggage at the back of a rather nice windowless automobile. He even opened the door for her. Night swallowed up the whole of London, but after a short ride, the darkness was cut back by the brilliance of magic.

The place was nothing like what Alvie had thought it would be.

CHAPTER 3

THE WHOLE ESTATE WAS lit with enchanted Gaffer's glass—bobbles of enchanted glass shining in muted colors of blue, pink, and orange. A good thing, for if Alvie had beheld the estate in the full light of the sun, she might have fainted.

Magicians were wealthy individuals, and Mg. Marion Praff was well esteemed in his field.

But *this*?

"It's a palace," she muttered as the automobile pulled up the drive. Gabled and conical roofing, bricked and tiled walls, and so many windows . . . She began counting those windows, her mind spinning with the growing number. Goodness, it had to be at least one window per twenty-five square feet of wall! And she thought she could see enchantments on some of them—perhaps to color the sunlight coming in, or to magnify the view.

The chauffeur snorted. "Hardly. But it *is* bloody giant." He parked the automobile but left the engine running, then came around to open Alvie's door. She stepped out, marveling.

"C'mon now," the driver said as he grabbed her suitcases. "There'll be plenty of time for that."

She nodded and followed him, only to notice the elaborate tiled path under her feet. Not ceramic tile. The glint of each square piece was metallic, and they *shifted* before her eyes, swirling in a dance of copper, silver, and gold. They stilled a few feet before the chauffeur stepped on them, and held their positions as Alvie crossed. Glancing over her shoulder, she noticed the tiles shifting once more about five feet behind her. Like a river of metal that iced over at the approach of footsteps.

It stole her breath away. There were magicians in Columbus, but she'd never seen such a display. It must have cost a fortune.

Gaffer lights hung around every door and window, glimmering an ever-changing pattern of blue, pink, and orange, like the capital grounds at Christmastime. There was a running fountain in the middle of a circular brick drive made for carriages. It was built of stone, but Alvie could make out a plastic form over its tiers. Polymaking! Did the plastic push the water up without pumps? Did it keep it cool, hot? Did it change the pattern in which it rose and fell? There were so many possibilities, and it made Alvie itch that she couldn't immediately decipher how the material had been used. Perhaps if she got closer . . . How much study would it take to be able to make such forms?

The chauffeur cleared his throat, and Alvie turned back to him, finally noticing the row of servants standing outside the door, all looking straight ahead at nothing in particular. It took another moment for Alvie to realize they'd lined up for *her*.

Coming out from the front door was a regal-looking man in a green uniform with a stiff collar and modest coattails. A Polymaker's uniform. Alvie knew from his biography that he was thirty-nine years old, but he looked younger. He was six feet tall, perhaps six one, and had short dark hair neatly parted to skirt his forehead, a straight nose, and eyebrows that pointed at the top. Clean shaven as of that morning, judging by the stubble coming in on his lip and jaw.

Alvie realized she was staring at Mg. Marion Praff, and subsequently kicked herself in the ankle.

"Welcome! Miss Brechenmacher, is it?"

He even said her name correctly. Alvie glanced at the pristine-looking woman beside him. His wife? She looked to be in her late thirties. "Uh, y-yes, sir. I-It's an honor."

Mg. Praff smiled and extended his hand. He had a firm grip. Alvie tried to return it, but her limbs were suddenly overcooked noodles.

The woman beside him said, "We were concerned something might have happened to you, dear."

"Oh!" Alvie pulled her hand back and twisted it in the other. "I'm so sorry. I was perfectly on time. That is, I followed the schedule exactly and made all of the mirrors and the boats and the train, but I got off at the wrong station. I wasn't paying attention to the engineer, and a man told me where to get off, but he was mistaken, and I was too dumb in the head to figure it out until—"

Mg. Praff laughed. "Quite all right. Miss Brechenmacher, this is my wife, Charlotte."

Mrs. Praff offered a small curtsy, not a hand. Was Alvie supposed to curtsy back? She attempted to.

"You've had a long journey." Mg. Praff motioned to one of the men standing in the stiff line outside the door—a footman, Alvie guessed. Without direction, he took the luggage from the chauffeur, who then departed back the way he had come. Alvie realized she hadn't asked his name. "You must be hungry. We've already dined, but we had something set aside for you."

"Oh, uh, thank you. So much. Um." She swallowed. "I've read all about you, Magician Praff. I really am honored to be under your, uh, tutelage."

She did not sound nearly as elegant as she had when practicing this speech in her mirror before leaving Ohio. In fact, she couldn't remember the next line.

He smiled. "The honor is all mine." He offered his elbow. Alvie hesitated, then took it, which must have been the right thing, for Mg. Praff glided over to the row of servants and introduced them one by one: the housekeeper, the butler, another footman, two maids. When the butler, Mr. Hemsley, looked down at her slacks, his brow knit together so tightly the two lines of hair became one. Perhaps slacks weren't the height of women's fashion in London, either.

"We've three children," Mg. Praff continued as he led his wife and Alvie into the house through the, uh, vestibule, Alvie thought it was called. A large, unblemished mirror hung on the right wall, and the walls were painted forest green with gold trim. "Lucas is studying abroad in Tokyo, of all places, and Maximus is at university. Our youngest, Martha, is recently married and has moved to the country. She's just a couple years your junior."

Eighteen and already married. Not that it was uncommon; it was just that Alvie had only been on one "date" her entire life, to a dance after graduating from secondary school, and she'd never so much as kissed a man, let alone been proposed to. She had the nagging feeling she and the Polymaker's daughter were very different vegetables.

As opposed to peas in a pod. That was the analogy to which she was referring. For herself . . .

Mg. Praff gave her a personal tour, his wife departing after the housekeeper whispered something to her. Being alone with Mg. Praff made Alvie more nervous, but as they walked from room to room—to room to room to room—Alvie gained a little more confidence, though she was still awed by the vastness of the house. Some ceilings had murals of cherubs or gardens painted on them; others had mantels decorated with elaborate wreaths of paper art, which Alvie thought funny, being near a fire and all. Perhaps a Pyre had enchanted the flames not to burn paper?

There were sofas galore and more chairs than windows, and each room had different carpeting and colored walls and fancy carvings on pillars and in corners. Alvie was sure the latter style had a specific architectural name, but—curse her studies—she couldn't fathom what it might be, and thus she didn't remark on it.

"Down there is the observatory, and this is the servants' hall, so you needn't trouble yourself with this area, at least," Mg. Praff told her.

"Are there many? Servants?" Was that a strange question to ask?

"Just enough to cover the needs of the estate. You met the main staff outside." Mg. Praff turned her around toward the stairs. "Briar Hall once belonged to a viscount, but the economy was not kind to him. And so it's in my family's name, though we have no formal title."

"Magician?"

"No title with the aristocracy," he amended.

They crested the stairs and took a turn. One of the maids from outside—Emma?—waited by the door to a room. A very tall door. When Alvie and Mg. Praff approached, she opened the door and stood inside.

"This is the green room, one of our guest chambers," Mg. Praff explained. "I thought it an appropriate choice for you." He gestured to his green uniform.

Alvie stepped in and ogled. It was a large room, with a very high ceiling—she couldn't fathom the purpose of such a high ceiling. Etched vines traced its periphery. A large bowl-shaped light hung from the center, its glass stained to look like leaves. The large bed, pressed up against the far wall, had a canopy with pale-green curtains and blankets bearing a golden sheen. There was a nightstand to the left of it and a bench at the foot of it. Atop the nightstand sat a bright Pyre-glass lamp—the brightest sort of magicked lamp, the kind that burned with magic-fueled flame on the inside and glowed with Gaffer's glass on the outside. This one emitted a golden-white light. Above the bed's headboard hung a bronze-framed painting of a forest littered with poppies. All the bedroom walls were painted the palest green, and darker green curtains covered what Alvie presumed to be a large window, and she itched to see the view. By the window was a strange piece of furniture she'd never

26

seen before, which looked to be half-bed and half-sofa . . . for lounging when one didn't wish to muss the bedcover? A smooth cherrywood desk sat just near the door. Alvie supposed the mirror atop it made it double as a vanity. And then there was a random tuffetlike thing in the space between the furniture. Alvie wasn't entirely sure what to do with that.

"It's lovely," she said, and that was the truth, for the room was grander than anything in her own home, as well as the dorm she had stayed in at the Jefferson School, and she had thought its furnishings fine. She looked down, admiring the complex floral patterns on the dark-green carpet.

"Brandon brought up your things," Emma said, and Alvie recalled Brandon was the name of the footman who had taken her suitcases. "With your permission, I can hang up your clothes."

She gestured to a closet nearby that Alvie hadn't seen. Goodness, it was its own room. A closet one could walk into! How unnecessarily fancy.

"Um, yes, thank you."

Mg. Praff gestured toward the door. "As I said, there's a meal waiting you, but if you're weary, we can ring to have it brought up here." He pointed to a cord on the wall near the bed. Did that go into the servants' quarters? Alvie would feel guilty ever ringing that, but the enormity of the house and her recent adventure across the Atlantic was beginning to clog her brain, so she nodded, and Emma hurried over and rang the bell.

"If I may ask," the Polymaker said, "have you ever considered getting enchanted lenses?"

Alvie looked at him. It took her a second to realize he meant her glasses. "They are enchanted, sir." A Gaffer's spell etched into the corner of each lens let the glass morph on its own if her prescription ever changed and helped make them thinner as well.

He blinked in surprise. "Do you mind?" He held out a hand.

"Um . . ." Shifting on her feet, Alvie grasped her glasses and pulled them off. The room turned into a blur of green. Mg. Praff blended into it surprisingly well.

"Goodness, they are." She gathered he was looking at the Gaffer etchings on the side of the giant lenses. "Do you mind if I fiddle with these? Just for a moment."

Alvie could barely tell if Mg. Praff was looking at her, but she didn't want to deny her mentor whatever plan he had, not when she had arrived so late to his house, and he had given her such a nice room. She nodded, and her tutor—master?—left the room, taking her ability to see with him. Someone else arrived, for Emma instructed the newcomer to bring in Alvie's dinner. Alvie's stomach gurgled in anticipation, reminding her that she hadn't eaten in some time.

"Do you want the slacks hung with the skirts?" Emma asked.

"Um . . . whatever you think is best. I usually keep them in drawers." She reached for the chair-blur at the desk, pulled it out, and sat, closing her eyes to turn off the disorientation of unaided sight.

Emma continued to work silently, and Alvie wondered if she was supposed to talk to her or ignore her or what. She'd never had servants before, and half the time she couldn't tell where the maid went, except for the sounds of footsteps and shuffling. Eventually another black-and-white blur arrived, or perhaps returned—there was no way of knowing for certain if this was the same servant from before—and set a tray on the desk in front of her. Alvie squinted, trying to determine what was being served. She punctured something with her fork and popped it into her mouth. Chicken. Very delicious chicken.

"All done," Emma announced when Alvie was three bites into her meal. "Do you need anything else? Help undressing?"

Alvie choked on her food. Swallowed. "Um, no. Thank you."

The Emma-blur bobbed and left. Alvie picked her way through some sort of savory pudding and what she thought were cinnamon pears.

A knock sounded at the door.

"Yes? Come in."

A green blur entered, and Mg. Praff said, "Here we are. I think I calculated it right." He held his hands out, and Alvie awkwardly grabbed his fingers before she found her glasses. She slipped them on, and the world became blissfully crisp once more.

She noticed a distinct lightness to her frames.

She touched the arms of the glasses and then pulled the glasses off. Put them back on. "I'm sorry, what did you do? I can't tell without the things on."

He smiled. "Plastic lenses."

Alvie gaped. Tapped her nail on the lens. It was almost glasslike. "Plastic lenses? We don't have those in the States!"

"They're relatively new, presented at the Discovery Convention last year. They're much lighter than glass but, at this point in time, also much more expensive. You'll find very few optometrists willing to sell them."

Alvie moved her head back and forth, savoring the lack of pain the spectacles caused her ears. "These are wonderful! Thank you."

He set a small cloth bundle on the desk. "These are your old lenses. I'm pleased you like the new ones. I haven't had many people to experiment on."

Alvie straightened. Stood. "Speaking of experiments, sir. Magician Praff. Am I to do the bonding tonight?" It felt like loose ribbons danced in her belly. Alvie hadn't actually bonded to plastic yet, which meant she could do nothing magical with it, though she was familiar with it thanks to her Basic Material Mechanics and History of Materials classes at Jefferson. *After* she bonded, she would never have the opportunity to cast spells with any other material. A bonding was for life.

"I promise to bond you in the morning. And show you the polymery."

Alvie clasped her hands together. "You have your own polymery?" How large would the lab be in an estate this extravagant? Her skin buzzed with excitement.

"Of course! And you will be welcome to use it. Starting tomorrow. We'll conduct your first lesson as well, if you're up for it."

"I will be, sir. I'd be up for it right now."

He smiled. "I do not doubt you. I admit I'm eager to begin—you seem much more enthusiastic than my last apprentice. He was a bit of a dullard."

Alvie didn't know what to say, so she merely nodded.

"I can send someone for the tray, if you're finished."

Alvie eyed her food, which she could now see. It looked like a child had picked through it. "Not yet. I can, uh, ring the bell?"

Mg. Praff nodded. "Until morning, then. Good night."

Alvie smiled, and Mg. Praff departed, closing the door behind him.

Alvie awoke to a face full of blanket and a sweet voice saying her name.

"Miss Alvie?"

She startled awake, blinking sunlight and blurry room from her vision, wiping her forearm across her mouth in case she had drooled. It took her a few seconds to realize where she was. Somewhat oriented, she fumbled for her nightstand and grabbed her glasses.

Emma stood at the foot of the bed. "So sorry to disturb you, but Mrs. Praff thought it best to check on you."

"Oh." She looked at the brightness of the window. Emma must have parted the curtains. *"Oh."* She searched for a clock and found none. "What time is it?"

"A quarter after nine."

Alvie slipped her hands beneath her new plastic lenses and rubbed her eyes. Sleeping in on her first day as an apprentice! She shuffled to the edge of the bed and slid off the mattress, but her foot caught in the sheet, and she tumbled onto the floor.

Emma grasped her shoulders and helped her up.

"Are you quite all right?" The maid released her and took a step back.

Alvie blew a mass of brown hair away from her face and straightened her glasses. "Oh. Yes. Um."

Apparently it was answer enough, for Emma turned back for the closet. "What would you like to wear today?"

Alvie followed her, her bare feet dragging on the carpet. "Uh . . . well, I'm going to the polymery today, doing my lessons. Hopefully some real work. So slacks and a shirt."

"A preference to your shirt?"

"Uh . . ."

Emma entered the closet and returned with two of Alvie's blouses on hangers: a white one and a lavender one. Alvie pointed to the second. Emma set it and a pair of black slacks on the foot of Alvie's bed, then set about straightening the coverlet for her.

"I can do that . . ."

Emma smiled. "It's what I'm here for. Do you want help dressing?"

Alvie hadn't had help dressing for fifteen years. "No."

Emma fluffed a pillow and tucked the blankets like a professional, then turned back to Alvie. "How about your hair?"

Alvie pinched some of the frizzy waves in her fingers. "Oh. There's not much that can be done with this."

"I have a serum we could try to smooth out the waves."

"Oh . . . if I'm working today, I thought I'd just put it up."

"What style would you like?"

"Not . . . styled?"

Emma smiled patiently. Alvie tended to get a lot of patient smiles like that. "If you change your mind, just ring the bell. Do you need anything else?"

"No?"

Emma nodded, offered a small curtsy, and left the room. Alvie noted that the room didn't have a lock, but servants usually knocked, right? At least when their charges weren't unconscious?

She grabbed the lavender blouse and stepped over to a long mirror nailed to the wall just outside the closet. Her hair was a lopsided, frizzy mess, as it usually was in the morning. Her glasses took up most of her face, which had never been especially pretty. At least, Alvie didn't think so, and she was certain the boys in secondary school and at the Jefferson School agreed. She did, however, have a nice figure. Her mother had said so, anyway. Alvie grabbed the seams of her nightgown and pulled them back to see it better, then tugged the gown off and dressed, cinching the waistband of her slacks at her navel and donning a pair of gray shoes with low heels. Alvie couldn't walk forward or backward in high heels, and she had never dared to attempt sideways. Fortunately, she wasn't short enough to really need them.

After twisting her hair up into a bun and tying her apron, Alvie creaked the door open and peered up and down the large hallway with its fancy carpet and dim, magical lights. She only vaguely remembered where everything was from yesterday. It had been a very long tour. She thought that, perhaps, she recalled where the kitchen was, so she might as well venture out for breakfast. Or was there a special room for breakfast? She couldn't remember.

Slipping from her room, she walked slowly and took in her surroundings, enjoying the adventure of navigating the halls. After finding the stairs, she went down two floors and emerged into the main hall, a giant of a room with a ceiling that went up two stories. Morning sunlight shined through domed windows at its top. She turned about for a moment before selecting a door. The music room, with a pianoforte and a harp that looked like it hadn't been used in some time. She began to retreat, but heard a man's muffled voice from the next room. Mg. Praff?

She crossed the music room and opened the door, finding a narrow hallway. Another door was cracked open across from her. The salon, if she remembered right. She pulled the door open and peeked in.

The only occupant of the room, which was furnished with cream-colored chairs and a matching sofa, was Mg. Praff, who stood in the far corner near a large, pristine mirror and elaborate candelabra. In the mirror was the image of an Englishwoman, perhaps in her late forties. Her hair was a similar color to Alvie's, but it was stick straight and pulled back in a painfully tight bun. Silver spectacles, small and dainty, sat on the bridge of her nose. She wore a dark-brown dress suit with a stiff collar and had her hands clasped behind her back.

"—paperwork is finished, and I expect things to go well," Mg. Praff said.

The woman in the mirror nodded. "I'm glad to hear it. We're striving to increase our foreign diplomacy, for lack of a better word, through these exchanges. I'm hoping to get a Folding apprentice here in a year or so, after the magician I have in mind is through her confinement." The woman's face turned to Alvie. "Seems we have a guest."

Mg. Praff turned around. Alvie was about to utter an apology, but he cut her off. "Alvie! You're up. Have you eaten?"

She hadn't even brushed her teeth. "Not yet. I thought to find the kitchen, but got lost."

"You'd startle the cook, no doubt. You need only ring the bell." He waved Alvie into the room. "Let me introduce Magician Patrice Aviosky, head of the Board of Education for England's Magicians' Cabinet."

"Oh." She was very important, then. "Um. Hello." Alvie tried for a curtsy.

"I'm eager to see what you have in store for us, Miss Brechenmacher," Mg. Aviosky said. Alvie wondered if she was a Gaffer or if Mg. Praff had merely paid a great sum to have a pre-enchanted communication mirror. Her father had promised to invest in one himself after hearing

Alvie was moving so far away. "Polymaking is a new frontier. There is much to learn, much to discover."

Alvie nodded. "I won't disappoint." What if Alvie created a new Polymaking spell? Wouldn't that be something? Her papa would polka with glee.

"Oh, Mg. Aviosky, I have a proposition for you." Mg. Praff turned back to the mirror. "Alvie arrived late last night; we're doing her bonding this morning. If you have the time, would you like to be the witness?"

Butterflies erupted up Alvie's throat, and she pressed her lips together to keep them from flying out her mouth. Someone from England's Magicians' Cabinet might be acting as her witness? Could this apprenticeship get any better?

Mg. Aviosky thought for a moment before saying, "I think that should work. I can arrive in an hour. It will give Miss Brechenmacher some time to eat."

"Excellent. I'll see you at the vestibule mirror."

Mg. Aviosky nodded, and her image blurred in a swirl of silver before the mirror stilled, reflecting only Mg. Praff and the salon behind him.

———

Later, Alvie ate in the breakfast room by herself, as the family had dined earlier. Mg. Praff had left the day's newspaper on the table, so she read that while helping herself to soft-boiled eggs and crumpets. Apparently another bill had been pushed to ban opposite-sex apprenticeships in England, but it was recently rejected, given that it would hinder new students from completing their apprenticeships if there was a shortage of teachers of either sex. What a relief—such a thing would have kept Alvie from studying here.

Finished, and unsure of what to do with the dishes, she left them on the table and wandered out of the breakfast room. The salon was adjacent to it, and a corridor separated the salon from a pretty flower garden, which also opened up to the main hall. She passed the butler, Mr. Hemsley, who eyed her slacks with a cross expression as he walked in the opposite direction. She watched him go, checked her slacks for spilled food, and, finding none, continued to the main hall. There wasn't much point to wearing a skirt when the family had already seen her in her travel-wrinkled clothes, was there?

She had good timing, for the moment she entered the large space, she heard the clicking heels of their visitor. Mg. Aviosky strode into the great room beside Mg. Praff. She was taller than Alvie had supposed, and she carried an air of authority that tied Alvie's tongue in knots, despite the fact that Alvie hadn't been trying to say anything. The best way not to look foolish was to stay silent, so she clasped her hands together and waited for the magicians to approach her.

"Ah, Alvie, perfect. This way," said Mg. Praff. He led them down a hall that hugged the salon, toward the back of the house, past some sort of greenhouse that, yes, looked to be made of plastic. As they approached a large back entrance, one of the footmen spotted them and hurried to open the door. He offered a bow as Alvie passed him. It made her feel far more important than she was.

A long path led across a manicured lawn and between two gardens of dwarf trees. It boasted the same shimmering, shifting metal blocks as the one at the front of the house, and the effect was even prettier in the sunlight. Mg. Aviosky, who did not seem easily impressed, commented on the skill behind the spell.

The path ended at a structure about the size of Alvie's home in Columbus. It had a much more robust exterior, made of brick, and each window bubbled out in a plastic dome that let in sunlight while obscuring the view. The polymery. Alvie's steps quickened with anticipation, and she stepped on the back of Mg. Aviosky's heel. Muttering an apology, Alvie inched over to the edge of the path and ogled the building. This was where she'd be working. This was where she'd make her bond.

The bonding. It was happening. Now. Her blood felt like air inside her veins. If only her parents could be here with her.

"Right this way." Mg. Praff pulled a key from his pocket. "I always keep it locked. You'll receive a key as well, Alvie, and Mr. Hemsley has one."

Mg. Aviosky said, "You've heard of the Turner break-in, then."

"I have." Mg. Praff unlocked the door. "Though it's always been my policy to safeguard my work."

Alvie glanced between the two magicians. "Turner break-in?"

Mg. Praff sighed. "There have been two polymery burglaries in the last year. The first was at the home of a magician near Liverpool. The second was at the Turner Polymery near Parliament Square—a lab that rents space to Polymakers and their apprentices."

"Neither of which seemed successful," Mg. Aviosky added. "Little was stolen."

Mg. Praff gestured inside, letting Mg. Aviosky pass through first and Alvie second. Alvie stepped into air that was almost too warm and smelled strongly of oils, lubricant, and plastic. The foyer was round in shape, with a few smaller rooms branching off from it and a set of stairs leading to a second floor. A large plastic mobile hung from the ceiling, and on it spun translucent shapes of circles and triangles, as well as some handcrafted birds and turtles. It turned without wind. There were a few tables and chairs in the large room, and a model skeleton crafted of plastic stood on a plastic stand. It looked real enough to move. There were model boats, model gliders, model automobiles.

The door to one of the larger rooms was open, revealing long counters atop drawers and cabinets. A large rectangular island with a granite countertop swallowed the middle of the floor, and a few stools were tucked under its ledge. An array of beakers and tubes took up a great deal of both counter and island space, and there were shelves and scales and vats and other things Alvie couldn't identify.

She wanted to know how *all* of it worked.

"This is incredible," she murmured.

"It is." Mg. Praff came to her shoulder. "And you will have access to all of it as my apprentice. There is only so much to learn, but a whole world to discover."

Gooseflesh danced across Alvie's skin. "Incredible."

"Your enthusiasm is a good sign," Mg. Aviosky said. "The sooner we have you bonded, the sooner you'll be able to start your studies. Have you set up everything, Mg. Praff?"

The Polymaker gestured to another side room, this one much smaller. It had a short counter with cupboards beneath, as well as two cupboards attached to the wall. A desk and chair were arranged along the opposite wall, and there was a small workbench with a magnifying glass and some empty vials. One of those bubbled windows let in light.

"This, Alvie, will be your personal workroom." Mg. Praff crossed the room's length toward the window while Alvie grabbed the counter to keep from fainting.

"This is for me? My own space?"

"Of course." Mg. Praff pressed his hand to the window and said, "Clarify."

The bubbled window cleared to an almost glasslike transparency. Outside, Alvie saw a well-trimmed hedge, some irises, and the edge of what looked like a garage. She moved to the window, taking in the view, the clear sky, and then the empty work space that would soon be filled with her own creations, her own knowledge. She could have cried for the joy of it.

"Haze will darken that again, if you prefer." Mg. Praff opened one of the high cupboards and pulled from it a short, thick piece of plastic and an easel. He set them both on the counter. "Here it is. Nothing fancy. Polymaking isn't a pretty magic like Folding or Gaffing, if you'll excuse the description, Magician Aviosky."

The woman simply nodded.

"I-I memorized the words." It was a requirement to graduate: memorizing the words that would permanently bond her to plastic. A bond that could never be undone. Her mouth went dry.

Mg. Praff stepped back. "Go ahead."

Alvie stepped up to the easel. Lifted a hand and pressed her fingertips to the cool plastic. She didn't hesitate. This was what she wanted more than anything else.

She took a deep breath. "Material made by man, your creator summons you. Link to me as I link to you through my years until the day I die and become earth."

The plastic warmed beneath her touch, and heat like a breath flooded her hand and traveled up her arm, cooling somewhere between her shoulder and her collarbone. The plastic tingled against her fingers.

She smiled.

She was a Polymaker.

CHAPTER 4

OR AT LEAST AN apprentice to one.

Mg. Praff had started to teach her rudimentary spells that first day, and now, a week after her bonding, she had five under her belt. An empty breakfast tray sat near the door of her work space. Mr. Hemsley always brought food out to the polymery now, since Alvie didn't want to waste time dining when she had magic to discover. It was Mr. Hemsley, and not Emma, who did the errands, for he was the only servant entrusted with a key to the polymery. For an openly friendly man, Mg. Praff was private about his work, but Alvie understood his reasons. Still, she'd rather have Emma venturing out to the polymery. Mr. Hemsley was one of the grumpiest men she'd ever met.

Alvie took a flat square of off-white plastic, tested its give, and savored the faint tingle it emitted under her fingers, reminding her of the new magic coursing through her capillaries. Mg. Praff had given her dozens of these squares to practice with, all with different levels of flexibility. Some snapped right back after she bent them in half, others broke apart like peanut brittle, and still others were so flimsy they'd bunch up and stick to themselves.

She eyed the apple sitting in front of her, saved from yesterday's lunch tray. She rested the plastic square, which had an area of about sixty-four square centimeters, atop its stem. The stems were the tricky part, she'd learned.

"Soften," she commanded, and the plastic gained flexibility. She wiggled it a little as she centered it on the apple, waiting for the dent of the stem to appear before speaking the next word. "Melt," she said, and the plastic warmed beneath her touch. Had she warmed it over a fire or electric bulb, it would have burned her, as Mg. Praff had so kindly demonstrated on her second day as his official apprentice. But the magic didn't hurt her. She imagined it was the same for Pyres, who wielded fireballs and made flames dance in elaborate shows of nonindustrialism. Granted, the warm plastic was nowhere near the temperature of a flame.

As the plastic drooped down the sides of the red apple, Alvie pulled her left hand away and scooped up the fruit, turning it slightly to help the plastic cover it. The Encompass spell danced on her tongue, but if the ends of the melted plastic couldn't "see" each other, they wouldn't merge completely, and she'd have another botched vacuum form. So she waited, watching the plastic slowly dribble down the sides of the fruit.

"Encompass," she commanded, and the melting plastic lurched forward to join itself. "Conform." And it sucked in close to the apple, as though she'd stuck a straw in its core and was sucking with all her might. "Harden."

The plastic turned hard once more. In her hand, she held a plastic-coated apple. The polymer hugged all its contours, though the very tip of the stem poked out from the plastic. Almost perfect. Almost.

She tossed the apple into a growing pile of vacuum-formed fruit near the window.

"It's looking well."

Alvie started and slammed her knee into the edge of her desk. Biting down on a curse, she turned toward the door and Mg. Praff standing in its doorway.

"I apologize for startling you."

"No, no, it's fine." She eyed her plastic fruit pile.

He followed her gaze. "No worries, you'll get it. If nothing else, they're well preserved."

A smile touched Alvie's lips.

"It's a slow-going magic." Mg. Praff stepped into the narrow room and folded his arms across his chest. "Not as slow as Smelting, of course, but not nearly as quick as Folding, Pyring, or even Gaffing. The spells drag out and take a good deal of practice to correct."

"I'll correct them." By tonight she would get the small-scale vacuum form right, and then Mg. Praff would teach her something else. Her blood tingled at the prospect.

"Then we'll move on to molds and plastic preparations. Every good Polymaker can process his—or her—own monomers. I'll deliver some reading to you this afternoon on that. But I came here to discuss your volunteer hours."

Alvie turned in her chair. "Volunteer hours?"

"A requirement for all of my apprentices." He held up two hands as though she had objected. "I know it's not standard, but volunteering keeps a person humble, and we can use a lot more of that in this world." He paused. "Or, at the very least, it forces them to leave the polymery."

"Ah." Alvie scratched the back of her neck. Since the bonding, she'd spent more time in the polymery than the house. Thus the breakfast trays. "Did you have many self-absorbed apprentices?" She wasn't self-absorbed, was she?

"Not really, no. But I met a Folder once who was as full of himself as a man could be, which gave me the idea. I require my apprentices to donate a minimum of two hours a week, and I can help with the arrangements. There's the poorhouses, food banks, hospitals, elderly homes, schools . . . I don't know if you have a preference."

"Could I be a chauffeur?"

Mg. Praff blinked. "I don't think so. Why ever would you want that?"

Alvie shrugged. "I know how to work an automobile."

"Really? America must be full of opportunity."

She smiled. "I wouldn't mind the hospital, sir." Once, while trying to construct a motor for a school project, she'd nearly sliced off her finger with a micro saw and had to go to the hospital. The staff there had been awfully friendly, and everything was so . . . tidy.

Mg. Praff rubbed his hands together. "Excellent. I'll see about getting you set up. Also, I'd like you to dine with the family tonight at seven; we haven't seen much of you, and we're expecting my daughter and her husband. Emma should have a dress prepared for you."

"A dress?"

"Mrs. Praff took the liberty of ordering you a few things." He chuckled as though embarrassed. "You'll have to forgive her meddling. She is very curious about you. Perhaps because I've never had a female apprentice, and she enjoys feminine company."

Alvie nodded slowly. "Uh, all right. Seven it is."

Mg. Praff nodded and turned for the door. "I recommend leaving the polymery by five."

"So early?"

He smiled, and left.

"Well, it's not the smartest thing," Alvie said, turning in front of her mirror.

"I think you look quite smart." Emma adjusted the gold belt around Alvie's waist. "You look like a lady."

Alvie sighed. "Sorry. I didn't mean to say it wasn't a fine dress."

Emma patted her shoulder. "And I didn't mean to say you weren't ladylike. Just I've never seen someone wear pants the way you do."

"Your work would be a lot easier with them. You should try it."

Emma laughed. "I doubt Mrs. Connway would approve the change in uniform," she said, naming the housekeeper.

Alvie studied her reflection. It *was* a fine dress, and her figure looked good in it. The gown was a gauzy light maroon over black, with gold embroidery about the hem and collar. Bits of material hung off the sleeves for a more ethereal effect, Alvie supposed. What a bother, to dress up for dinner. What if she spilled food on it?

"You should wear it when Mr. Lucas Praff comes home from Japan. Maybe you'll catch his eye," Emma teased.

Alvie snorted and adjusted her glasses. "I doubt that's a possibility."

"What do you mean?"

Alvie just shrugged and stared at the mirror. Took her glasses off and squinted, but without them, she couldn't make out her face well at all. She slipped the things back on and sat at the desk vanity, tolerating Emma's handiwork and serums for her hair for about ten minutes.

The Praffs' main dining room was large, and they had a considerable table to fill it, though there were only five of them seated at one of its ends. Footmen brought around trays of tarts and fancy vegetables, and Alvie had to watch the others to figure out how she was supposed to serve herself. She did, indeed, drop a piece of pheasant on her skirt, but she thought no one noticed.

"So, Miss Brechenmacher," chimed Mrs. Martha Peal, Mg. Praff's newly married daughter, "tell me about your family."

Alvie had food in her mouth and stopped chewing, trying to decide if she was to spit it out, talk over it, or swallow. She chewed very quickly and swallowed with a sip of wine, but felt the silence stretched just a little too long. "It's just me and my parents. We live in Columbus."

"That's New York?"

Mr. Peal answered, "Ohio."

Alvie nodded. "Yes, Ohio."

"Oh." Mrs. Peal laughed, though Alvie wasn't sure what was funny. "And is your father a magician?"

"No . . ."

Mrs. Peal nodded, like that was a splendid place to end the conversation, and returned to her pheasant.

Alvie turned to Mg. Praff. "I've noticed you don't have any electric lights in your home." Electric lights were cheaper than magical ones, at least in the States.

Mrs. Praff answered, "I prefer the luminance of enchanted lights, and Magician Praff humors me." She touched her lips with a napkin. "Technology is the uneducated man's magic, and I do mean to do Briar Hall justice."

"Oh, I disagree," Alvie said, and both the Peals ceased their eating. "Technology requires a great deal of education, possibly even more than the magical arts. Or at least a different kind of learning."

"Hmm." Mrs. Praff settled her hands on her lap. "A different kind of learning, certainly. It would take a different kind to develop a *technology* Gaffers and Pyres have been perfecting for centuries."

Alvie's stomach tightened, as did her shoulders. "Are you familiar with the Jefferson School of Material Mechanics, Mrs. Praff?"

Mrs. Praff hesitated, perhaps thrown by the change of subject. "I am, though more so with the Praff school."

"Then you're aware the tuition is incredibly expensive. Some twelve thousand dollars a year, or whatever that is in pounds." In the States, the government subsidized a large percentage of the tuition for immigrants or those willing to move out West. Alvie had not qualified for the subsidies, nor had she been granted any scholarships.

Mrs. Praff nodded.

"I was able to attend on the fortune my father made by developing the very technology you seem to think redundant. Not everyone can afford a Gaffer light, and the light bulb can illuminate places where no magician has ever stood. That technology is the very reason I'm here."

Mrs. Praff blushed just a little, or perhaps that was a trick of the magical lighting. "I didn't realize."

"You're very eloquent tonight, Alvie," Mg. Praff said, and Alvie realized she'd said too much, or perhaps said it the wrong way. She'd never excelled at judging conversation.

Her gaze dropped to the table. Perhaps she'd been too forward. After all, she barely knew these people.

She finished her meal in silence.

———————

Alvie went to the polymery early the next morning, eager to break away from the house and dive into her work. She was to get a new lesson today; best to be prepared. After tucking herself away into her small work space, Alvie vacuum-formed a pencil and turned to the reading Mg. Praff had given her. *Chemical Binding of Monomers* was a dry book, and one that had not been written specifically for Polymakers, but it certainly had its interesting moments. Alvie turned a page and studied a diagram there. Perhaps she could write an updated book specifically for plastic magicians once she officially became one. *The Basics of Polymerization for Polymakers*. Volumes 1 and 2. The thought made her smile.

A soft knock sounded at the door, and Mr. Hemsley opened it. He balanced a breakfast tray in his free hand. "Yet another one."

"Thank you." Alvie offered him a smile before taking the tray and setting it beside her. Mr. Hemsley left with a muted sigh.

She turned back to her book. Retrieving a piece of paper and melting the plastic from her pencil, she drew the outline of the diagram herself to learn it better. The scents of cinnamon, apples, and eggs, however, drew her attention to the tray. Pushing her work aside, Alvie pulled the tray over and picked up the fork, only to notice a copy of *Discovery Today* tucked under her plate. She slipped the magazine out and studied its cover. It boasted an image of a skeleton, very much like the one in the polymery's foyer, only made of paper. Intriguing.

Alvie flipped through the pages, wondering if Mr. Hemsley had picked up the magazine for her or if Mg. Praff had sent it along. Likely the latter. Alvie read the article about electricity and the one on telephones, as well as an advertisement for the annual Discovery in Material Mechanics Convention. Alvie stared at the print, mesmerized. She knew about the Discovery Convention. While open to all magical disciplines, it was the largest showcase for Polymakers in the world, and next year it was to be held in Oxford. Magician inventors of all backgrounds went to present their creations and share their knowledge. Scientists could get grants, and magicians could make their names known—just as Mg. Praff had done. Would Mg. Praff let her go? She'd need to watch her tongue more around the family if she wanted that.

She turned another page to see a black-and-white picture of a familiar dark-haired man with a receding hairline and a mustache. The style of his jacket was a magician's uniform. The caption beneath read "Magician Roscoe Ezzell, Polymaker." She racked her brain for a moment before name, photograph, and memory collided into one—he was the man she'd spoken to on the train. The one who had directed her to the wrong station.

Alvie turned her gaze to the article. Seemed Mg. Ezzell was experimenting with using color-changing plastic for thermometers. Fascinated, Alvie read the article to its end, but it appeared no solid breakthroughs had yet been made. Alvie hummed to herself. She wanted to learn the spells the Polymaker was tinkering with.

She heard the door to the polymery creak and opened her own door with her foot, spying Mg. Praff in his work clothes. She grabbed the magazine and hurried to meet him.

"Have you seen this, sir?" she asked, holding up *Discovery Today*.

He planted his hands on his hips. "Yes, I have, and I wanted you to see it, too. Find anything interesting?"

"All of it is interesting! Telephones, thermometers, the Discovery Convention—"

Mg. Praff snapped his fingers. "That is a wonderful convention. Coming to England next year. Certainly an excellent opportunity for an apprentice."

Alvie squeezed the magazine in her hands. "Truly? We'll go?"

"I try to go every year," Mg. Praff said, though the excitement in his voice wavered. He gestured to the lab ahead of them, where Alvie had her lessons, and led the way to its heart.

"You presented the Imagidome at the 1904 convention," Alvie said. He had not discussed his most popular invention with her yet, and she was hoping he'd do so now.

He smiled and nodded. "So you've heard of it."

"Anyone who reads has heard of it."

He chuckled. "Kind of you to say. A lot of work went into it, and it was received well."

Received well? It had been the star of the convention! It was said the bundle of spells created a feigned reality and that a person could step into the Imagidome and feel as though they were somewhere else completely. "And this year?"

"I made some adjustments and presented it again. I impressed a few, but . . ." They reached the large granite-topped island in the lab, and Alvie took a seat on one of three stools tucked against it. "Well, I admit I've nothing to present for the convention in the spring. I'm in a bit of a rut. Our craft . . . it's so new, and there are so many leaves to be overturned, but I've been unable to discover anything new, or reinvent anything old. I'm hoping that reviewing the basics with you might lead to an idea or two."

"I'm sure you'll think of something. The convention is still months away." Today was September 26, and if Alvie remembered the advertisement correctly, the convention would be on March 19. That was . . . 174 days away. How many lessons would Alvie have in 174 days? Right now she averaged two lessons a week, and there were about, oh . . . twenty-five weeks until the Discovery Convention. Fifty lessons. Surely there would be something in there to spur Mg. Praff's creativity! And she learned two to three spells per lesson, so she would know . . . let's see, how many spells by March—

"Alvie? Are you listening?"

Alvie perked up, noticing the lab around her as if awakening from a slumber. "Oh. Um, no. I'm sorry. I was thinking about the numbers."

"What numbers?"

"Um. Nothing important." She smiled. Smiling usually helped alleviate any distress caused by her tendency to drift into her thoughts.

Mg. Praff leaned his elbows on the stone countertop. "As I was saying, I'm sure some more study would be good for both of us. I need to think outside the box, and for now, you need to think within it." He straightened and moved to one of several drawers arranged beneath his lab equipment—vials and tubes Alvie still hadn't learned to use—and pulled out several ruler-shaped bits of plastic. He set them before Alvie. "I thought today we could learn some shaping spells. Take one of these—yes, there you are. Now, with shaping spells, you have to use the Soften command first, else the plastic will just shatter. Like so." He concentrated on the plastic in his hands and said, "Curl."

The plastic shuddered and split into three uneven pieces.

He made a point of looking at Alvie before picking up a new piece. "Soften," he commanded, followed by, "Cease. We don't want it *too* soft, else we'll just have a mess. Curl."

The plastic twisted like a pig's thickened tail.

"Harden," the Polymaker said, and the plastic stiffened under his fingers, cementing its new shape. "And there you have it. You try it, and then I'll show you how to adjust the tightness of the curl."

Alvie did as Mg. Praff instructed, pleased to see her curl resembled his on the first try. The plastic tingled slightly under her fingers, as all plastic did since her bonding.

"Most excellent. Now, you can make a tighter curl by saying just that. Tight Curl, Tighter Curl, Tightest Curl. That last one hardly allows any space between the loops. You must say the modifier before the command, or the plastic will simply curl into its usual shape and ignore the rest. The softer the plastic, the tighter it will curl. You'll need to practice to get used to it."

Alvie nodded and wrote down his instructions.

"For straightening—"

"A quick question?"

"Go ahead."

"When will I learn about color changing? That seems basic enough, doesn't it? You see, the magazine talked about using color-changing plastic in thermometers . . ."

Mg. Praff chuckled, but his expression didn't seem humorous at all. "Ah yes, Mg. Ezzell's work."

Alvie studied his face for a moment, trying to determine if the displeasure was with her or not. "Do you know him?"

"Oh, Mg. Ezzell and I are well acquainted. We're, well, sort of rivals, you could say. At least, he would say as much."

"Rivals? Really?" Had the mistake on the train been intentional? Hadn't Mg. Ezzell said Alvie would be disappointed with Mg. Praff?

Mg. Praff pulled up a stool and sat. He laced his fingers together and rested his chin upon them. "Because Polymaking is so new, it's not flooded with magicians. Not yet, and most Polymakers are not incredibly experienced, either. It's easy to view the expansion of the discipline as a sort of race. A contest to see who can discover what first. Who can earn the most merits."

Alvie grinned. "Exciting."

"Some may think so."

"You don't?"

The Polymaker's lip quirked. "Ah. Well. I do try to play the humble scientist, but, yes, I think it's exciting. If I didn't, I wouldn't be so concerned about the Discovery Convention."

"I don't know of any Polymaker as renowned as yourself, Mg. Praff." Alvie pushed her glasses up her nose. "If you don't mind me saying so."

He smiled. "I don't mind. But problems arise with the competition. Two, three, even four Polymakers could pursue the same theory and end up creating similar inventions, or discovering the same spell. Whoever registers theirs first gets the glory, meaning all the hard work the rest put into reaching the same end is wasted. It can build bitterness between men who were once colleagues."

She processed that. "Like Magician Ezzell."

A nod. "Like Magician Ezzell. He and I have similar interests, and our paths have crossed on multiple occasions. I think I dropped the coffin into my grave when I presented the Imagidome at the Discovery Convention two years ago."

Alvie drew her brows together and waited for him to explain.

Mg. Praff pressed his palms into his thighs. "Both Magician Ezzell and I—and another fellow named Smith—were pursuing possible applications of visual cues for plastic. The year I presented the Imagidome, Magician Ezzell had created a sort of enchanted kaleidoscope—something very similar in theory to the Imagidome, though the visuals were made with a single tile and changed between three pictures when the scope turned. I'm afraid he was . . . overshadowed."

Alvie frowned, trying to imagine herself in such a predicament. "That must have been disappointing . . . but yours was the better invention. You transcribed a single image over *hundreds* of tiles, with movement and everything."

A weak smile pulled on his lips. "Yes, and I dedicated enough time to it that Charlotte threatened divorce." Alvie blanched, but Mg. Praff only chuckled. "We're all well now. Don't you worry. But once you become a leader in your field, there's an enormous amount of pressure to stay that way, and an increasing number of people who want to take the lead from you." He let a long breath out through his nose. "Let's just say Magician Ezzell has not yet learned the art of subtlety. I suppose he's trying to make these thermometers his next great jump, but from what I know of the thermodynamics of polymers, it won't work. Not the way he wants it to. He hasn't displayed anything particularly grand for some years now. I wonder if he's becoming desperate."

Alvie straightened in her stool and grabbed a piece of plastic from the stack. "Well, Magician Praff, I am ready to learn. I'll help you discover something new. That's the whole reason I chose plastic, you know. The chance to discover."

A smile warmed the Polymaker's face. "Glad to hear it. In that case, let's cover straightening. Then, if that quick mind of yours has space for it, we'll go over the steps for color alteration."

CHAPTER 5

WITH THE CHAUFFEUR BUSY taking Mrs. Praff on errands, Alvie hired an automobile—or a "buggy," though Alvie would always associate that word with a horse and carriage—and had it drop her off at the Woosley Hospital of Special Care a few minutes before nine in the morning. Alvie still hadn't gotten the hang of English currency, but Mrs. Praff had counted out everything for her beforehand, with the stern warning, "And don't let him take anything more. This will cover every mile."

Fortunately, her driver did not demand more than the coin she handed him, so all was well. Alvie was incredibly grateful the Praffs had allowed her to take a buggy, since the train ran past the hospital. She did not want a repeat of her first night in London.

The hospital was a large building; Alvie thought Mg. Praff had said it was an abbey at some point. It was wide and rectangular, with narrow windows embedded in the yellowish brick exterior. She walked up the steps to the building and opened the heavy door leading inside. The room was built of dark wood in need of a coat of polish, but was otherwise clean and well kept. A secretary manned a desk to the left of the entry. There sat a sofa with an exposed frame and a few chairs for waiting to the right. A tall broad-leaved plant squatted in the far corner, where the room opened into a hallway.

"May I help you?" asked the secretary. She looked about the age of Alvie's mama.

"Uh, I'm Alvie Brechenmacher. I'm here to volunteer."

The woman looked down at a book and flipped a few pages. "Oh yes. One moment." She selected another book, this one with paper torn at the bottom. Alvie recognized it—a mimicry communication booklet, made by Folders. The pages were each torn in half, and whoever possessed the other half of the booklet would receive any messages written therein. The secretary turned to a page with a line of writing at the top and crossed it out. Beneath it she wrote, *Volunteer for Nurse Padson has arrived at the front desk.* She waited a second for the ink to dry, then closed the book. Perhaps the other half of that page was tacked to a bulletin board somewhere.

Alvie took a seat on the couch, fiddling with the straps of the small bag that contained her money, her identification, a few plastic beads— just in case—and her key to the polymery. She didn't need a key to the house; there was always a servant ready to answer the door at any given time.

She studied the hem of her pin-striped slacks. She hadn't worn the apprentice's apron today. Mg. Praff had said it wasn't necessary. *"Your time there is about the patients, not about your magic."* Good enough reason.

"Oh, you're Magician Praff's new apprentice?" Alvie looked up as a nurse in a light-blue dress, white apron, and white cap strode into the room with shoes that clacked prettily against the floor, though Alvie thought nice shoes and white aprons were inappropriate for work that involved a lot of standing and blood. She rose without making the comment aloud and extended her hand.

"Yes, I'm Alvie. Here to volunteer. With . . . I'm not sure."

The nurse smiled. She wore faded red lipstick, and her skin was tanner than that of most Englishmen, but Alvie thought it becoming. By appearance, the woman was no more than five years Alvie's senior. The nurse shook her hand and said, "I'm Nurse Padson. It's very good to meet you, Alvie. A German name, yes?"

She nodded.

"Come right this way. We won't have you do anything too intense, don't worry. Except mopping the floor." She laughed. Alvie didn't quite get the joke, but she smiled nonetheless. "A lot of our patients are receiving intensive care or have sustained terrible injuries. What they need more than anything is cheering up. Socialization. That's the best thing you can do."

"Socialize?"

Nurse Padson held open a door to a room with two sinks and shelves full of towels and soap and other amenities. "Yes. And seeing to their comfort. I'll give you a tour so you'll know where we keep bedding, food, water, and the like. We have a small library as well, and our patients borrow books from it. If they make a request, you have permission to retrieve the items for them. There's a limit to snacks, and you can't handle any medication, but most of our patients know that and won't try their luck. Here, wash up to your elbows."

Alvie went to the sink and rolled up her sleeves, washing well. She kept her sleeves rolled after drying off and tied on the white apron Nurse Padson handed her. They proceeded to the tour, as promised. Alvie noted with relief that Woosley Hospital was much smaller and easier to understand than Briar Hall, especially since she was only per- mitted in a small, easy-to-memorize area.

"Try not to disturb sleeping patients." Nurse Padson led Alvie into a large room with a dozen beds, six against each wall. White curtains stretched between them, providing privacy from other patients, but the beds were still exposed to nurses and visitors. "This is the recovery room, where you'll be spending most of your time. Sometimes no one is in need of anything, and it's best to just pace until someone calls for you. There's always laundry to be done and floors to be swept if everything is a little too quiet. Dishes, too."

Alvie nodded, spying between the partitions. One man, who appeared to be sleeping, had a bandage around his head and one of his eyes. The sight made Alvie shiver, but she tried not to show it. She'd requested the hospital, after all. Another man had no visible ailments—though a blanket covered a good bit of his body—and was reading a well-worn book. Alvie couldn't see the title without being obvious. There was a woman with a blond braid whose eyes followed Alvie as she passed, and then another man with bandaging around his neck. An older woman in a smart violet hat and jacket sat on a chair beside him, talking gently.

"Any questions?" asked Nurse Padson.

Alvie paused and turned about, taking in the room. "Only . . . where will you be, if I have one?"

"I'll be in and out of the recovery ward. If it's crucial, and I'm not here, you may go upstairs and speak to a nurse there. At eleven I'll be back in the pantry to help provide lunch. You're welcome to assist."

Alvie's hours were technically over at eleven, but she nodded. "All right. Sounds easy enough."

Nurse Padson offered a smile and strode from the room, her heels clacking as she went.

Alvie walked the rest of the hall. Two more patients sleeping, another reading. One was sitting up in bed, penning a letter. The two at the end had moved their partition and were deep in conversation, laughing over something about Napoleon. Turning around, Alvie retraced her steps, pacing as instructed. At least she'd get some good exercise out of this.

"You're a volunteer?"

Alvie slowed to see the blond woman with the braid. "Yes. It's my first day. Can I help you with something?"

She smiled. Alvie guessed her to be about Nurse Padson's age. She was a little pale and tired looking, but otherwise pretty. "I'm sure I could think of something to need."

"A book?"

She sighed. "Not much up for reading. Hard to hold the book."

She lifted her left arm from the blanket, and Alvie tensed her stomach muscles to keep a gasp of surprise from escaping her. The poor woman's arm ended just below the elbow. Her forearm and hand were gone, replaced by a bundle of off-white bandages.

"Oh dear. I'm terribly sorry," Alvie offered.

She shrugged and rested her arm back against the mattress. "Everyone is."

Seeing a chair near the bedside, Alvie sat upon it. "My name is Alvie."

The woman smiled, just a little, and it warmed Alvie's insides. "Ethel. I like that you wear slacks. I only wear breeches when I'm working, but I have to change into them there. People around here aren't as sensible as they are in the States."

Alvie nodded, remembering that her accent gave away her homeland—something she'd need to get used to. "They're not very popular back home, either." She considered for a moment. "Where do you work?"

"*Did* work," the woman corrected with a small frown. "My father owns a Siping factory. I worked there. I wanted a job, and that was one of the more exciting options."

"Your father is a Siper?"

"Oh no," she laughed. "He just runs the factory that makes supplies for them. Rubber buttons and strings, tires, that sort of thing. I supervised the assembly lines. Got mixed up with a new hire who wasn't practicing the best of safety. Too close to the machine, and . . ." She raised her stump again.

Alvie frowned. "I'm sorry. Was the new hire okay?"

"Yes." She seemed a little relieved at that. "Yes, I heard he was."

"Are you right-handed?"

"Thankfully, yes. But I do love to play, Alvie. The pianoforte, that is. And that needs both hands."

"Oh." Alvie scratched her knee, trying to think of something to say. A few too many seconds passed before the words came. "Well, you'll be better at the piano with one hand than I am with two."

Ethel chuckled. "Not a musician, then."

"Oh no. I don't have the ear for it, or so my mother says. I'm actually apprenticing to be a Polymaker."

"Really?" Ethel pushed herself more upright in bed. "That's exciting. My brother is an apprentice, too."

"Oh? What discipline?"

A masculine voice startled Alvie. "Sorry I'm late, Ethel. I just wanted to—oh, I'm sorry. Am I interrupting?"

Alvie turned in her seat to see a man in a clean white shirt and pressed brown slacks, holding a bouquet of pink carnations under one elbow. His short, straight hair looked like sunshine over the dark brown of his eyes.

Alvie blinked. "You!" She hadn't thought she'd run into him again, knowing he lived in a different area of London. England was much smaller than she'd realized. Her smile was so broad it pinched her cheeks.

Bennet's face softened. "I know you. Euston Station, right? Alice?"

"Alvie," Ethel corrected. "This is my brother, Bennet. The one I was just talking about."

"Folding," Alvie said aloud, answering her own question. Bennet raised an eyebrow. "I mean, that's what I was asking your sister just now. What you did for your discipline. But I already know because you told me. But I didn't, uh, know it was you. Ethel's brother." She swallowed and rubbed the back of her neck. "Younger brother?"

Bennet smiled and stepped around to the other side of the bed, offering his sister the carnations. She took them with her right hand, beaming. "Younger, yes. Ethel here turns twenty-six next month. I'm twenty-two."

"I hope to be out of here by then, but, well, we'll have to see." Her smile faded.

Alvie stood from her chair. "Would you like a vase, Ethel? I can fetch one."

"Oh yes, please. Thank you, Alvie."

Alvie nodded and hurried from the room, slowing her steps so she wouldn't get lost. She remembered where the vases were from her tour and found one, which she filled halfway with water. When she returned, Bennet was still standing, obviously reluctant to take Alvie's seat. Alvie rearranged a few things on a small table by Ethel's head and set the vase down, then snuck by a sleeping patient to borrow the chair at his bedside.

"Here," she said, setting the chair down for Bennet.

He looked surprised. "You didn't have to—"

"I'm a volunteer. It's my job."

She offered a smile, and her stomach fluttered just a little when Bennet smiled back.

"You don't need to leave," Ethel said to her. "I like you. I don't get a lot of female conversation outside of how I'm feeling or my pain level."

The fluttering died. Softly, Alvie asked, "Does it hurt an awful lot?"

Ethel shrugged. "Sometimes. Sometimes I just . . . I feel my hand still there, and it aches, but I can't do anything about it because, well, it's . . . not."

A pained look came over Bennet's face, creasing his forehead. Alvie had the urge to smooth out the lines, but of course that would be silly. Right? Yes, silly.

"The doctor said it will get better with time." Bennet drew his gaze from his sister to Alvie. "It's only been a week."

"Eight days," Ethel said. "They had to cut off more in surgery—oh, Alvie, I'm sorry. You probably don't want to hear that."

"I don't mind at all," Alvie said, "if it's what you want to talk about. It's oddly fascinating, in a way." She blanched. "Oh, I'm sorry. I shouldn't have said—"

Ethel laughed. "No, don't worry about it. Everyone tiptoes around me. Please don't do the same. I suppose it is oddly fascinating. I just wish . . ." She didn't finish the sentence, only looked at the space where her arm and hand should be.

And then it struck.

The idea.

The idea.

Alvie's shoulders tingled, and the sensation spread down her arms and chest, clear to her legs. That was it. The discovery. She didn't know enough to do it, but Mg. Praff did. Was such a thing possible?

"Alvie?" Bennet asked.

"Um. I'm sorry. I need to write something down. But I'll be back soon." The last bit was for Ethel. "You two, uh, have some privacy for a bit."

Should she curtsy? No, this was a hospital. And . . . oh, bother it. It didn't matter!

Alvie scurried from the room, begged some paper from the secretary, and began to draw.

"Magician Praff!" Alvie shouted as she ran from the hired buggy up the drive to the front doors of Briar Hall. She pulled open the heavy door and sprinted through the vestibule, startling the butler, who scowled as she passed. "Magician Praff!"

Mrs. Connway, the housekeeper, ran in from the gallery. "Miss Alvie! What is the matter?"

Alvie danced. She couldn't hold still. "Where is Magician Praff? I must speak to him."

"Well . . . I think I last saw him in the den . . ."

Alvie raced down the main hall, stopped, and turned around. "Where's the den, again?"

Mrs. Connway pointed, and Alvie ran through the halls until she found it. She knocked on the door. No answer. Peeked inside, but the den was empty. Swiping hair from her face and pushing up her glasses, she ran back the way she had come, checking the music room and the salon. Then she sprinted across the Smelted path to the polymery so quickly the shifting spells on the metal tiles could barely keep up with her.

The building was unlocked. She burst in. "Magician Praff!"

"Alvie?" he called from the main lab. Alvie sprinted to the door. He met her there.

"Are you quite all right?" He looked her up and down, concerned.

"I'm perfect! Magician Praff, I have a wonderful idea for the Discovery Convention! I met a woman at the hospital—Ethel Cooper—and she lost an arm in a factory incident."

"Terrible, but—"

"And she plays the piano. You can't play the piano with just one hand. Not well, you see."

"Yes, but—"

"Magician Praff." Alvie grabbed both his elbows and looked hard at his face. "Plastic is light and flexible and can be enchanted. Don't you see? We could make her a prosthetic hand! Something to give her mobility again. Something to help her feel normal, and if the parts move right, and if we can find the right spells, well, it might move just like a real hand. Like that paper skeleton from the magazine!"

Mg. Praff's face was blank.

Alvie shook him. "Well? I can't do it by myself; I don't know enough! I have a rough sketch, some ideas, and—"

"*Alvie.*"

Alvie snapped her mouth shut and, noting that she was still clawing at his arms, quickly dropped her hands to her sides.

Mg. Praff moved stiffly, looking from her, to the lab, to the front door, and back to her. Slowly, *so* slowly, a smile split his face.

"Alvie, you are a *genius*." He hurried past her to the plastic display skeleton against the wall. He grabbed it and hoisted it off the ground, carrying it at an angle back toward the lab. Alvie hurried to the counter of the island, where she shuffled through her bag for her scribbled notes and sketches.

"Prosthetics. I've never even considered prosthetics." Mg. Praff set the skeleton beside the island. "Arms, hands, feet, legs . . . the leg is the simpler construction—"

"Ethel doesn't need a leg."

Mg. Praff made a pointed look at Alvie. "Ethel aside, the leg is a good place to start—"

"The leg is less complex." Alvie walked the length of the lab and back, pointing to her foot. "The ankle, the toe . . . their mechanics are more simple, not like a wrist and fingers. Important, yes, but"—she considered her words—"easier. Not as groundbreaking."

Mg. Praff watched her strides for a moment, then formed his thumb and index finger around his chin. "Yes, you're right. The complexity of a hand and wrist . . . re-creating *that* would be the greater opportunity. That's where science and medicine haven't ventured yet. But"—he looked at the skeleton—"it will take a great deal of work. I have some ideas already. We'll need to form a hand first, unenchanted. Learn more of how it works. Hmm . . . that new Gordon Museum? Maybe? Oh, better yet, the morgue!"

"Morgue?" Alvie repeated, the word heavy on her tongue. Mg. Praff didn't seem to hear her.

He slid Alvie's notes over. They were far simpler than whatever brewed inside his head, she was sure. He nodded. "There is a book," he said, making his way to the stairs in the foyer. He took them two at a time, and Alvie lost her breath trying to keep up. A modest library filled one of the three rooms on the second floor. Mg. Praff studied the shelves for a long moment before reaching for a gray textbook above his head. "This. Here. Read this, specifically the sections on muscle movements, joints, hands, and arms. I believe it's all in there. And then we'll venture out tomorrow morning."

Alvie took the heavy book and read the title: *Anatomy of the Human Body*, volume 1. She'd never been more eager to read. "You'd have me be part of it?"

He looked at her as though she'd grown horns. "Of course you'll be part of it. You're my apprentice. And this was *your* idea, Alvie. I expect many late nights from both of us to stay up to the task. The convention is six months away, and I'd like to present at least a partial sample!"

A shrill squeal erupted from Alvie's throat. She clamped her hand over her mouth, almost dropping her textbook. "Yes, of course," she said through her fingers. "I'll get to reading right now."

"There will be a test."

"I hope so!" Clutching the book to her chest, Alvie hurried back down the stairs and flung open the door to her workroom. She set the anatomy book on the counter and flipped to the table of contents. She remained standing; her blood pumped too quickly for her to sit.

She scanned, found what she wanted, and flipped pages. Adjusted her glasses.

"Chapter four," she read aloud. "'Workings of the Inner Body: Musculature.'"

As promised, she did pull a late night. It would be the first of many, surely.

CHAPTER 6

Mg. Praff had been all seriousness when he'd mentioned the morgue the evening before. He and Alvie left bright and early and drove into the city, just past a large cemetery to a very square building that looked like it was made of giant cubes of concrete. Mg. Praff must have mail-birded or telegrammed ahead, because the mortician was expecting them.

"This is rather unorthodox, but we do have a body donated to science, and the medical students at Oxford didn't seem much interested in the hands." He led them down a staircase to a room lit with Pyre lights as opposed to Gaffer ones. Most Pyre lights were still encased in glass, but the glass didn't have any magical properties. Alvie assumed the morgue used them to allay the chill. The basement was terribly cold.

"If you'll stay with me and answer my questions," Mg. Praff said, "I don't think I'll do any damage."

The mortician gave Alvie and Mg. Praff each a pair of gloves and went to a sort of chest in the wall. He opened it and rolled out a pallet, upon which a body rested beneath a white sheet. Alvie's stomach tightened a little. She'd seen dead bodies before, of course. She'd been to two funerals. But while it was tempting to take this opportunity to study anatomy unhindered, it felt a little . . . unnatural to her.

And the smell wasn't pleasant.

She watched as the mortician uncovered only a pale left hand, explaining how the rigor mortis had subsided. He talked about the working of the joints in the fingers and wrist as Mg. Praff picked up the limb and worked it this way and that, pressing his hands into the knuckles in a way that looked painful. Thus the requirement for a deceased specimen.

When he finished, he asked, "Do you want to see, Alvie?"

To which she answered, "I think the skeleton back home will be sufficient for me, sir."

Gloves off, Mg. Praff wrote several notes and assaulted the mortician with a dozen questions. After that, they were ready to go.

"Fred," Mg. Praff said to the chauffeur once he and Alvie got inside the automobile, "would you stop by the warehouse? I need to pick up a few things before heading home."

Fred nodded and turned the automobile about.

"Warehouse?" Alvie asked.

"The West London Polymer Depository. It houses all the textiles a Polymaker should need for his, or her, experiments." He chuckled. "I only half know what I'm doing, I admit. I want to make sure I have a wide range of plastics to work with to best imitate those knuckles. And it's a good place for an apprentice to visit. At least two future lessons will be held there. They added a new wing a couple years ago, so the building has got quite large."

"Really? Are there many depositories for Polymakers?"

"No, unfortunately. But West London will ship."

It was about thirty minutes to the depository. The place wasn't as large as Alvie had imagined. It had a brick front with several windows—perhaps it had been a factory once—and from its back stretched a much-newer-looking wing with brick that didn't quite match the original. There was even a small paved lot in front of the warehouse for automobile parking, though Fred pulled the automobile up to the doors to minimize their walk.

The whole building was open on the inside, clear to the ceiling, where giant Smelted fans spun of their own volition to manage the temperature. There were enormous shelves stacked with boxes and pallets and drawers and bags. A simple desk sat just inside the door. Behind it, an overweight man with glasses not dissimilar from Alvie's said, "Magician Praff! Come on in, you're cleared. Want the paperwork for this one?" He nodded toward Alvie.

"Not just yet. Thank you, Harry."

The man nodded to Alvie as she passed. To think, if she stayed in London, she might walk into a place like this and have the workers know her by name. As for the paperwork, she assumed she'd need it if she ever came here without a renowned escort.

"The knuckles," Mg. Praff said as they approached the first shelf, "will need to allow extension and flexibility."

"Condyloid joints," she said.

He paused. "I . . . yes, that's what the mortician said. You were listening closely."

"I did read that book, sir."

He raised an eyebrow. "All of it?"

"The section on hands."

He nodded with a smile. "You're proving to be more and more valuable, Alvie."

"It's exciting, sir. To think we could be changing an entire facet of medicine—"

Mg. Praff held his hand up to stop Alvie and said to the space behind her, "Hello, Roscoe. Always a pleasure."

Alvie spun around to see the man from the train approach, a scowl twisting his lip. He looked as though he'd been caught doing something. Eavesdropping?

Alvie pressed her lips shut as if she could trap the words she'd already spoken behind them. This project would stun everyone at the Discovery Convention . . . *if* they managed to keep it secret. Had she said too much?

Mg. Ezzell gave Alvie a dismissive glance before settling hard eyes on her mentor. "Setting your sights for something large, Marion?"

"Just here to show my apprentice the ropes."

"Hmmph. Always coy."

"And you are very light on your feet, if I may say so."

Alvie's gaze darted between the magicians. The room warmed a few degrees. She glanced up to make sure those magicked fans were still spinning.

The magicians were silent as an employee in a blue smock walked by. The moment he stepped out of earshot, Mg. Ezzell jutted his pointer finger toward Mg. Praff and muttered, "Your reign is coming to an end. Thought I'd warn you now, so you can prepare. I'm going to turn that convention on its head and make the world forget about Marion Praff. Your uncle's name will only carry you so far."

Mg. Praff straightened. "If it makes you feel more secure to believe my achievements are merely accolades for Tagis Praff, you are welcome to continue to think so."

Mg. Ezzell turned a bright shade of crimson, but his countenance remained stern. "We'll see, Marion."

He turned on his heel and marched for the door, barking to an employee to bring his items out to the auto. Alvie watched him go.

"What an ornery fellow," she said. "I certainly hope I never have a rival."

Mg. Praff sighed. "As do I. Best to keep our voices down in public, just to be sure." He glanced toward a warehouse worker leaning toward them who, upon being spotted, busied himself arranging boxes on a shelf.

"But I can tell Ethel, yes?"

He smiled. "Of course. We'll need her cooperation."

Her shoulders sagged in relief. "Excellent."

"Now, on with our tour. Over here you'll find vacuum-form-ready sheets . . ."

"But you *can't tell anyone.*" Alvie punctuated the warning with a stiff wag of her finger. She'd nearly burst with anticipation, waiting the four days until her next shift at the hospital. Mg. Praff had kept her so busy she couldn't so much as steal away early for a visit.

Ethel leaned on the elbow of her good arm, staring at Alvie with wide brown eyes—the same color as Bennet's. "You really think it's possible? A magic-fueled arm?"

"I hope so. I don't know all there is to know about Polymaking, of course, but I know a lot about mechanics and how things work. My papa used to let me tinker in his workshop. If nothing else, it will be an advancement on what's available today." Not that Alvie knew what sort of prosthetic arms were currently available. Mg. Praff had assigned himself the task of learning about the "competition." Hopefully he'd bring back samples.

Ethel rested back in her bed. Her eyes glistened, but she didn't cry.

Alvie's throat tightened. Maybe she shouldn't have said anything. What if she couldn't make the arm the way she wanted to make it? What if by telling Ethel her plans, she was getting her hopes up for nothing?

"I think you can do it, Alvie," the injured woman said. A smile touched her lips. "I really do. We don't know each other terribly well, but I see your drive. People with drive do amazing things."

Alvie knotted her fingers together. "I hope you're right, Ethel. For both of us. And Magician Praff, of course."

Ethel chuckled. "I'll keep him in my prayers! All the help you can get, right?"

Footsteps neared the bed, and Alvie turned to see Bennet approaching, this time with a carrier's bag. "Good morning," he said, his grin as bright as his hair. Alvie's heartbeat picked up, and she pressed a hand to the side of her neck as though Bennet would be able to see the pumping of the artery there. "I'm running an errand for Magician Bailey and thought I'd swing by. Alvie, nice to see you."

She nodded. "I didn't even get lost."

He chuckled. "Glad to hear it."

"Bennet, you won't believe what Alvie told me," said Ethel.

Alvie dropped her hand and whirled on the patient. "I said not *anyone*!"

"Bennet is part of this! We can't keep him in the dark." Ethel moved to push herself up in bed, only to teeter to the left. She gripped the mattress with her right hand and lifted up what remained of her left arm. Her countenance fell. "I forget sometimes."

Alvie felt like a puddle on the floor. "I'm sorry. Of course you can tell him. Your family should know."

"Tell me what?" he asked.

Ethel's features brightened just a bit as she told Bennet Alvie and Mg. Praff's plans for the prosthesis in hushed tones. Bennet's lips parted as he listened, and every so often, his eyes darted over to Alvie. He really did have pretty eyelashes. Was it strange to think a man's eyelashes pretty? Best not to say anything about them.

"Really, Alvie?" He focused on her. "You think you could?"

"We're going to try. I've calloused my eyes reading up on anatomy and plastics animations." Mg. Praff was teaching her the basics of animating plastic creations today, something that hadn't been on her original study schedule for another eight months. Bennet kept staring at her, so she added, "I, uh, could probably change its color, too. If you want a green arm. Or pink. Or . . . what's your favorite color, Ethel?"

Ethel laughed, and Bennet broke his gaze. Alvie, unsure what to do, took off her glasses and cleaned them on her blouse.

"Blue, actually." Ethel pushed a lock of hair out of her face. At least, that's what Alvie thought her blur was doing. "Though I don't think I'd like a blue arm."

Alvie pushed her spectacles back over her ears. "Might be fun for, uh, a party?"

"Are those different?"

Alvie shifted her focus to Bennet. "Huh?"

"Your glasses," he said, then chuckled and rubbed the back of his neck. "Are they different from before? I remember at the train station their being . . . well, having a much stronger prescription."

Alvie laughed. "Magician Praff gave me plastic lenses that make me look a little less muscid. Or, uh, bug-eyed. They're much lighter, too."

"Miss?" called a patient from across the aisle. "Miss, could I get some water?"

"Yes! Coming." She stood and brushed off her slacks. These were new ones—deep maroon that gathered about the ankle, so that if Alvie stood with her feet together it *almost* appeared as though she were wearing a skirt. Her mama had sent them through mirror-delivery after Alvie tried and failed to find women's slacks locally. "I'll keep you updated," she said to Ethel and, turning to Bennet, added, "And I warmed up that chair for you."

Bennet laughed, and Alvie silently excused herself to wait on the other patients.

———

A couple of weeks later, Alvie found herself amid ruler-shaped strips of foggy plastic littering the island in the lab. Mg. Praff held one between his fingers and said, "Soften . . . Cease."

The plastic dropped in his hand.

"Now, if this were a Folding spell, so long as the creation is anthropomorphic, a simple Breathe command would be enough to make it come to life." Alvie nodded, but didn't write it down. She wasn't a Folder, after all. "But you can't just create a frog or a fish with plastic and expect it to move. Plastic is too hard, and softening it would ruin the shape of the creature. The creature has to move in parts, and the parts construct the whole." He grabbed the tip of the droopy plastic—Alvie noted that he'd only softened the center—and moved it back and forth. "Memory," he said, then, releasing the end, added, "Breathe."

The plastic moved on its own, exactly the way Mg. Praff had directed it.

"Fascinating." Alvie reached forward, and Mg. Praff handed her the bobbing plastic.

"This works best for joints. I'll instruct you on how to form a ball joint tomorrow, but I want you to practice this first. We're jumping around a bit, and I don't want to risk your education for the sake of innovation. Questions?"

Alvie glanced at her notes. "I think I've got it." Focusing on the bending plastic in her hand, she said, "Cease," and it stilled, returning to its solemn, droopy form.

"Excellent." Mg. Praff stood and tucked his stool close to the island. "Now, come this way, and I'll explain how this portion of the lab works." He moved to the counter that boasted a great deal of chemistry equipment. "This is for the creation and purification of plastic—it's easier to buy the plastic premade, of course, but oftentimes a Polymaker needs certain specifications in his—or her—materials, and it's quicker to do it yourself than to special order it and hope someone else gets it right. Now, this"—he gestured to a tall beaker—"is called a—"

A knock on the open lab door directed their attention away from the equipment. Mr. Hemsley, the butler, stood erect and proper with his hands clasped behind his back and his nose turned slightly up.

"Beg your pardon for the interruption, Magician Praff, but there's a visitor here for Miss Brechenmacher."

"Me?" Alvie asked. Who on earth would be visiting her?

A chill coursed up her spine as her brain whirled through the possibilities. Had she unknowingly snubbed a buggy driver? Or worse, could it be Mg. Aviosky? Perhaps she'd erred in sharing her studies with the Coopers and someone had overheard her at the hospital and reported her . . .

"Alvie?" Mg. Praff tapped her shoulder.

"Uh." Alvie looked from her mentor to the butler. "Who is it, exactly?"

"Young man, said his name was Bennet Cooper."

Alvie dropped her notepad. She stooped down to snatch it up and bumped her hip into Mg. Praff, who, in turn, hit a flask with his elbow, knocking it over. Alvie blurted a string of apologies as she retreated, tucking her notes under her arm.

Bennet Cooper? Here? To see *her*? Whatever for? Was he upset about her getting his sister's hopes up? Did he wish to see the work for himself? She didn't have anything to show him, not yet . . .

"M-May I go? I'm sure it will be quick," she said, trying to smooth her hair.

Mg. Praff nodded. "Yes, go ahead. There's something I wish to examine, besides. Hemsley, you'll escort her?"

"Of course."

Mr. Hemsley departed without so much as a glance at Alvie. She hurried after him, pausing only to set her notes in her own workroom. The butler waited at the exit and, with a sniff in the general direction of her wardrobe, opened the door for Alvie.

Alvie had the distinct impression that Mr. Hemsley did not like her, though she couldn't fathom why. Perhaps because she took so many meals out in the polymery and that made him go out of his way. Or perhaps it was simply because she wore slacks. That seemed like such a silly reason to dislike a person, but no one looked at her legs as much as Mr. Hemsley did, so it was a viable option. All the same, with the weather starting to cool, she preferred slacks to skirts more than ever.

Alvie's mind couldn't stay on Mr. Hemsley, however, nor on the magicked path shifting about her feet as she followed the butler to the house. Her thoughts bounced between Bennet Cooper and his reason for being here. Bennet Cooper and his poor sister in the hospital. Bennet Cooper and his sunshine hair and smiling eyes.

She adjusted her glasses as Mr. Hemsley led her to a set of stairs.

"Where is he?" she asked.

"The sitting room. That is where we receive guests."

"Oh." She vaguely recalled where it was. A room just for sitting seemed excessive. Then again, Briar Hall was excessive.

The butler stopped at a door and opened it, then kept it open with the heel of his foot. Alvie started to follow after him, only to have herself announced. "Miss Brechenmacher." Mr. Hemsley gave her a hard glance. Was she supposed to wait to be announced before coming in?

She tripped over the toe of Mr. Hemsley's well-polished shoes. Quickly straightened. Pushed up her glasses.

The sitting room had been on Alvie's tour, of course, but she hadn't returned to it since. Its walls were made of polished wood carved into squares like some cherry checkerboard, except at the very top, where there was some enormous ivory-colored wainscoting, so elaborately carved Alvie couldn't tell what the designs were supposed to be. There were two fireplaces—two!—and Indian-looking carpets beneath an array of furniture made for sitting. Thus the name of the room.

Bennet was indeed within the sitting room and had selected a forest-green chair to sit in, though he stood when Alvie entered. Had he seen her trip? Probably.

The door shut behind her, giving her a start. Mr. Hemsley had departed. The sitting room suddenly looked rather large.

"Um, hi," she said, tucking waves of hair behind her ears. The locks popped back out again. Any space behind her ears was taken up by the arms of her glasses. Her heart beat a little too fast, and she tried to shush it, but her body didn't obey her the way plastic or machines did. Bother.

"Forgive me for not writing ahead," he said, wringing the edge of a hat in his hands. She'd never seen him wear a hat. Why would someone with hair as cheerful as his ever want to cover it with a hat? She almost said as much, but Bennet continued, "I knew you studied under Praff, so it wasn't hard to find you. Though I could have sent a bird."

A mail bird, he meant. Folders could Fold paper into all sorts of creatures and send them off into the world. Complex spells, those mail birds, but useless in bad weather.

"Oh no, it's no trouble." To be honest, when she went to the hospital for her volunteer hours and Bennet wasn't there, she was disappointed. Not that Ethel wasn't pleasant company. Quite the opposite. She was probably the best friend Alvie had in London so far, and they hardly knew each other. The thought made Alvie a little homesick. She'd left twenty years' worth of socializing behind her. Now she had to start anew without the excuse of school or neighborhood parties to prompt mingling.

Bennet smiled. "I'm glad."

"I mean, wouldn't it be a bother for you? It's out of the way. You must really like trains."

Bennet laughed. "I don't mind them, though I came in my mentor's auto."

"Really?" Alvie perked up like a tulip in the morning sun. "You drive?"

"I do."

She took several steps forward, closing the yawning gap between them. "What sort of auto does he have?"

"He owns a couple; I brought the Benz."

"A *Benz?*" Alvie clapped her hands together. "Really? Here?"

His hands loosened on his hat. "Outside, yes."

Her muscles grew antsy. "Oh, Bennet, could I see it? Would you mind terribly?"

He grinned. "Not at all. Lead the way—I'm not sure I remember how to get back to the drive."

Alvie resisted jumping with glee and hurried from the sitting room, Bennet behind her. She found the stairs and took them down to the main hall.

"Does Magician Bailey have a large house? That was his name, right?" she asked as they moved toward the vestibule.

"He does, yes. More modern in design, fewer servants. He's strange that way."

Alvie glanced to his face. She liked his profile. "Is he nice?"

Bennet snorted. "He's very . . . competent."

That was an evasion if Alvie had ever heard one. She dropped the subject.

Sure enough, a 1901 Benz sat out on the drive, beautifully framed by a background of yellowing autumn trees. It was white, with a covered engine and sleek fenders and a leather—no, that was Sipered rubber—top that lay over the back like an accordion. A built-in spell would bring up the roof in case of rain. It boasted leather covers on the steering wheel and clutch. All the exposed metal was polished, even the spark and throttle lever rods.

Alvie approached it slowly and touched the Gaffer headlamps. "This . . . is the most beautiful automobile I've ever seen."

"Would you like a ride?"

"I'd like to see the engine!" She whirled around. "May I see the engine?" The engine was in the front rather than the back. Intriguing.

He hesitated a moment. "Sure."

Alvie squealed. Bennet moved to lift the hood, but Alvie knew where the latch was and did it herself. A marvel of machinery winked back at her. The radiator was the smallest she'd ever seen in an automobile. It and the fan were pushed against the front, above the breather pipe and commutator. The pipes, the crankcases, the combustion chamber—they were all set up for optimum efficiency. And none of it was enchanted. Pure technology.

She leaned over the radiator filler flange and pushed her hands into the engine, feeling for the carburetor.

"Don't take this the wrong way," she began, wiggling her hands free and finding footing on the ground, "but I'd love to see this thing strewn out on the lawn."

"What?"

"It's like a puzzle. Take it apart, put it back together."

"Ah." Bennet nodded. "I understand the sentiment, though I have a feeling your expertise surpasses my own. You surprise me, Alvie. Oh dear, your hands."

Alvie glanced down. Smears of black and brown covered her fingers and one of her wrists. She crouched and wiped them on the grass just as Bennet fetched a handkerchief.

"Oh, sorry." She lifted her hands up. Clean enough. "That wasn't very ladylike of me."

He laughed. "I don't mind."

"But I would enjoy a drive. See how she works." Her thoughts spun with automobile organs. Her papa would be so jealous when she told him.

"Of course. Though I did come here with a purpose, Alvie."

She blinked. Stepped away from the automobile as though it had transformed into a giant spider. "Oh, I'm so sorry. I didn't even ask after that. You see, I don't have anything solid to show you for Ethel yet, but when we do, there will have to be a fitting, and I'll—"

"You're kind to think of her, really." Bennet was wringing his hat again. He'd ruin it, doing that. "But I'm not here on behalf of Ethel. You see . . ." His neck reddened just a bit, which was funny, since it was a cool day. The sky was more cloud than blue, as it often was in

England. "Well, I was wondering if you'd like to spend an afternoon at Green Park with me tomorrow. A picnic of sorts. I can even take you in this, if you'd like."

He gestured to the automobile, but Alvie's gaze was vacuum-formed to his face. She knew her mouth was gaping, but she couldn't seem to close it.

Was Bennet Cooper asking her . . . on a *date*?

No one asked Alvie on dates. Boys didn't spend time with her unless they needed something fixed or help with schoolwork. Men only looked at her legs if they were disapproving her choice of clothing.

Bennet shifted the hat behind his back. "That is, only if you'd like. I'm being forward, I know, and I understand if you'd prefer to keep this, well, on a more acquaintance level—"

"Oh. No. I mean, yes. I mean, yes to the park and no to the acquaintance level." Her words spilled out like overcooked noodles. "I would really like to go to the park. With you. And the Benz. But not just because of the Benz . . ."

Bennet laughed. His shoulders relaxed, and the hat reappeared. "Well, that's a relief. I can stop by at three o'clock?"

Alvie locked her now-jittery fingers together. "Oh, I have a lesson at three. But I could cancel it—"

Bennet raised a hand to stop her. "I don't want to interrupt your studies."

"What about your studies?"

He laughed. "Magician Bailey schedules my studies out a month in advance; I know exactly when I'll have free time. It's mostly review right now."

"Oh! Because you're testing soon!"

"Or so I hope." He smiled. "How about we make it an evening venture. Six?"

A grin pulled on Alvie's lips. "Yes. That sounds perfect."

Bennet put his cap back on. "Do you still want a ride?"

"Oh yes!" She scrambled for the automobile. It was wide enough for two in the front and had a second set of seats in the back. She itched for the driver's seat, but perhaps it was better—and politer—to let Bennet demonstrate first.

He cranked the automobile and released the brake before getting in, then pulled levers and pushed pedals to start the engine. Alvie imagined all the parts working together, the oil and fuel pumping through, the carburetor mixing in the . . .

The . . .

That was it. A pump. Air or liquid, but it would move the fingers, wouldn't it? Was there a spell that would work like a pump, or a carburetor, to add function to the prosthesis? Make it more like a real hand?

"Here we—"

"Wait!"

Bennet pushed down the brake pedal and looked at her.

"I just had a wild idea!" She leapt up from the seat. "I have to go!"

"But—"

"It's for Ethel! I believe I know how to make her hand work! Tomorrow at six, yes?"

His features softened. "Yes. And you'll have to tell me what's got you so excited."

"I will. I will. But I have to figure it out . . . diagram, but Magician Praff—"

He chuckled. "Go, Alvie."

She waved her thanks with both hands and leapt from the automobile, running through the main hall toward the polymery. She needed to research her idea before presenting it to Mg. Praff . . . but if it could work, they would be one *big* step closer to helping Ethel.

And that much closer to prevailing at the Discovery Convention.

CHAPTER 7

ALVIE PRESSED A RULER against the parchment on her desk the next morning, slowly tracing its edge with the point of her pencil. Such was her concentration on that line that when Mg. Praff knocked on the door, Alvie jumped and nearly rammed the pencil butt right into her eye. Fortunately, her Polymade glasses protected her from anything more than a smudge.

"Alvie?" the magician called, cracking the door open. "We had a lesson scheduled for ten thirty . . . What on earth are you up to in here?"

Straightening in her chair—her back popping once in protest—Alvie tried to see her workroom through Mg. Praff's eyes. The over-flowing waste bin and crumpled paper littering the floor, the pencil shavings dusting the counter between uncapped pens, the left hand of the skeleton that she may or may not have wrenched from its display late last night.

"Um." She wiped her sleeve over the smudge on her glasses. "Is it past ten thirty?"

"It's eleven . . ." Mg. Praff stepped into the workroom. A balled-up piece of paper crunched under his foot. He picked it up. "What is all of this?"

Alvie smiled. She couldn't help it. "I've discovered a missing piece of the puzzle, sir. It's the carburetor."

"The what?"

She turned back to her drawing, frowning at the slipped mark of her pencil. Lining up the ruler, she finished her line, then made two more. Mg. Praff waited by the door. Finished, she handed the not-quite-complete sketch to him. "I was looking at the engine of an automobile yesterday. A Benz! That Bennet Cooper who came to see me—did I mention he's Ethel's brother? Also a Folder. Or, almost. Anyway, he came by in a Benz and let me look at it, and it's a fantastic piece of machinery—well kept, pure—"

"Alvie."

"Oh. Uh, but I saw the carburetor, and it gave me an idea. You know how carburetors work, don't you, Magician Praff?"

His eyes lit up. "Yes. Yes, I do." He studied Alvie's sketch again.

"What if we could use the same principles in this prosthesis? I'm trying to draw hollow chambers, like straws, that run up the forearm and into the fingers, though I'm not sure how to best implement them in the knuckles. I wanted to figure that out first. But if we could use pressurized liquid or air—"

"To open and close the fingers," Mg. Praff finished for her. He rubbed his chin. "That . . . yes, that would be something, wouldn't it? But to create a motor like that, so small . . . and we couldn't connect it to the nerves of the arm. Such a feat is beyond magic and technology. But perhaps there's a way around it. Perhaps we could pressurize liquid polyethylene. An enchantment . . . this requires a great deal of experimentation!"

Alvie jumped from her chair. "You think it might work?"

"I think we'll need lunch brought to the polymery." The Polymaker grinned. "I ought to send that Magician Jefferson a bouquet of roses for delivering you here, Alvie. You're exactly the spark this place needs!"

Alvie warmed. "Th-Thank you, sir." Thoughts of lunch naturally led to thoughts of dinner, which sent her heart fluttering. Tonight was her picnic with Bennet. She still couldn't fathom it. A man—and a man as stunning and kind as Bennet Cooper—wanted to spend time with her. It *was* a date, wasn't it? What if she was mistaken? But how could one mistake an invitation to a picnic?

Should she wear a skirt?

Mg. Praff had said something to her that she missed and left the room. Alvie was grateful for his excitement and the opportunity to explore this new path toward an operational prosthesis. It kept her mind off things she couldn't quite understand—or might not dare to believe.

Alvie came to the lab, where Mg. Praff was going through drawers. He lifted a sack full of pale plastic beads, which he dumped onto the island counter. Several fell to the floor, but he didn't seem to notice.

"I'm going to show you some shaping techniques, Alvie. Very similar to vacuum-forming. Melt, Soften—no, I didn't mean you!" A bead had melted in his hands, thinking the command for itself. Mg. Praff ordered it to harden again and tossed it into the sink in the corner of the lab.

Taking one of the model skeletal hands he'd been creating over the last week, the Polymaker made several measurements and then constructed a tube that would fit within the confines of an average adult hand. It looked something like a very skinny test tube with a flat bottom. Alvie watched, mesmerized. She'd never seen Mg. Praff work so quickly before. Would she be able to move like that in years to come? To craft and bend plastic the way he did, without a second thought, without checking her notes? He used some commands she didn't understand. She itched to learn them.

"Unyielding," Mg. Praff said to the long, narrow cylinder. He looked at Alvie. "That will keep this mold from heeding the commands you give to the plastic you work around it. Think of it as a spell to make a mold incredibly stubborn. Only a Yield command, said while moving your fingers along the shape, will break that spell."

Alvie nodded, repeating the instruction three times in her head; she hadn't brought her notebook with her and didn't wish to slow Mg. Praff's work.

Mg. Praff went on to show her how to form the plastic to the mold, creating a long, thin straw. Thinness was important, but the shapes couldn't be too thin, either. They would determine the exact measurements later. A Flex spell made the finished product malleable without softening the plastic.

"Make these. Make many of these. I'll work on creating a hollow version of this." He held up the model arm and hand.

"Yes, sir!" Alvie pulled her chair up and got to work. She botched her first attempt, but her second was usable, and her third and fourth better than that. She got a little quicker with each one. A good thing, as Mg. Praff frequently grabbed a straw from her pile and used it with the plastic fingers he was molding, often cursing under his breath before discarding the thing and grabbing another. He seemed to utter only English curses, and thus Alvie didn't mind the language at all. She still didn't quite grasp why it was so awful for something to be bloody.

Lunch was served in the polymery by Mr. Hemsley, who was mostly ignored by both Alvie and her mentor. The food itself went untouched until the bread for the sandwiches was nearly stale, and then Alvie or Mg. Praff would take a bite between measurements and melting. Alvie moved from making straws to studying *A Glossary of Polymaking Spells through 1904*, hoping that perhaps she'd find something useful. She did write down a few potential spells, one of which she then heard Mg. Praff utter under his breath. She crossed it off her list.

"Aha! Alvie, come wear this. Quickly."

Alvie hurried to her mentor's side, only to have him shove a rounded, hollow forearm and hand over her own. He positioned her fingers with her thumb, forefinger, and middle finger straight, and her ring and pinky fingers curled in. She held the position for a very long time while he molded the plastic around her. Then he pulled the thing off and stuck it full of straws. Alvie hurried back to the cylinder mold to make more. Watching Mg. Praff work, she started adding rivets along the straws. They were flexible, yes, but this would allow them to bend more without cutting off the flow. Mg. Praff must have approved, for when he started using them, he didn't complain.

"Pressure. Pressurize. Push. Hmmmm." The Polymaker had a beaker full of melted plastic and a syringe he used to push it through the straws. "There's got to be a spell here we're not finding. Alvie, go upstairs and find me a thesaurus!"

"Yes, sir!" Alvie hurried out of the lab and made her way up to the library, which she had become well acquainted with over nearly a month of training. She found a thesaurus on the far wall and hurried back down to the lab, only to see Mr. Hemsley walking in with another tray of food.

Alvie froze halfway down the stairs. Her eyes shot to one of the plastic domed windows. "Hemsley!" she cried, racing down the stairs. "Hemsley, what time is it?"

Hemsley sighed. "When I left the kitchen, I believe it was five minutes to seven."

Alvie felt all the pigment drain out of her body. She rushed over to the butler and grabbed his sleeve, nearly toppling over the dinner tray. "Bennet! Did Bennet come? Is he here? He was supposed to be—"

"Miss Brechenmacher." Her name was sharp and hard on Mr. Hemsley's lips. He jerked his arm free of her grasp. "I came to the lab over an hour ago to announce your guest, and you ignored me." He sniffed. "Both of you did, so I returned to my usual routine."

Now Alvie's stomach plummeted to the floor. "Y-You did? I didn't hear . . ."

"No, you didn't. You're quite good at ignoring the spoken word. If you'll excuse me, it's my duty to see that Magician Praff does not starve." He pushed by her, taking his tray to the lab.

Alvie was still as a church on Monday for a long moment. Then, dropping the thesaurus, she ran from the polymery.

The cool evening air swirled around her as she bolted down the path, making a mess of her hair. She burst into the house, startling a maid, and cut through the music room, the main hall, the vestibule. She stumbled down the front steps to the drive, the brilliant colors of a sunset greeting her.

There was no automobile. No sign of him. He'd already left.

Alvie dropped to her knees. If only she hadn't been so absorbed in her work. If only she'd paid attention to her clock. If only she could have escaped the confines of her own head long enough to hear Mr. Hemsley's announcement!

She grabbed the thick rim of her glasses and pulled them off, not wanting to smear the lenses with tears. She breathed deeply and gritted her teeth, but a few drops still squeezed out.

Stupid, stupid girl. What must he think of her? He came all this way yesterday just to ask . . . and she had ignored him to make plastic straws. No wonder no one ever wanted to date her—she was impossible. Her chest hurt in a peculiar and awful way. She rubbed the edge of her sleeve over her eyes.

What if Bennet told Ethel—and they were so close, Alvie was sure he would—and she didn't want Alvie's company anymore? She had finally started to make friends in this place halfway across the world, and she'd ruined it. Maybe even ruined something more. All to make some straws that easily could have been made tomorrow.

Oh, how Alvie ached for her easy, familiar life in Columbus. How badly she wanted to fall through a mirror and appear in her own bed, far away from this ache. Any desire for creation and the lab had fled her entirely.

She sat there on the edge of the drive for a long time, watching the sun set until clouds settled over the waning light and cold nipped at her nose and her fingers. Then she picked herself up off the bricks and turned back for the house.

For the first time since arriving in London, Alvie went to bed early.

CHAPTER 8

SHE STILL WOKE EARLY. However, instead of heading out to the polymery, Alvie asked Fred to take her into town. She'd requested permission from Mrs. Praff since Mg. Praff was *still* working in the lab. An
apology to her mentor would be in order when she got back, but there
was another apology she owed first. She wrung her hands the entire way
to the post office. It was a small comfort that she rode in the back of the
automobile, where the chauffeur wouldn't see her.

She could go to the house, she was sure. The Bailey house, that was.
Look him up the same way Bennet had looked up Mg. Praff's residence.
But the thought of trekking up, uninvited, to another giant mansion
to seek an audience with a person who very rightly didn't want to see
her made Alvie's skin burn. And Bennet had mentioned having a strict
schedule. What if she interrupted? What if she made it *worse*? Besides,
Alvie wasn't the most eloquent person with words. She needed to think
them out in order to get them right . . . which was precisely why this
slightly more cowardly plan she'd developed would work. Hopefully.

Alvie had decided to go to the post office and use her stipend to
buy every single mail bird they had in stock. She would figure out the
eloquent words, gush her sorrys, and send them all dancing into the

sky. It would be a grand spectacle, and Bennet was a Folder, wasn't he? He liked paper. With luck, he would be charmed into forgiving her.

At least, that's how it played out in her head.

Fred pulled the automobile up to the post office, which was a bit larger than Alvie had anticipated, and quite a bit busier. She stepped inside and saw a short line at the front. The side wall boasted a large bulletin board covered in cards offering services, fliers for lost persons or pets, and advertisements for various wares. There were also cubbies along the wall for those who liked to pick up their mail, Alvie supposed, and a shelf that had paper, pens, boxes, and the like for sale. Alvie didn't see any mail birds on it; they must have been special order.

Wringing her hands, Alvie inched around the post office until she found a thick book to the left of the front desk. The word "Addresses" was typed across the front, and beneath those bold letters were the words "Sort: (By Name)." This was an enchanted book, then. Good, that would make things easier.

Alvie touched the cover of the book and said, "Sort: Bailey."

The book popped open as though by invisible hands, the pages shuffling until parting on a page in the B section. Alvie frowned. There were a good deal of Baileys listed. What was Bennet's mentor's first name, again?

Chewing on her lip, Alvie closed the book. Considered the conundrum. Said, "Sort: Folders."

There were much fewer of those.

The book opened to a section closer to the back, labeled "Magicians." The section for Folding took up one-third of a column. Mg. Pritwin Bailey's name sat at the top.

Sighing in relief, Alvie pulled a pencil and her ledger from her bag, jotted down the address, and joined the line stemming from the front desk. She bounced on her toes, trying to think of sincere things to say. Or perhaps clever. People liked clever things. Alvie was terrible at jokes, though. Could she think of something clever that wasn't a joke?

Was there even space on a mail bird to write out a joke? The jokes she knew—the ones her papa told—were very long, and often didn't seem like jokes until he got to the end—

"Miss?"

Alvie blinked and glanced up at the postal worker behind the desk. He resembled Mg. Jefferson, sans mustache.

"Oh, sorry." She closed the gap between herself and the desk. "I need to buy mail birds. A lot of mail birds. How many do you have?" *And will you help me count out the money for them?* For all her credits in math, she still hadn't memorized the conversion rate of dollars to pounds.

"I'm sorry, lass," the worker said. "We're fresh out of birds. But letters work just as well."

Alvie's skeleton seemed to crinkle in on itself, making her feel a great deal shorter. "All out? You're sure?" She couldn't make a grand magical gesture with envelopes. And mail delivered in person took longer to arrive . . . she couldn't let Bennet go days thinking she'd snubbed him!

The worker tilted his head to the side and offered an apologetic smile beneath his mustache. "I'm afraid so . . . ah, wait! Looks like we're in luck. Morning to you, Magician Thane."

Alvie spun around just in time to see a woman reply, "Good morning, Marcus." She was a couple inches shorter than Alvie and had vivid orange hair pulled back into a French twist. She didn't *look* like a magician, though Alvie supposed magicians didn't have a particular look. She did, however, appear ready to burst at the middle. The woman had to be a full nine months pregnant.

She held a sizeable parcel resting atop her round belly. Marcus, the postal worker, readied to come around the desk, so Alvie said, "Here, let me," and took the parcel from her. It was astonishingly light. She set it on the desk, and Marcus pulled a small knife from his pocket to cut the strings.

"Magician Thane here delivers our mail birds," he explained. "So looks like I'll have some after all."

Alvie's skeleton straightened itself out. "Really? Can I buy all of them?"

Marcus paused in his cutting and eyed her. Beside her, the small, round Mg. Thane laughed.

"Here," she said, taking Alvie's elbow. "The line is getting long, and I can tell you're not from around here. I've got paper in my bag; I'll make you some for free."

Alvie's glasses slid a millimeter down her nose, but she hesitated to correct them. "Are you sure? I can pay for—"

"All one hundred I just brought? And then they'll be out again!" She smiled. "I don't mind. Come this way."

Alvie eyed the woman's stomach but obliged, letting Mg. Thane pull her away from the line and over to a bench. The Folder settled down a little lopsidedly, then let out a long breath and rested a hand on her stomach. Looking at Alvie, she said, "Mind grabbing that table? I've run out of lap space for Folding."

Alvie looked across the way and saw a short table near the shelves of supplies for sale. She quickly crossed over to it and grabbed its sides. It was much heavier than it looked, and when Alvie dragged it, its feet scraped loudly against the stony tiles of the post office floor. But the Folder needed a table, and Alvie needed a grand gesture, so she kept tugging that screeching table across the room to the bench, trying to ignore the looks that followed her and the two children who covered their ears and wailed to their mother. Alvie couldn't hear their exact complaints over the table's screeching.

Mg. Thane looked a little surprised when Alvie finally reached her—she wasn't sure why—but the smile returned. "So you need a great number of mail birds. They don't fare well across the ocean, unfortunately."

"Oh. No. I'm not writing home." Alvie plopped down beside her. "I'm writing to someone in town. Well, close to town." She pulled out the address and showed it to the Folder. "I got caught up in my own head, you see, and I may have missed, uh, well, a date, and I just feel horrible about it, and I thought, well, since he's a Folder, maybe he'd appreciate . . . Folding?" Mg. Thane had an interesting look on her face, to say the least, so Alvie added, "Unless you think that's a silly idea."

"Oh no, not at all. It's just, well, I know this residence. I wouldn't have thought Magician Bailey the dating type, is all! You must have really—"

"Oh. Oh no. It's for his apprentice. His name is Bennet Cooper. I'll be sure to address them all to him." Alvie paled at the thought of her grand gesture going to the wrong person. *Oh, hello, Bennet. Not only did I forget about your dinner, but I'm apparently crazy for your mentor. La-di-da, something British.*

A strange knowing smile spread on Mg. Thane's face. "That makes more sense. Let's see." She pulled a short stack of square papers from her bag. Half were white, the rest multicolored—orange, yellow, pink, green. "I can do four types of birds, as well as a butterfly. Those are the standards, at least."

"All of it, if you can. I was thinking . . . twenty?"

Mg. Thane nodded and reached into her bag.

"I can pay you—"

"Oh, hush, I don't need it. I'm all for the furthering of romance." She smiled and handed a stack of roughly twenty papers to Alvie. "Start writing, and I'll Fold them after."

Alvie nodded. "Thank you. Really." She took out her pencil and wrote the first thing that came to her head. *Bennet, I'm so sorry I missed you yesterday. I had truly looked forward to the evening. My head got caught up in the polymery, and I missed the hour. Please forgive me.*

She took up another sheet. *I'm so very, very sorry!*

And another. *I will swear off magic until Christmas if you'll forgive me. Oh, this is Alvie, by the way.*

Alvie glanced up to Mg. Thane. Her hands worked deftly, carefully lining up the sides of the paper and creasing the edges, forming wings and a tail. Alvie marveled as she formed a songbird, then a crane, then a butterfly. How different this magic was from her own!

Folding was one of the oldest forms of magic. How many spells did it have, while Polymaking was still so new, so untried?

Alvie grabbed another paper, and another, scrawling apologies across them all. On one she drew a picture of herself looking sad. Was that silly? But she didn't want to waste Mg. Thane's paper or her generosity, so she handed it over. Mg. Thane chuckled when she Folded that one.

"All right," the orange-haired woman said once she'd finished. Folded creations filled the table and the stretch of bench between them. "I've included the spells already, so all you have to do is say, 'Breathe,' and then recite the address. Write Bennet's name on the wings first, though."

Alvie nodded. "I will. Oh, thank you, so very much. I really—"

A man's voice interrupted her. "'Just a moment,' she said. 'I'm only dropping it off,' she said."

Alvie glanced up to see a man standing a few feet in from the entrance, his arms folded across his chest. He looked to be in his thirties, with wavy black hair that couldn't decide if it wanted to be short or long. He wore an unusual indigo coat.

"I stumbled upon a friend of Bennet's," Mg. Thane said, grabbing the edge of the bench and hauling herself to her feet. "She needed mail birds."

The man smiled, though the expression enlivened his eyes more than it did his mouth. "Is that not what was in the box?" He eyed the mess on the bench.

Alvie said, "It's for a grand gesture."

The man nodded and let his arms fall to his sides. "Ah. I am not one to stand in the way of a grand gesture." He offered his elbow to Mg. Thane. "If you're ready, love."

Mg. Thane smiled and took the man's arm. Turning back to Alvie, she said, "Good luck!" and departed out the door.

Alvie watched the couple go, then turned back to the spells scattered around her. How incredibly fortunate she had been to run into a Folder at the post office! Since the table was already here, Alvie went ahead and scrawled Bennet's name on all the mail birds' and butterflies' wings, then scooped them into her bag, careful not to crush them. She then got back in line and took out a few pence from her wallet.

When she reached Marcus, he said, "Anything else, miss?"

"Just one of the mail birds, if you don't mind."

He fished behind his counter and offered her three styles of bird. She selected the crane and handed him nine coins; he returned one.

Thanking him, Alvie sidestepped to the address book and again looked up Folders. She found two listings under Thane, but both resided at the same address. "Unfold," she told the pre-enchanted spell, and the spell opened to a heavily creased square. Upon it, Alvie wrote, *Thank you for your help at the post office. —Alvie Brechenmacher.*

She commanded the bird, "Refold," and watched its edges and creases crinkle and warp until its body was restored. Alvie hurried outside, not wanting to make Fred wait too long. Finding a spot down the street where there were fewer people, she dumped all of Bennet's mail things on the ground and said, "Breathe."

To her delight, every single creature animated, coming to life as though they were flesh and blood. Birds hopped over the cobblestones, and butterflies fluttered around her crown.

Alvie recited the address, and the small army of spells took to the sky, heading west in unison. Grinning, Alvie shielded her eyes and watched them go. She pulled out the purchased bird and was about to send it off to Mg. Thane when a man said, "Miss Brechenmacher, just who I wanted to see."

Gooseflesh rose on her arms, and she turned quickly enough that her glasses slid down her nose. She shoved them back up and took in Mg. Ezzell walking toward her on the pavement. He was well dressed, expensively so, and had a tailored coat buttoned around his waist. He hid his hands in its pockets.

Her stomach squirmed. She glanced behind him, spotting a man and woman walking arm in arm on the pavement, but they were moving away, not toward. A boy rode past on horseback, eyes glued to the road. "I was just leaving." She tucked the mail bird under her arm and turned away from the Polymaker, heading back toward the post office and Fred.

"Wait, wait, no need for rudeness." Mg. Ezzell picked up his pace and circled around her, blocking her path. "Has your mentor painted me so foully that you won't even say hello?"

"Magician Praff doesn't talk about you."

It happened again—the tightness around his eyes, just like on the train. She was very certain now that he had knowingly sent her to the wrong stop, and he had no doubt taken pleasure in it.

He smiled. It looked almost feral. Forced. "Oh, I'm glad to hear it. Tell me, what does Praff say?"

He put a hand on her shoulder. She shook it off. "Nothing of consequence. My driver is waiting for me." An automobile engine sounded in the distance, then faded.

"Listen, dear." He leaned in and lowered his voice. "What would you like, hm? Just for a few whispers of what goes on in that polymery. Money? Name your price." He pulled out a wallet stuffed with bills and began counting them.

Alvie made a noise of disgust—a noise her mama hated—and stepped around him, charging up the street. Someone crossed the road ahead of her, glanced her way, and disappeared into the post office.

Maybe she should have called out to him. But what would she say? *Help! This man is trying to have a conversation with me, and I don't like it!*

Mg. Ezzell caught up and walked beside her. She contemplated shoving him into the ornamental bushes lining the walk, but she didn't exactly excel in upper-body strength. "Not money? How about a copy of the Polymaker's test?"

She stopped. He continued half a step before halting.

Gritting her teeth, she said, "I'm not telling you anything. I'm not going to associate with you. Please leave." Her heart was beating faster now, and her hands were cool and moist. She gripped the strap of her bag until her knuckles whitened. Part of her wanted to swing it into the side of the Polymaker's head. Another part of her wanted to run away and hide behind the shrubbery.

A scowl devoured the false smile. "Listen, you little—"

"I will scream."

He said nothing more, only raised both hands as if in surrender. A young man was coming down the walk behind him, and an automobile had just passed them on the road. Alvie wondered if Mg. Ezzell felt the eyes of passersby. The last thing a prestigious magician would want was a record.

He nodded. "Good day." And with that, he pushed past her, bumping his shoulder into hers. She turned and watched him go, waiting until he was a safe distance before running up the street and around the corner to where Fred waited. She opened the door and jumped into the automobile before he could even stir from his seat. "Let's go," she said. "Please."

He nodded and started the engine.

Reaching her hand out the window, Alvie set the mail bird for Mg. Thane free, watching it spiral skyward until the driver pulled away.

CHAPTER 9

THE HARDWOOD FLOOR PROMISED bruises as it dug into Alvie's knees, but she scrubbed vigorously anyway, making sure the brush's bristles flicked through every crevice and cranny. Today she was thankful for the apron the hospital gave its volunteers, and she'd piled her thick hair in a bun atop her head—a style her mother often likened to a bird's nest. Even with the lighter lenses, the motion of scrubbing made her glasses slip off her nose, and more than once she'd gotten suds on her face trying to push them back up. When she returned to Briar Hall, she'd assemble some sort of band to wrap from one arm to the other, fastening the spectacles to the back of her head. No more slipping. She knew enough Polymaking to do that on her own.

Upon arriving for her volunteer hours, she had asked to be assigned to something other than rounds in the recovery room. She was grateful for the hard work, for in the days since sending off her army of paper birds, she had received no reply from Bennet, and Mr. Hemsley probably hated her even more for all the times she'd asked after the mail yesterday. But of course inundating a person with letters wouldn't instantly guarantee their forgiveness. Or maybe the birds hadn't made it. Or maybe she'd annoyed Bennet and/or his tutor into loathing her permanently.

"Bah." She dunked her brush in the bucket of soapy water. Better to stay away from men, anyway. She had to focus on her studies.

Mg. Praff hadn't been too disgruntled about her sudden departure. He was too absorbed in the work—one of the reasons Alvie had yet to tell him about her encounter with Mg. Ezzell. At least there was one person on this island who understood the draw of creation the way Alvie and her papa did. It was hard finding people who understood her. And if she understood Mg. Praff, it was better to wait for his genius to come to a stop on its own than to interrupt it with stories about his rival.

Her thoughts shifted to Ethel, and she scrubbed with renewed vigor. She hadn't so much as stepped into the recovery room today. She'd asked for a different task specifically to avoid the Coopers, for fear her gesture had failed and Bennet had remarked poorly on her character to his sister. She was withering inside, however, wondering how it'd gone off. Wondering what either of them thought of her. Surely she couldn't leave without checking on Ethel. For all she knew, her friend was about to be discharged.

She dipped her brush. The whole point of this invention was to help Ethel, wasn't it? She had been the catalyst, the inspiration. What kind of an inventor—and *friend*—would Alvie be if she didn't actually follow through on her promise? Maybe Ethel's cheeriness would be dampened by the episode with Bennet . . . but there had been such hope in her eyes.

"Blazes blasted this whole stupid bloody thing." Alvie hardly understood the meaning of half the sour words she'd picked up since moving to England, but there was no one around to hear her. She finished the hallway, washed out the bucket, scrubbed her hands, and changed into a clean apron. She only remembered to let down the nest of her hair a few steps before entering the recovery room.

The man in the first bed, a newcomer, spied her and asked for water. Alvie fetched a cup. Seeing him cared for, she tiptoed to Ethel's bed. She had a visitor, but it wasn't Bennet. This was an older man with a big round circle of baldness atop his head and long graying muttonchops. He had an open chest of arms next to him. Fake arms, of course. It wasn't likely an Excisioner would sit around with a stolen limb or two on display. The thought gave Alvie chills. Excision was the one practice of magic illegal across all continents. Some debased person long ago had discovered a dark secret: since man-made things could be enchanted, so too could humans themselves. Man made man, after all. It was magic at its darkest.

"Alvie? Did you hear me?"

Alvie came back to herself, noticing Ethel sitting up and staring at her for the first time. The man with the chest of arms also cocked an eyebrow at her.

"Oh. Uh, no. Sorry. I was thinking about arms."

Ethel laughed. A dozen weights fell off Alvie's shoulders at the sound of it, and it suddenly felt like she could float right up to the ceiling.

"You're a nurse?" the man asked.

"Just a volunteer."

"Well, we're about done here." The man held a thick sleeve that looked to be made out of red rubber, with a joint at the end that Alvie assumed connected to the fixture of a false hand. He set it atop the arms made of wood in the chest and closed the chest. "Do you know where a lavatory is, m'dear?"

"Oh, uh." Alvie pointed out the way she'd come. "Go past the reception room to the end of the hall. It's on the right."

He nodded his thanks and left, leaving the chest by the bed.

Alvie eyed that chest.

"I don't think he'll mind," Ethel said.

Grinning, Alvie got down on her sore knees and pulled back the lid, picking through the false arms. They were heavier than she'd thought they would be. Heavier than a true arm, certainly. Who wanted to go around with a false arm that felt like a club?

She picked up a wooden one with some joints and studied it.

"It will move if I turn my . . . stump . . . certain ways," Ethel said, frowning. "But it will only respond to really jarring movements."

Ethel looked toward the ceiling and took in a deep breath, blinking rapidly. Oh. Of course this would be hard for her. If the prosthesis salesman was here, Ethel was likely being discharged soon.

Alvie dropped the fake arm and shut the chest lid. "I'm sorry, Ethel. But Magician Praff and I are still working on the project. I think it's coming along rather well, though I've nothing to show, yet."

A small smile worked its way to Ethel's mouth. "I'm so glad to hear it, Alvie. If not for me, then for the next poor soul who occupies this bed."

"Of course it will be for you. I'm not that slow. That is . . . if we can work out the spells." It had to have magic to mimic the functionality of a real arm, unless Alvie could somehow advance science a couple of centuries.

"I'd love to see it sometime."

"You should!" Alvie leaned forward in the chair. "When do you leave?"

Ethel's face fell again. She touched her stump as if uncomfortable. "Tomorrow."

Alvie frowned to match her. "But you'll get to go home, and sleep where strange men can't sit up and watch you. That's a perk, right?"

Ethel laughed. "Yes, I suppose so." She sighed and lifted her stump. "But here, this is normal. At home, with my friends . . . it isn't." She stared at the space where her arm used to be. "It still feels like it's there. I have dreams where it's there. If I didn't dream about it, maybe it wouldn't be so bad."

A chilled, unpleasant tingling ran up the side of Alvie's neck. She held back a frown. "I don't know how to stop your dreams."

"No one does. I suppose I'll just have to make a lot of new memories so I can dream about those instead. There's not much excitement inside this place. Nothing worth dreaming about."

"Oh. I suppose I could, uh . . . cause some excitement . . ." Maybe knock over the trash receptacle or start singing a Bob Cole song, though she had a terrible voice. Such a thing might only encourage Ethel's nightmares.

Ethel smiled. "No need. Tomorrow's excitement will be enough for me. Maybe too much."

Alvie nodded, and silence fell like snow between them, bit by bit, magnified by the chatter of other patients.

Ethel began to say something, but Alvie blurted out, "I snubbed Bennet, and I'm really sorry about it."

Ethel's mouth snapped shut with a click of her teeth. Her delicate brow furrowed just slightly. "Snubbed Bennet?" Her eyes sparkled. "Did he seek you out?"

Alvie's chest felt too hot in her blouse. "Uh, well, he did come over."

Ethel slapped her hand against the bed frame. "He did? He didn't tell me!" Her dark eyes darted back and forth, reading Alvie's face. "Oh no. Not good?"

"I'm such a dunce, Ethel." Alvie slouched in the chair. "We were going to go on a picnic, but I lost track of time. My head was stuck in the polymery. I mean, the rest of me was, too. That is, I could have left. I'm metaphorically stuck, or was."

Ethel nodded. "I figured as much."

"I sent him a letter"—Alvie decided not to disclose how *many* letters she'd sent—"but I haven't heard back."

With her good arm, Ethel reached over the bed and grabbed Alvie's hand. "Bennet isn't one to hold a grudge. If you'd like, I'll put a good word in for you."

"Really?"

Footsteps announced the return of the salesman. He smiled at them and hefted the chest. "I'll leave an order sheet and brochure with the front desk that you can take home."

Ethel nodded, and the salesman excused himself.

Alvie cleared her throat. "Really?"

"Really. I like you, Alvie. And Bennet doesn't get out as much as he should." She wrinkled her nose. "That mentor of his is a real stickler, which hasn't helped. I bet he'd be livid if he thought Bennet was dating."

Alvie's whole body became a shiver. "But I sent the birds to Magician Bailey's house."

Ethel chuckled. "Oh, I'm being dramatic. But I hope Bennet puts his foot down and actually tests out of his apprenticeship soon. He's thinking in the spring. Used to say winter, but he's pushed it back again. That boy needs to build up his confidence."

Nurse Padson walked by, and Ethel released Alvie's hand. "Ah, Alvie," the nurse said. "There you are. Could you help us organize some supplies?"

Alvie stood. "Of course."

Ethel said, "I'll leave my home address with the front desk for you, Alvie. Come visit when you can, with or without the . . . project."

Alvie beamed. "Thank you. I will."

Nurse Padson cleared her throat, and Alvie scuttled away from Ethel's bedside, offering a wave good-bye as she went.

Alvie was crossing the yard to the polymery, Ethel's address in her back pocket, when she heard a great booming voice that seemed to shake the very foundation of the earth.

"Eureka!"

A few birds flitted out of a nearby ash tree, sending several of its orange leaves spiraling to the ground.

Alvie paused for only a moment before running the rest of the way to the polymery. She nearly stumbled over a tube of plastic as she entered the foyer. It was narrower on one end than the other. Ah, a forearm. And there was another, and another. Several of them had spilled out of the lab, and the floor inside was swimming with them. She picked her way around them, making a path to Mg. Praff at the island.

"Magician Praff?" His hair was a wild mess, and a few smears of oil marked his lab coat and chin, which had a good two days' worth of beard growth on it. He looked up at her, a loony smile splitting his face. His eyes were wide and bloodshot, eyelids baggy.

"Alvie! *Alvie!* I've done it! I've found it! Come, come!" He ran at her like a madman, plastic bits and pieces parting around his footsteps like unraked leaves, and Alvie was a little cowed before he grabbed both her wrists and hauled her into the lab. This time she *did* trip over a forearm, but Mg. Praff's surprisingly strong grip kept her upright.

He released her and swept his arm over the island, knocking more debris to the floor.

Alvie pushed up her glasses. "Did it?" She perked up. "Did *it?*"

"Yes, *yes!*" The Polymaker grabbed a forearm-shaped tube with plastic straws half melted along its length. With shaky, sleep-deprived movements, he filled each of the three straws with liquid plastic, then pinched off their ends with the side of his hand.

He looked at her, wild-eyed, then at the straws. "Compress," he commanded.

Alvie leaned forward as the plastic swirled and bubbled inside the straws. The forearm began to quake like a rodeo bull under Mg. Praff's hands. He moved his hand, and the liquid shot out from the tubes and splattered against the wall, beside a few other, older splats.

Alvie's jaw fell. Her gaze darted from the wall to the forearm to Mg. Praff's hand.

"You discovered a spell to pressurize it."

"Yes! *Yes!*" He raised both fists in triumph. "It's not done, no . . . but we have something to work around. That spell alone will blow away the convention . . . we need to make paths for the pressure, and learn to harness it so the hand doesn't explode—"

"Explode?" Alvie pictured Ethel walking down the street, her prosthetic arm suddenly combusting. Yet she smiled. "We have it. You have it. The beginning."

"This is the middle, Alvie." Mg. Praff grabbed her shoulders. "This is the *middle*. We have the middle! Compress!"

He began laughing manically, grabbing the partial prosthesis and holding it over his head like he had just won the pie contest at the fair. He even twirled, once.

"Enough to start the paper." He set the experiment down. "How are you with papers? This is yours, too. You could write the paper."

Alvie blinked. "Uh . . . I'm functional, as a writer. I'm better with my hands."

"Hands. Yes, good. I need you to replicate a few parts for me. I'll start on the paper—"

"Magician Praff."

The Polymaker had begun rooting through a drawer, but he looked up. The short hair at his crown was mussed.

Alvie took a deep breath and grinned. "This is a marvelous moment. But I think it would be best if you get some sleep before you try to write academically. And, perhaps, bathe."

Mg. Praff blinked several times. He straightened, looking around the polymery, which appeared as if a tornado had touched down and decided to stay the night. "You are right. A few hours would do me good. I'll . . . send for Hemsley."

"I'll get started on the cleanup."

Mg. Praff nodded, smoothed his hair back, and started for the door.

"And, sir?"

He glanced back.

Alvie gave him a short round of applause. "Congratulations."

———————

With the polymery cleaned up, Alvie was able to settle in and truly absorb the excitement of her mentor's discovery. Not only had Marion Praff discovered a new Polymaking spell; he had also found the key to making a prosthesis that would operate more like a real hand than anything on the market. She got to work molding the parts Mg. Praff would need to continue testing the spell and its functionality within a prosthesis, namely, controlling the pressure at a very small level. To think what such a spell could do on a larger scale . . . but that was a question to be answered later. A question that would be asked by all Polymakers, after the presentation at the Discovery Convention.

Alvie grinned as she measured and cut patterns out of a long sheet of opaque white plastic. A first-year apprentice, and she'd stand beside a renowned magician at the Discovery Convention. Her! Not only would she get to bask in the creativity and intellect of creators from all over the world, but her résumé would sparkle.

She'd begun shaping the tip of a ring finger when a knock sounded at the entrance to the polymery. She looked up from her stool at the lab island. As she moved to stand, however, the door opened, and none other than Bennet Cooper stood there.

"Bennet!" Alvie exclaimed, leaping from her stool. Unfortunately, her toe caught on the foot ring, and she tripped before even finding the floor. With her feet, anyway. She found it quite thoroughly with her left knee.

She muttered a curse—a very American one—as Bennet hurried across the polymery to her side.

"Are you all right?" he asked.

Alvie grabbed the seat of her stool and pulled herself up, wincing as she straightened her leg. What was Bennet Cooper doing here? And her desk was a mess. There were plastic beads all over the floor, and half the cabinets were ajar! Not to mention he wasn't allowed in the polymery . . . then again, he wouldn't have known where to find her unless the butler or Mg. Praff had shown him . . . that meant the visit was sanctioned, yes?

"Um." She stumbled. "Just a bruise." She sat in her chair to prevent further tumbling. "I've got lots of them, and from clumsier things than that."

"You're sure?"

She nodded, perhaps a little too quickly. "Why are you here? Did you get my letters?"

A lopsided smile crossed his lips, and he reached forward to straighten Alvie's glasses. She hadn't realized they'd tilted. Jitters like electricity shot down the arms and into her neck. "Yes. I've never received so much mail in my life. And I got the message from Ethel, as well."

Alvie almost asked what Ethel had said, but perhaps she didn't want to know.

"I'm sorry for the interruption," he continued, "but when I rang the bell, the butler seemed perturbed at me and told me to go around to the polymery myself. So I did." He stepped back and looked around, taking in the lab. "This is very different from Folding."

"I suspect it is. Um." She smoothed out her blouse, not that it needed smoothing, then did the same for her slacks. And her hair, which likely *did* need smoothing. "So. You got my letters . . ."

"They were quite extravagant, yes."

"I really am sor—"

Bennet chuckled. "Goodness, Alvie. If you apologize one more time, my ears will start ringing. I thought it might be a good idea for us to try again."

Alvie straightened, then winced at the protest of her knee. "Again? Picnic?"

"Well, it might be a little cold for a—"

"Let's go *right now*." She grabbed his hand and tugged him out of the lab, her whining knee be damned.

"Right now?" Bennet repeated.

She let go of him and spun around. "Yes! I can't miss it if we go right now!" She paused. "Unless you want me to wear a skirt, in which case I'll need a few minutes. I was planning to wear a skirt the first time, you know. Picnicking in them is horrid, but I wanted to look ladylike. Have you ever picnicked in a skirt?"

He smiled. "I can't say I have."

"Doing anything in one of them is a pain in the a—ahem. But if you don't mind, let's go right now. I'll even walk. Wherever you want to go."

"No need for that. I brought the Benz—"

"Did you really?" Alvie jumped. "Then what are we waiting for?"

He laughed. "All right. But at least let me escort you." He took her hand and looped it through the crook of his elbow. The touch of his warm skin through his shirtsleeve ignited giddiness inside Alvie, like her belly was filled with popcorn kernels and Bennet was the fire beneath them. He reached over and picked a small plastic bead from her hair.

"Do you need to talk to Magician Praff?"

"Oh no." She let him lead her through the exit, stopping only to lock the door behind her. "He's still resting by orders of Mrs. Praff. He went crazy."

Bennet paused. "Pardon?"

"Not real crazy. Temporary crazy. Oh! It's wonderful, Bennet. We've made a remarkable discovery to help create Ethel's prosthesis. You see, after I studied your carburetor—that is, Magician Bailey's carburetor—I had this idea that if we could only pressurize the hand to give a natural movement to the fingers . . ."

CHAPTER 10

ALVIE STILL ITCHED TO drive the Benz herself, though she didn't have much experience, but she sat in a ladylike manner in the passenger seat as Bennet pulled the beautiful automobile around the drive and into the city. He was a good driver and only ground the gears once, after he had to stop for a long line of school children crossing the street. A few of them pointed at the Benz as they passed. Alvie wasn't sure if it was appropriate to wave or not, so she merely sat on her hands.

The city was busy at the lunch hour, the streets full of buggies and horses and a few other privately owned vehicles. Bennet parked the Benz on the side of a street near Parliament Square and again placed Alvie's hand on the crook of his elbow. It made her forget the cold autumn breeze blowing about.

Big Ben gonged noon, startling Alvie. She eyed it, examining its architecture. "It's not as big as I heard it was."

Bennet glanced over to the clock. "I suppose in America, everything's bigger."

Alvie considered that and agreed. The roads were wider and the houses larger, as were the spaces between them.

He took her to a small restaurant on the square called St. Alban's Salmon Bistro, hesitantly asking at the door if she liked fish.

"I like everything," she said. And it was true.

The waiter sat them at a small table in the back corner, a cozy spot where Alvie could see the interior restaurant and still glance out the window at the bustling square. It was a very pretty square, sort of old looking, though she had no idea how old it actually was. Everything in Columbus had been made to be useful, not to be pretty. Alvie tended to prefer function to beauty.

She scanned the restaurant. It had electric lights, to her surprise, not magicked ones. It could fit about thirty people, and with some rearranging, she suspected it could fit fifty . . . but, no, she wasn't going to let herself get carried away with the measurements, not while she was on a *date*. She did note, however, before turning back to Bennet, that a splotch of paint on the wall looked brighter and newer than its surroundings, as though something had somewhat recently taken out just a small chunk of it. Curious.

"Do you dance, Alvie?"

Her eyes darted to his. He was buttering bread. Oh, there was bread on the table. She took a slice. "No."

For some reason, he appeared surprised by her answer. "No?"

She shook her head. "I've never been good with it. I mean, it's all patterns, and patterns are simple enough, but then I have to follow someone who knows the patterns that I don't, and even if I learn the patterns, the other person is bound to put in a flourish or a spin of some sort that throws it off, and it's all just nonsensical." She shrugged, thinking of the only other date she'd ever been on—the dance in secondary school. "And then he gets mad when you step on his feet, like it's your fault that he broke the pattern."

Bennet grinned. "You're different, Alvie."

She buttered her bread. "I know."

"It's a good thing."

She glanced at him and smiled.

A waitress came by and took their orders—Alvie asked for shrimp with tartar sauce, since she'd never had that. Setting her bread aside, she pulled out her wallet and started counting out coins.

"Oh, Alvie, you don't need to do that."

She glanced up. "Hm?"

He laughed. "That's not how these things work. I'm paying for it."

"Oh. But you don't have to. I have a—"

"Alvie."

She paused, then slid the coins into her wallet and dropped it into her purse. "Sorry. And thank you. I've just never really dated before."

"Really?" He took a sip of water.

She shrugged again. "Just once, back in Columbus. I mean, I'm a little scatterbrained and not the prettiest . . . I'm fairly certain he only asked me because he liked how I looked from the neck down, and, well, it was a dance, so you're supposed to stand close—"

Bennet choked and whipped his arm up over his mouth, protecting Alvie from any possible spew. She offered him her paper napkin, but he waved it away as he composed himself.

"Sorry," she repeated.

He recovered and managed to laugh. "No, no, you just surprised me." He wiped a knuckle under his eye. "I have a feeling I'll never be bored with you."

That might have been the nicest thing a man had ever said to her, and she beamed.

He cleared his throat. "I, uh, well, I think you're pre—"

The waiter returned with their food just then, and Bennet swallowed whatever he had been about to say, and after the waiter left, the topic moved on from Alvie's awkward once-date to plastics and France and guest speakers at Cambridge. Alvie was halfway through her shrimp when she remembered her earlier conversation with Ethel.

"Are you taking your test soon?" she asked.

Bennet slowed the twirl of his fork in his pasta. "My Folding test? Yes. Spring. Maybe."

"Why maybe? Do you know the spells?"

He studied his pasta. "Well, it's just that I think I do, and then something pops up that I don't know as well as I should, and, well, I'd like to pass the first time."

"Ethel said Magician Bailey is a bully. Well, she didn't say *that*. I'm paraphrasing."

Bennet sighed, set down his fork, and leaned back in his chair. "He's honest, is all."

"Just take the test. I'm sure you can do it."

"But how can you be? You've never seen me Fold."

She gestured to his napkin. "That's paper."

He picked it up, considering, then took another napkin and brought it down to his lap, out of Alvie's line of sight. He worked quietly and, a minute later, presented her with a lovely, if napkin-limp, paper blossom. He whispered, "Breathe," and the petals unfolded into a lily.

She grinned and accepted it. "This is beautiful."

"Thank you."

"I pass you."

He laughed. "If only it were so simple. But . . . spring. I'm sure I'll set the test for spring. That gives me time to prepare."

"The Discovery Convention is in the spring. Oh, Bennet, you should come if you can. It's going to be wonderful. And you could come as a full-fledged magician!"

"Have you been before?"

"No, but I know it will be. I've read about it." She skewered a piece of shrimp, but didn't raise it to her mouth. "And once Magician Praff and I get everything assembled, we're going to make a splash. We won't only be helping Ethel; we'll be changing an entire facet of medicine."

His features softened. "I truly am thankful, Alvie."

A flash of light caught Alvie's attention—sun shining off the glass-inlaid door to the bistro as it opened. She almost ignored it, but a very familiar hairline appeared, and Alvie's stomach dropped.

Mg. Ezzell.

She averted her eyes. Glanced back. Was he here by chance? He had to be. There was no point in pursuing her. Besides, he couldn't possibly know she was here . . . unless he was watching the house. But that was preposterous.

Or was it? He'd found her outside the post office, hadn't he? Had that been happenstance, or had he known she would be there? A shiver ran down her spine.

"Alvie?" Bennet's soft voice penetrated the fog of her thoughts.

"Um," she said.

Bennet watched her a second before turning around in his seat. Mg. Ezzell glanced over, then quickly diverted his gaze to the headwaiter.

Alvie set down her fork.

"Do you know him?"

"His name is Magician Ezzell. He's, uh, Magician Praff's rival. I'm fairly certain he's the reason I got off at the wrong station. Not that I mind, in the end." She wouldn't have met Bennet otherwise. Well, she would have at the hospital, but they might never have gotten to talking . . .

He nodded knowingly. "Magician Bailey has one of those."

She rolled her lips together. Did every magician have to have an enemy?

Was Mg. Ezzell also going to be hers?

A waitress approached Mg. Ezzell and began leading him toward their table. Alvie glanced around—there were two empty tables near them.

"Oh bother," she whispered.

Bennet eyed her, then Mg. Ezzell. He scooted out his chair and offered her his hand. Alvie glanced at him, wondering.

"Come on," he said. "We'll pay up there and leave."

"You don't have to—"

"Do you want to go?"

She hesitated. The waitress sat Mg. Ezzell right behind Bennet. She nodded.

He offered her a sympathetic smile, and she let him lead her to the front of the bistro just as the hateful Polymaker took a seat at the table across from theirs.

She refused to look back to see if Mg. Ezzell was watching.

Bennet bid farewell to Alvie outside Briar Hall. Alvie wasn't entirely sure what was expected after a date—after that dance, the fellow had hugged her, walked off, and never contacted her again. But Bennet didn't even touch her. He just sort of looked around and rubbed his neck, complimented her shoes, and then drove home. Alvie had thought the outing a relative success . . . could she have misinterpreted it?

Don't think about it right now. She sighed as she slipped through the front doors, forgoing knocking or ringing the bell so as not to disturb Mr. Hemsley. Perhaps the lighting had been the problem. Even Alvie knew it was awkward to hug a person when the sun was unclouded in the sky, sitting there, watching with all its brightness. Stupid sun.

Scuffing through the main hall, she spied Emma dusting a pedestal.

"Emma? Is Magician Praff still in bed?"

"I believe he's in the salon with a guest. Are you well?"

She nodded, though there was little energy to it. "Thank you." She crossed the hall to the music room and entered the short hallway leading to the salon. The door was cracked open, and Mr. Hemsley stood guard outside it in a chair, a newspaper spread before his face.

Seeing her approach, he said, "Magician Praff is occupied," to which Alvie merely nodded and found another chair. Mr. Hemsley watched her for a moment, then clicked his tongue and returned to his paper.

To her relief, she only had to wait about fifteen minutes before a man she didn't recognize stepped out of the salon, Mg. Praff beside him. The two exchanged a few pleasantries, and Mr. Hemsley rose to attention and offered to escort the guest out.

When he was gone, Mg. Praff, who looked rested and much more groomed, asked, "What's the trouble, Alvie?"

"Who was that?"

"Old friend. Grew up together, and he was in town."

"He's not in London?"

"Moved to Liverpool after he got married."

She nodded once. "I saw Magician Ezzell at the bistro today. That is, Bennet and I just went to this place at Parliament Square."

"Oh dear." He folded his arms. "I hope he didn't give you any trouble."

"No. Not then. We left before he could."

The fold of his arms loosened. "Not *then*?"

She told him about the post office—a story she'd neglected to mention earlier, what with all the work and study there was to do. When she'd finished, Mg. Praff wore a frown that made him look his age.

"I see. That's rather . . . nefarious of him. Though . . . when did you say this was?"

Alvie counted in her head. "Two days ago." She didn't think Mg. Praff would care for the hours and approximate minutes.

"Ah, I see. Have you been reading the paper?"

The question made Alvie blink. "I, uh, not recently. Was I supposed to be reading it? If you have the old issues, I can catch up—"

Mg. Praff chuckled softly. "No need for that. But Magician Ezzell's polymery was recently broken into."

She sat up straighter. "Another one?" There had been two already— Mg. Praff and Mg. Aviosky had spoken of the burglaries the day Alvie bonded to plastic.

Mg. Praff frowned. "I'm afraid so. There weren't many details, but plans and supplies were taken. Unfortunate." He sighed. "Though I am not fond of Magician Ezzell, perhaps that was why he was in a foul mood when you met him. I'm sorry you have to be involved with him at all." Mg. Praff tapped his chin. "He's quite the gentleman when he wants to be."

Alvie snorted. "A gentleman, indeed. Gentlemen speak kindly, sir. Magician Ezzell is a pistol, and his words are his ammunition." He should have been a Smelter. They could do all sorts of things with bullets. "Though I am sorry to hear about his break-in."

A small smile turned Mg. Praff's mouth. "An accurate description. And I do thank you for your integrity."

"My papa said that the world can take all it wants from a man, but he has to give up his integrity freely."

"Your father is a wise man." He sighed. "As for Magician Ezzell . . . obviously it would be beneficial for us to share our project and aspirations with the medical community, at least, but the rivalry in Polymaking is fierce, and it's easy to be undermined. Better to wait until we have a usable prototype, and the Discovery Convention is the best way to expose the technology and garner interest." He strode toward the music room. "But if you don't mind cutting your free time short, there are a few spells I'd like to teach you. All this pushing for the convention and Ethel's prosthesis has made your education . . . well, not exactly linear. There are still rudimentary things you need to learn." He rubbed his eyes. "I shouldn't be weighing you down with all this convention nonsense."

"Oh, please do. I love the weight."

He chuckled. "Good. But we're getting ahead of ourselves. To the polymery."

———————————

Alvie studied in her bedroom that night, wanting something more comfortable and lazy, and it was also getting dreadfully cold outside, especially after sunset. It was a short walk between the polymery and the house, but a chilly one.

She sat on her too-big bed with a pair of her half boots in front of her. She'd affixed plastic aglets to the laces, little more than narrow tubes. Practicing the spell Mg. Praff had taught her, she said, "Heed: Pattern," to one of the shoes, then went on to tie the laces, this time in a double knot. When she had finished, she said, "Cease."

She untied the shoe and set it before her. "Heed: Direction."

To her delight, the shoe tied itself. This was the seventh time she'd done the spell with shoelaces, but it still fascinated her. Why, she wouldn't need to bend over to tie her laces ever again! Perhaps that would lead to less tripping in her future. And corsets! Perhaps Alvie could invest some magic into that industry . . .

After enchanting the second half boot, Alvie slid off her bed and sat on the floor. She'd collected a few plastic things—a wheel she'd made earlier, a hanger from the closet, a boat of Mg. Praff's making, and a simple sheet of plastic. She lined them up, making sure her hands touched each one, and said, "Propel."

All the items moved forward at once, as though racing against one another. The wheel went the fastest, rolling across the carpet until it hit the wall beneath the window. Then the boat, then the hanger. The piece of unformed plastic dawdled behind. She called out, "Cease," and all four items stopped at once, lifeless. It made sense that the wheel and the boat, which had propellers, had gone the farthest with the forward-projection spell. Minimal friction. The hanger had less surface area against the floor than the piece of unformed plastic, which was undoubtedly why it had moved more swiftly.

A knock sounded at the door. Alvie stood and began gathering her collection. "Come in."

Mg. Praff opened the door. "What have we here? It's nine thirty, and Alvie is actually *in* the house?"

"Might occur more often once it starts snowing." Though she'd heard Ohio got a great deal more snow than London did.

"I won't interrupt too long, but I thought you'd like to know that the abstract was accepted at the Discovery Convention." He held up two paper-clipped sheets.

"Really? That's excellent!" Not that Alvie had ever doubted they'd be accepted. She went to the door and took the papers from her mentor. At the front was a short telegraph announcing the acceptance. The abstract was only a page long, but it was all the convention required to judge whether a project would be accepted; the full paper would be written later. She studied the cover page and its delicate typeface. "The Use of a Newfound Pressurizing Spell in the Movement of Prosthetic Limbs," it read. Beneath the title, in smaller type, was, "By Magician Marion Praff and Alvie Brechenmacher."

Alvie stared at her name. And stared. And stared.

"Well?" he asked.

She glanced up at him. Pushed up her glasses. In a voice weak as a mouse's, she said, "Y-You put my name on it."

"Of course I did. It was your idea, after all. I've only helped bring it to fruition."

Her mouth went dry. "But . . . the Compress spell was all your doing."

"Well." He made a show of straightening his vest. "That's why my name is on it, too."

Alvie grinned hard enough to hurt. Her heart felt like a spinning ball bearing, and her eyes moistened. "This means . . . a lot to me, sir. I'm . . . thank you, so much."

He accepted the papers back. "I should be thanking you. You're going to make quite the mark on the world, Alvie. I'm honored to be at the beginning of your journey."

She wasn't sure what to say, so she just nodded. Mg. Praff mirrored the gesture and slipped away, closing the door behind him.

CHAPTER 11

ALVIE PUT ON HER nightgown in her closet for some privacy while Emma turned down the blankets of the bed and tidied the room. Once Alvie was dressed for sleep, she walked to her window. Through it she could see the polymery. The extinguished lights made her strangely sad, and it occurred to her that she'd stayed up working enough nights that she wasn't particularly tired now.

Glancing out the window again, she said, "I'm not terribly tired. Maybe I'll head back to the polymery."

Emma scurried over and glanced out the window. "I don't know, miss. Might rain. Best to stay in tonight."

It was too dark for Alvie to tell if it was going to rain or not, but she was a foreigner here, so she nodded and climbed into her bed. Emma wished her good night and slipped away.

Alvie struggled to sleep. Excitement over the abstract and the Discovery in Material Mechanics Convention, most likely. Or, per-haps, because Emma had changed the sheets on the bed to flannel ones instead of cotton, and Alvie had never slept on flannel before.

Whatever it was, Alvie dreamed about plastic arms and the conven-tion when she did sleep, and when she didn't, she stared at the blurry starlight edging her curtains and wondered why she wasn't more tired. Around two thirty in the morning, when she found that she was staring quite a bit more than snoozing, Alvie threw back the covers and got dressed. That was one nice thing about living in a house that employed servants—Alvie hadn't done her laundry once since arriving, yet her clothes were always clean and pressed and ready to wear. She'd need to remember to thank Emma for that when the sun was up.

Thankfully, it was *not* raining, so her late-night venture would leave her no worse for wear. She ran a wide-toothed comb through her jungle of hair before twisting it atop her head. She donned her jacket—her hardy Ohio coat had been too large to fit into her suitcases—grabbed a Gaffer lamp, and slipped out the door.

She stayed late in the polymery more often than not, so this was not her first time wandering the house at night. But that was always coming in, not going out, and for some reason, the two felt very different. Like she was getting away with something. She rechecked her pocket for her polymery key and whispered, "Brighter," to her pre-enchanted lamp so that it filled the fancy corridors with its glow. She didn't want any stirring shadows to startle her. She hadn't the slightest idea when the servants got up, though she knew Mrs. Praff liked to sleep in.

She turned the glow down to its lowest setting when she reached the back door and slipped outside. The shifting mosaic of metal tiles looked like water in the moonlight, rippling and twisting with unseen aquatic life. Alvie watched it for a moment, marveling. If only she could study more than one form of magic! She imagined Smelting involved a great deal more sweating than was required of Polymaking.

She stepped onto the path, watching the movement of the tiles pause for her as though frozen by the autumn chill. For some reason, that made her think of Bennet. Would he see water in the shifting tiles? Did he ever wake up in the middle of the night, only to feed the desire to work? Folding hadn't been his first choice, but he seemed to like it.

He would have been a Polymaker, or so he'd said at the train station. That made her like him even more.

A couple more steps, and Alvie paused. Yes, he'd been very kind at the train station, hadn't he? Nice from the start. At the hospital, at the house, on the date. That's the sort of person Bennet Cooper was. The nice sort.

What if he's just being nice?

It would be a silly thought for someone like, oh, Emma to think. Emma, who was petite and pretty, pretty in a way that didn't need cosmetics or fancy dresses or special serum to tame her hair. But despite what her parents said, Alvie wasn't exactly pretty, was she?

She touched her heavy glasses. Not a lot of young people wore glasses, and if they did, they weren't glasses like hers. Big, ungainly things that could compete with a headlamp. Alvie had tried smaller frames once—frames like Mg. Aviosky's. But they hadn't worked for her. Her original lenses were too thick for small frames—they'd constantly popped out. Besides, the narrow frames gave her a narrow window through which to see the world. It seemed God had given her a high-functioning mind as trade for good eyesight. At least Mg. Praff had thinned out the lenses so she didn't look so bug-eyed anymore.

A cold breeze bit her exposed ears, so Alvie continued down the path, shivering. Prescription eyewear aside, it was just that boys—men—didn't tend to take an interest in her. That was a scientific fact. So why would Bennet Cooper, a dashing specimen of a man, suddenly bend the numbers?

Her stomach squirmed and made her chest feel heavy. Reaching for her key, she tried to push thoughts of Bennet away by wondering if there were any snacks in her workroom, but that only made her wonder what sort of snacks Bennet liked, and it frustrated her to be thinking more about a Folder than about plastic.

"Bother," she muttered.

But then Alvie heard something that sounded off. Even this late there was plenty of ambient noise—a cold breeze rustling the gardens or a skittering rabbit or a buggy out driving late—but this was markedly the shuffling of feet, followed by the breaking of something distinctly plastic.

She froze, the metal tiles swimming a few feet in front of her. "Cease," she whispered to the light, and it went out. Darkness swallowed the yard. Alvie blinked rapidly, trying to adjust her eyes.

No noise. Had she imagined it?

She stepped off the path, letting the enchanted tiles return to their watery swaying. The noise had come from the polymery, had it not? There was nothing else that had plastic in this direction. Only the polymery—

There was a distinct tapping of a hammer—chisel?—being worked. But Alvie could see the polymery now, and none of the lights were on. Anyone who belonged in the polymery would have turned the lights on. At the very least, they would be carrying a Gaffer light.

A new chill tingled over Alvie's skin.

Good heavens, were they being burglarized?

She froze, clutching her extinguished Gaffer lamp, mind spinning. Was there a spell she could . . . of course there wasn't, and she had no plastic on her, anyway. She should run back into the house, but by the time she roused someone, what if . . . Ethel's arm was in there! All their prototypes, what if . . .

She thought of Mg. Ezzell and his scowls and did the one thing she hoped might help.

She screamed.

Alvie had a number of talents. She could factor large numbers in her head, for one, and she could write in shorthand with incredible speed if she didn't heed her penmanship. She knew almost all the rudimentary spells for Polymaking, and she was fairly certain she could disassemble and reassemble the engine of an automobile in six hours and four minutes without having to consult a manual.

She was also, apparently, very good at screaming.

The noise hurt her own ears, it was so loud and high. Evenly pitched, enough to stir a slumbering bird from a nearby tree. And though Alvie wasn't an orator or singer, she screamed for a very long time. Seemed that, beneath her well-endowed chest, she had a remarkable set of lungs.

She screamed loud and long enough that several lights went on inside Briar Hall. When she finally ran out of air, her throat tingling, she thought she saw a large shadow beside the polymery move very quickly toward the fence bordering the estate.

So she screamed again.

Several policemen lurked about the polymery in the wee hours of dawn, along with Mrs. and Mg. Praff, Mr. Hemsley, and Mrs. Connway. A few other servants lingered by the back door, trying to peer over one another to get a better look at the scene. Alvie was quite cold, but evidence needed to be collected, so she couldn't go into the polymery, and she couldn't bear to return to the manor before hearing what the policemen had to say.

So she huddled inside her jacket, cold hands pressed into its pockets. She'd let her hair down, and that helped.

One of the policemen, carrying a clipboard, stepped out of the polymery and approached Mg. Praff. Alvie hurried in that direction, her cold toes aching in her shoes.

"Doesn't seem like anything was stolen—none of the things you mentioned," the policeman said. "The burglar didn't get very far. He entered the workroom through the window on the north side and got as far as the foyer before fleeing. It's a mess, but the damage won't be too expensive to set right."

Alvie sighed. *Her* workroom, then. What a bother. But they were so fortunate the crook hadn't made it to the lab.

The policeman took a pen from behind his ear. He turned to Alvie. "You're the witness."

"Yes, sir."

"Did you make out anything about the individual? Individuals?"

She shook her head. "I *think* it was only one. I just heard it, and saw a shadow."

The policeman nodded, jotting something down. "Can you describe this shadow?"

"Um. Black and shadowy?"

He glanced up at her.

Alvie shrugged. "I'd bet twenty dollars—er, quid—that it was Magician Ezzell."

"Alvie." Mg. Praff's voice had a note of warning in it.

"What?" she asked. "He's practically threatened to overturn your work and tried to bully me into sharing your secrets."

The policeman seemed interested. "Is that true?"

Mg. Praff sighed. "I'm afraid so."

"I don't know that we have any evidence to pin the man, but we can question him. Magician Roscoe Ezzell, I take it."

Mrs. Praff asked, "You know him?"

"His polymery was also recently burglarized."

Alvie pressed her lips together. Perhaps it wasn't him . . . but circumstances told her otherwise.

The policeman adjusted his cap. "Seems to me it'd be much easier to simply melt one of the plastic windows and enter that way. Silent, quick. Effective."

"If one were a Polymaker," Alvie pointed out. *Which the burglar probably was.* "Of course, anyone could melt plastic with a torch or the like, but the light would give them away . . . unless there's a tool that could impart heat without direct fire . . ."

The policeman blinked a few times. "Er, yes, I suppose."

Alvie pushed up her glasses. "Even so, if the window *had* been melted, the likeliest perpetrator would be a Polymaker. Magician Ezzell would have known better than to use a Melt spell."

"Alvie." Another warning from her mentor.

The policeman added, "Any evidence pointing to Ezzell at this time would be circumstantial at best. We can talk to him, miss, but we cannot assume he had any part of this."

I *can still assume,* Alvie thought, huddling into her jacket.

To Mg. Praff, the officer said, "I'll see if we can finish up in there and get the men out. Make sure to record and report anything strange that you might find, anything missing."

"I will do that. Thank you." Mg. Praff seemed haggard. Possibly from lack of sleep, probably from having his lab broken into.

"Miss?"

Alvie jumped. Emma stood beside her, looking tired herself, though her maid's uniform was neatly pressed. Everyone looked tired. Mr. Hemsley would topple over snoring any moment now, Alvie was sure of it.

"Sorry." Emma apologized and offered a quick curtsey. "Are you all right?"

She nodded as Mg. and Mrs. Praff walked off with the officer who'd been questioning them. "Just a little frazzled is all."

"But the polymery is safe?"

She nodded. "Just a mess. The burglar didn't get far."

Emma smiled. "I'm glad to hear it. Do you want help? With the mess?"

A sigh passed through Alvie's lips. "I haven't even looked at it yet. It'll be all right." She started toward the polymery.

"Are you sure that you don't want a hand?" Emma hesitated, chewed her lip. "And that . . . it's safe in there?"

Alvie's shoulders relaxed a little. "I'm sure. The police have already been through it. Thank you, Emma. We'll work it out one way or another."

Though as Alvie turned back for the workshop, she frowned. The motives seemed quite obvious to her, as did the crook, but there was little she could do to prove the latter. At least the hands and arms hadn't been found. At least, as far as she knew, Mg. Praff hadn't written down the newly discovered spell, even in the abstract he'd submitted to the convention.

If anyone wanted that, they'd have to crack open his—or Alvie's—head to get it.

———

Alvie spent that morning straightening her workroom while Mg. Praff personally installed new locks on the polymery door and windows. The burglar hadn't meddled with any of the old locks, but Alvie figured it was more for Mg. Praff's peace of mind than anything. When she'd finished tidying, she stepped around to the front door where Mg. Praff was twisting a final screw into a hardy Smelted knob.

He spoke without looking up. "These are specially enchanted to withstand Smelters. There's an Unlatch spell those magicians can use that releases nearly any lock, unless it's either exceedingly complicated or enchanted to withstand it." He tightened the screw and stood up. "There."

"Looks expensive."

He chuckled. "It is."

She grabbed the knob and turned it. Just an ordinary door handle from this end. "I suppose a plastic one wouldn't do." Though if Mg. Ezzell was the culprit, that would be a *very* poor choice of lock.

"No. Even the strongest plastic can't hold up to the durability of metal. And I'd still need a key. The Unlatch spell isn't included in a Polymaker's repertoire."

He pocketed his screwdriver and stepped into the foyer. "Come. I set something up for you last night. Fortunately, our burglar didn't get far enough to meddle with it."

Curiosity piqued, she followed him up the stairs, past the library, and into the larger room over the lab. When she entered, she beheld a massive igloo of plastic formed from thousands of tiny hexagons. Three could fit snuggly in her palm. The thing was taller than she—about eight feet high—and took up two-thirds of the room. It looked like a strange sort of carapace—a celestial turtle, maybe. The edges of each tile seemed to glimmer, as if the magic were letting her know it was there.

Her jaw dropped, and she pressed her hands over her mouth.

Mg. Praff grinned. "Recognize it?"

"It's the *Imagidome!*" Alvie said through her fingers, walking around the beautiful monstrosity, taking in its opaque structure. It would take months to construct something like this, but she could see faint lines delineating sections. It came apart in wide pieces, then, not as individual hexagons.

This. This was the creation that had turned the Discovery Convention on its head two years ago. This had been the main feature in every magazine her papa subscribed to for months.

"Can I touch it?"

Her mentor laughed. "Of course you can touch it. I want you to try it."

She tried to suppress a nervous giggle and only half succeeded. She poked the structure. It was firmer than expected. She traced the tiny hexagons with her index finger. They tingled beneath her skin.

"Can I really?" she asked, winding around to the door. It was only about four feet high, and also made of hexagons.

He gestured inside. "After you."

Squatting, Alvie shimmied inside the dome and stood erect within it. The plastic let in a bit of muted light, but once Mg. Praff came in and shut the door, the space was almost entirely dark.

"I'll teach you how to program it yourself before the convention," he said.

"You will? You're bringing it?"

"Of course I'm bringing it. It might be old news, but it's not boring yet!"

She saw the outline of his hand against the wall of the dome. "Image Memory: Starry Night."

The light snuffed out all at once, then built up in dark-blue hues. Above her head, small, false stars burst to life, twinkling across the Imagidome's ceiling. She gaped. She couldn't make out the hexagons anymore. She felt as if she stood somewhere else, staring up at a true night sky. Around the base of the dome formed silhouettes of grass, expanding out until they met the "horizon." A field. And . . . over there, a tree. The grass and the tree's branches waved in a breeze Alvie couldn't feel. The lit heavens rotated slowly around one star immediately above her head.

"This is . . . amazing."

"This is four years of work," Mg. Praff said. "Revealing it was one of my proudest moments. I hope we'll have another moment like that, come March."

"The hand," she said, turning and taking in the loveliness of the scene around her, "is very important. But this is exquisite. Magical."

This was the gap that technology couldn't fill. This was the stuff magicians were made for.

This was what she could create.

"But in the end, it's pandering, really." Mg. Praff touched the edge of the starry sky and murmured, "Cease," and the otherworldliness of the spell blinked out, opening a strange sort of longing inside Alvie's chest. She rubbed at it.

Mg. Praff continued, "It's art; it's entertainment; it's an escape. But society can go on without those things. What we're doing now, Alvie, is making the fundamentals of life—movement, capability—better. What we're doing is restoring functionality to a young woman who thought those things were lost. Think of what we could do for veterans alone."

Alvie dropped her hand. The dreaminess of the Imagidome enthralled her, but she very much liked Mg. Praff's speech. If they could push a little harder, work a little longer, they truly could better the lives of those who had lost limbs. And what next? Her mind spun with the possibilities.

Alvie still swam in thought when she returned to the house on a break enforced by Mg. Praff. It was nearing the dinner hour, and Alvie would be eating with the family tonight, which she did a few times a week, now, usually without consequence. As far as she knew, none of the Praff children would be joining them this evening.

As she began to ascend the stairs to her room, Mr. Hemsley coughed loudly behind her. She turned around.

"A letter for you." The butler held up a silver tray that had an orange crane perched on it. It was large for a mail bird. Alvie's heart instantly began to pitter-patter.

"Thank you." She hurried back down the stairs and grabbed the crane by its neck. Holding the bird to her chest, she hurried up the flight of stairs and darted into the privacy of her bedroom.

Checking to make sure Emma wasn't hanging laundry in the closet or the like, Alvie plopped down on her desk vanity chair and unfolded the bird. Her hands trembled just a bit as she did so. A smaller white songbird fell out first, blank, for a return message. The inside of the orange bird read:

> Alvie,
>
> I heard about the break-in at the polymery—Mg. Bailey subscribes to the local news telegrams. Are you all right? I heard the burglary was unsuccessful. I hope all is well.
>
> Bennet

Alvie reread the letter. Not even twenty-four hours had passed, and people were already talking about it. Of course it would be news; Mg. Praff's name carried weight.

She wished the letter were longer. In fact, she turned the unfolded crane over just to check. But he'd written her, and that made her happy. She read the note a third time, then carefully unfolded the songbird and wrote:

Nothing stolen, nothing important broken. We're all okay.

She thought about adding her suspicions about Mg. Ezzell, but neither the police officer nor Mg. Praff had seemed pleased with her suggestion, so she decided against it . . . at least until she could find concrete evidence to support her theory. She thought for a long moment and, trying to match Bennet's tone, wrote:

How are your studies?

She stared at it for a long moment before commanding the bird, "Refold," and hurrying to her window. Alvie had never tried to open it, but it *did* open, with a little leverage. A burst of cold air coughed onto her. "Breathe," she told the pre-enchanted spell, and the bird came alive. It must have already known where to go, for it hopped off her hand and into the cold night without hesitation.

Alvie looked up at the sky. She hoped it wasn't going to rain. Given how poorly mail birds did in wet conditions, it was a wonder Londoners used them at all.

She shut the window and returned to Bennet's letter, reading it a fourth time. Something squirmed inside her.

It wasn't precisely the most romantic letter, was it? Very straightforward. Nothing poetic or flowery. Just a note from a friend. Or someone eager to make sure his sister's arm hadn't been lost.

Alvie set the letter in her lap and slouched over it. The squirming feeling turned sharp, and she knuckled the sore spot between her breasts. Rolled her lips together.

She really liked him, didn't she? She rubbed the spot harder. *Oh bother.* She'd almost forgotten this uncomfortable feeling of liking someone. She'd liked boys before, of course, but none of them had ever looked her way twice.

But Bennet wasn't like those other boys, was he? He had written her, after all. And he'd taken her out . . . but maybe he really had done it just to be nice. For all she knew, Ethel might have asked him to—at least the second time. Alvie wasn't charming. She knew that.

Sighing, she tucked the letter into a drawer of the desk and crossed the room to the closet, where the tall mirror stood. She pushed up her glasses and looked in it. Retucked her shirt into her pants. She had a trim waist, didn't she? Surely Bennet liked trim waists.

She combed her fingers through her hair—or tried to. They caught on several knots. There were almost always knots in her too-thick, too-wavy locks. Plain and brown, not bright and blond like Ethel's or bold like those of the Folder she'd met at the post office. Brown hair, brown eyes. A face half eaten up by glasses.

She took them off and stepped closer to the mirror, so close her nose almost touched it. Fuzzy shapes comprised her face. She squinted, clearing them a bit, but she hardly looked right squinting. She put her glasses back on. She didn't have any pimples or wrinkles. That was a point in her favor, wasn't it?

She stuck her tongue out at her reflection. What a bother. She didn't need a distraction now, not with the Discovery Convention looming ahead of her. And she had to plan her trip home for Christmas, besides. It was a little more than a month away.

If only her heart would agree with her.

Emma knocked at the door and poked her head in. "Would you like help choosing a dress for dinner, Alvie?"

Alvie sighed and backed away from the mirror. "Might as well."

Emma smiled and crossed the room. It was easier to let her pick something from the closet, though Alvie still insisted on dressing herself. She was twenty, after all.

Twenty, with two whole dates under her belt. Twenty, and never been kissed.

She wondered if Emma had been kissed. Surely she had. But that was probably an awkward question to ask, so she didn't.

Emma pulled out a slim black dress with thick lace around the collar and sleeves. "I know Mrs. Praff is wearing blue tonight, so let's go with this one. Best not to match."

"Are we having guests?"

"Well, no . . ."

Alvie smiled. "Whatever you think is best."

Emma nodded and set the dress—and matching shoes—at the foot of the bed.

"Emma?"

"Hm?"

Alvie glanced at her reflection. "Do you think you could do my hair tonight?"

Emma grinned. "I'd be happy to."

CHAPTER 12

THE LEAVES WERE THOROUGHLY autumn colored at the end of November, and dripping with freezing rain the afternoon Alvie asked the chauffer to take her to see Ethel. Alvie had finally invested in a good English coat, and even an English hat to match. Though Fred assured her he knew where he was going, Alvie paid special attention to the route, occasionally glancing down at the address in her hand. If London would only allow public mirror-transport, she'd be there by now, and without the need of a coat or hat.

They wound up at a modest home toward the outskirts of the city, not too far afield to be in the country. Two stories, with russet brick and white trim. It had a small porch with a short fence, and two white pillars guarded either side of the door.

Hauling her large bag of supplies with her, Alvie stepped out of the automobile and waved for the chauffeur to go on his way; she would be an hour, at least. As the automobile drove off, however, a prickly sensation danced across Alvie's neck. She turned around, scanning the street. She had the oddest feeling she was being watched, but the weather had driven everyone else inside, as far as she could see. It must have been the rain stirring her hair.

She hurried up the steps and knocked. A woman with pale blond hair, graying at the temples, opened the door. She wore a high-necked brown dress and had blue eyes—a stark contrast to Ethel's and Bennet's rich brown. Glancing at Alvie's bag, she said, "Yes, she's just through that hallway."

"Um. Thank you." Alvie slid by her, trying to be small, but her bag knocked the woman's knees—a woman whom Alvie presumed to be Mrs. Cooper. Alvie's glasses fogged instantly in the warmth of the house, and she struggled to wipe them clear with her sleeve while avoiding a collision with the blurry furniture.

"Alvie?" Ethel's sweet voice eased the stress building in Alvie's shoulders. Following the sound, Alvie stepped into a small sitting room of sorts. It had two cream-colored chairs and a cream-colored couch, two windows, and a very small oak writing desk. Faded-blue wallpaper with a fleur-de-lis design running through its middle coated all four walls.

Ethel sat on the couch, her knees up, holding open a book with her right hand. Alvie wondered if she and Mg. Praff would be able to create a prosthesis finely tuned enough to turn pages. Ethel's hair was pinned up in a stylish pompadour, and she wore a floral-printed dress that seemed too cheery for the weather.

"Don't mind Mum." Ethel gestured to a chair, and Alvie sat, setting the heavy bag down in front of her. "She's unsure about all of this."

"Why?"

Ethel shrugged. "Because you and Magician Praff aren't doctors."

"Oh." A valid point. "But Mg. Praff is communicating with one. I saw them chatting through the salon mirror earlier this week."

Ethel smiled and put down the book. "It's good to see you again. It's stuffy inside this house. Not many people come to visit."

"Why not?"

Another shrug. "Guess they don't know what to say."

"Well, your brain isn't gone, is it?" Alvie opened her bag and pulled out a ledger, a pen, and a seamstress's measuring tape. "And you could go outside."

The rain picked up, pattering against the window.

Alvie frowned at it. "I suppose it's not the best season for recovery."

"It makes my arm hurt. The rain." Ethel rubbed her stump. She no longer wore bandaging, just a painful-looking scar.

"My mama says that about her knee."

"I always thought it was a joke, but it's true. The weather has an effect on the body, even when you're not standing in it."

Alvie held up the measuring tape. "Do you mind?"

"Oh. No." Ethel sat up and held out her half arm. Alvie began measuring it, jotting the numbers down in her book. She'd measure the right arm, too, for comparison.

"I heard about the burglary," Ethel said.

"Oh yes. It wasn't *really* a burglary. Nothing was taken, fortunately."

"Still. Scary to think what might have happened."

Alvie straightened, keeping her thumb on the measuring tape to remember the number. "The case is more or less closed. There's no evidence to point toward who the intruder could be. But . . ."

"But?"

"Well"—Alvie glanced to the door—"you see, there's a Magician Ezzell who doesn't like Magician Praff at all. He's rather unlikeable."

"Oh, the one at the restaurant."

"I—yes." Had Bennet told her about that? What had he said? That Alvie was awkward? That he'd decided there was no spark between them after all?

"You think it was him?" Ethel guessed.

Alvie sighed and jotted down the measurement. "*I* think it's him, yes. He certainly had the motivation, but there's no evidence. Unfortunately, he has a sound alibi. He was at home, and his wife confirmed that he was in bed during the break-in, and his chauffeur never left the house. Or something like that. I didn't get to hear the full report. But his own polymery was broken into a while back, so . . ." She got off the chair and knelt before Ethel so she could measure her right arm.

"And nothing else has happened since?" A pause. "Alvie?"

"Hold on. Math."

"Oh, sorry."

Alvie looked toward the ceiling, adding fractions in her head, and jotted their sum in the ledger.

"Nothing else has happened?" Ethel tried again.

"Oh no. We've been much more careful. Magician Praff changed the locks and put up some wards and the like, just in case. And he's started locking up the prostheses at the end of every night. It's a bother, but safe is better than sorry. Four polymeries have been broken into in the last year, and no one knows who is doing it or why." She sighed. "What are you reading?"

Ethel picked up the book. "*A Tale of Two Cities*. Just started it this morning. Have you read it?"

"No. I don't read a lot of fiction."

"Never? You're denying yourself, Alvie!"

Alvie took her ledger back to her chair. "I did read *Heart of Darkness* before prep school."

Ethel laughed. "I wouldn't have pinned you for a lover of gothic romance."

"I suppose I'll have to read at least one more in the genre to know if I am."

Ethel leaned close, her eyes taking on a feline light. "*Speaking* of romance. How is my brother? He's too private for my liking."

"Uh . . ." Alvie glanced away and cleared her throat. "I don't know. You must see him more than I do."

Ethel's face fell. "You haven't seen him?"

"Not in the last couple of weeks, no. But he sends me mail birds every couple of days. He seems committed to his Folding test, at least."

Ethel nodded. "At least. Don't take it to heart, Alvie. That mentor of his keeps him on a tight leash, and he's a little shy with women."

"Take what to heart?" He *was* sending her notes, but they were still . . . unromantic. Not that Alvie knew a great deal about courting, but she could write something at least a little romantic. Even if Emma had to help her with it.

Needless to say, she hadn't had the courage to send *that* bird.

Ethel studied Alvie's face. For what, she wasn't sure. Part of Alvie wanted to blurt out, *Do you know if he cares for me that way? Would he ever? Does he talk about me? Do you think it would work?* But she kept her lips firmly sealed. She'd rather not make a fool of herself today.

A mischievous grin lifted Ethel's countenance. "Would you like to see his room?"

"H-His room?"

"He's not there, of course. He lives with Magician Bailey. But his room is still here . . ."

Ethel looked ready to jump off the couch.

Alvie nodded.

Grabbing Alvie's hand, Ethel tore back through the hallway to the stairs. Halfway up them, her mother called, "You need rest!" Advice that Ethel did not heed. She took Alvie to the second room on the left and opened the door.

"*Voilà!*" She lifted her good arm up in show, and tucked her stump behind her.

It wasn't anything remarkable. A simple room, small, equipped with the basic necessities. Clean, as it was currently unoccupied. Bennet's bed had plaid covers on it, and it tucked right under the window. On the sill rested a small telescope—did he like the stars? He had a very tall dresser, atop which sat an assortment of paper creations he must have left there during visits home—a fan, a frog, a flower similar to the one he'd Folded for Alvie at the restaurant. She'd kept it on a shelf in her workroom, but the burglar had knocked it off, and the delicate paper had unfolded itself.

There was a ship in a bottle on his nightstand—did he like the sea?—and a very old model of a Gaffer lamp. His closet doors were shut. Alvie wondered what lay behind them. Had he always had such a modest and pristine taste in fashion, or was that something he'd acquired recently?

"What are you doing up there?" Mrs. Cooper called from the bottom of the stairs.

"Coming down!" Ethel grinned. She took Alvie's hand again and led her back to the sitting room, much slower than they had left it.

When the two were once again settled, Alvie forced her mind back to Polymaking and pulled out a few cups of plastic, which she had shaped yesterday. She softened the plastic and formed it over Ethel's stump, then used a Heed: Pattern spell and asked Ethel to move her arm in different directions. If the stump created any pressure points in the plastic, they could use those to activate movements in the prosthesis. She repeated this exercise several times. A wider range of samples led to a better product, or so Mg. Praff had told her when he helped her pack her bag. Lastly, Alvie vacuum-formed Ethel's right wrist and hand, creating several copies in different positions. Mg. Praff would use these to create a finely tuned model to work with.

"You didn't say what you thought," Ethel said as Alvie packed up.

"I think it will fit well, when we're done with it."

Ethel lightly smacked Alvie's arm. "About Bennet's room."

Alvie brushed a lock of hair from her face. "Well, it's not like I'm sleeping in it."

"Not yet, anyway."

Her face heated. *Ethel.*

Ethel laughed, and Alvie found she didn't mind the teasing quite so much. It was good to hear her friend laugh.

Alvie sighed. "I do like him, of course. I really like him."

Ethel bounced on the sofa. She almost clapped, then remembered, and stopped herself. Her smile faded.

"But," Alvie amended, "I don't think it will go anywhere. I don't think . . . Bennet is going to pursue me."

"Why wouldn't he?"

"I've had lots of time to think about it. Compile evidence, sort the possible outcomes. The current hypothesis is—"

"Alvie."

Alvie closed her mouth.

Ethel leaned her stump and elbow on her thighs. "You can't science up love like that. Men don't ask women on dates and send them letters just for nanty narking."

"For *what?*"

"For fun."

Alvie shrugged. "My chauffeur is probably waiting outside."

Ethel frowned. "I haven't pressed too hard, have I?"

"Oh no. Not at all. I don't mind, really."

Ethel took her hand. "You're a good friend, Alvie. Even without all the magic."

Alvie squeezed her hand. "You are, too, Ethel. Even without the arm."

The older woman's eyes watered just a bit. "I think that, today, that's something I needed to hear."

Ethel saw Alvie to the door, and, sure enough, Fred was parked in front of the house. As he came around to open the passenger door, however, Alvie again got that prickling sensation—and the rain had stopped, for the time being.

She looked around, peering into the old green trees lining the street to the west. Searched the neighboring homes. She didn't see anyone.

Yet as she slid into the auto, she couldn't shake the feeling that someone had been watching *her.*

Chapter 13

Alvie opened a second box on the island in the center of Mg. Praff's lab. Today they were bringing supplies to the Woosley Hospital to fulfill a special order from the coordinator of staff. The adhesive bandages and canisters for storage carried no enchantment, but in addition to those, Mg. Praff had created a variety of casts that could be formed to any broken limb, making the work of bodily mending a much smoother process. She added syringes that would fill to the desired, spoken amount without bubbles, as well as vinyl sheets that would fit any mattress, specially treated to prevent tearing.

"I'll show you the difference between transferable and non-transferable vacuum-forming when we return. You'd be surprised how many people want to purchase vacuum-forming spells for food preservation." Mg. Praff set a thin strip of transparent plastic over the top of the already-filled box and commanded it, "Adhere." Alvie finished the second box and got a strip of her own, repeating the spell to seal it.

Two footmen came in to carry the boxes out to the automobile, where the chauffeur awaited them. Alvie and Mg. Praff followed, but as the footmen strapped in the boxes, Mr. Hemsley came out of the manor with the announcement, "Miss Brechenmacher, the mirror is for you."

"Me?" Alvie asked. Her parents hadn't said they'd be calling today. It was always a challenge when they did—the Gaffing magic that allowed communication between mirrors couldn't stretch all the way from Columbus to London, so it had to be bounced about other mirrors across the Atlantic, which resulted in blurry images and garbled sound. Still, it was faster than a letter. She usually spoke to her parents once a week, on Sunday afternoons. Today was Friday.

Mg. Praff said, "Thank you, Hemsley. Go on, Alvie. We're in no hurry. I need to check that we didn't leave the polymery unlocked, besides."

Alvie nodded and scurried past the ever-frowning butler to the house. She waved to Emma, who had been watching the loading through the window, and hurried down the main hall into the salon. Sure enough, the oval mirror in the far corner shimmered with magic. It was not her parents' blurred faces that filled it, however, but Bennet's crisp one.

"Oh!" She quickened her step, subsequently tripping over the back of her own heel.

"Alvie?" the mirror asked. Fortunately, Alvie didn't think Bennet could see all the way to the salon door.

"Here, here, coming!" She picked herself up and walked to the mirror at a safer pace. "You didn't say you'd be calling." She hadn't gotten a bird from him in four days, as a matter of fact. She had begun worrying that Ethel's encouragement had been misplaced.

Bennet rubbed the back of his head. "Yes, sorry. I've a knack for just showing up, don't I?"

"I don't mind at all!" She cringed at the excitement in her own voice. *Easy, Alvie.* "But the butler probably does."

Good job, Alvie.

"Oh, sorry."

"Oh no, he just minds everything. Don't worry about him."

A small smile brushed Bennet's lips. "I know the type, believe me. In fact, I don't have long to use this mirror, so I'll get to the point. I was wondering if you were going home for Christmas."

She nodded. "I'm leaving on the fifteenth. Until . . . well, I'm departing from the States late on the second, so with the time change, it might be the third . . ."

"The fifteenth," he repeated with a nod. "Going back the way you came? The station?"

"Well, yes."

"Would you mind an escort?" He shifted, as if he was wrestling with his hands or the like, though the mirror cut off too high for her to see for sure. "That is, you're quite capable."

Alvie didn't realize she was smiling until her cheeks began to ache. "I did get lost."

"Not of your own volition."

"I would very much like an escort. Even without the Benz."

Bennet let out a breath. She wondered at that. "Excellent. I'll speak to Magician Bailey . . . we've been terribly busy. The holidays demand every paper decoration you can imagine. Magician Bailey generally works in textbooks, but there's a shortage of Folders. I figure I need the practice as well. I can Fold twenty-one types of stars . . . doubt that will be on the test, though."

Alvie's lips formed an O. "I'm sure they're lovely. My parents get the chains—the ones that unravel themselves as they count down to Christmas."

"Ah yes. Those are fairly simple."

"Do you have the test questions yet?"

A new voice sounded in the distance of Bennet's mirror. "Bennet!" The sharp words were garbled, but she heard how the invective ended: "—and the delivery!"

Alvie frowned. "Is that Magician Bailey?"

He ran a hand back through his sunshine hair. "Yes. He's . . . stressed. I should go."

Alvie offered a heartening smile. At least, she tried to make it heartening. "I'll see you on the fifteenth, then. I'm taking the one o'clock train."

Bennet nodded. "I'll arrive early."

His hand moved outside of the frame, and the vision of him rippled silver until Alvie stared only at her own reflection.

Woosley Hospital's delivery entrance was located at the back of the old building. A narrow road ran past it, and an ambulance blocked part of it coming south, so Fred circled around the adjacent block until he could find a decent parking space not terribly far from the hospital.

"We'll be just a moment, Fred." Mg. Praff slipped out of the vehicle and circled back to the rear, and Alvie slid across the bench to follow. Another automobile, one of the older models, passed by as he went, splashing through a puddle from a recent rainfall. Muddy droplets sprayed the door and Alvie's shoes, as well as the hem of Mg. Praff's slacks.

She stuck her tongue out at the offending vehicle. "Rude."

Fred turned around in his seat. "That one's been behind us since Mayfair."

"Really?" Alvie asked. The same one? She wondered where they were headed.

The chauffeur nodded. "Even around the block." The automobile in question turned onto the next adjoining road, out of sight.

Alvie stepped gingerly onto the road and took one of the boxes from Mg. Praff, though her eyes were on the street ahead of them. The box was light, another benefit of plastic.

As Mg. Praff led the way down the street, Alvie asked, "Why isn't the demand for Polymakers higher? Plastic is lighter and more durable than glass, and it seems it could replace a great deal of metal—machine parts, maybe. Silverware."

Mg. Praff laughed. "Plastic silverware?"

"Plasticware. Why not?"

"I think the demand for plastic will increase as time goes on, and as we continue to prove ourselves useful. And not just materials from Polymakers. Many of the things you're talking about can be fashioned by regular people. Perhaps, one day, in factories."

They turned a corner. Alvie stepped in a puddle she hadn't seen thanks to the large box in her arms. "To think, how different the world might be in just ten years—"

"Stop right there," a gruff voice said. Mg. Praff halted immediately; Alvie stopped just behind him.

The click of metal sent a chill up her back. She'd heard that sound before, on the shooting range near the Jefferson School.

She turned to see two persons behind her. They wore common English clothes, but both had brown cloths tied around their faces, exposing only part of their eyes—just enough to see. The taller one held a pistol in his hand. The shorter, slimmer figure had a knife drawn and a tight hat tugged over his head.

Her body went cold.

"Now, now," Mg. Praff said, very slowly turning as well. They were on a narrow one-way road that connected with the street behind the hospital. No houses, no witnesses, unless another automobile drove by. These thieves must have come from the automobile the chauffeur had mentioned, the one that had followed them all the way from Mayfair.

"We've nothing of use," Mg. Praff said slowly, "just hospital supplies."

The taller robber waved the gun, and Alvie flinched. Her mind buzzed with possibilities of how to get away . . . but they all died before really forming. She didn't have a weapon. She didn't have any combat skills. She didn't know any spells to help . . . and even if she did, Polymaking was the second slowest magic there was. She doubted either robber was going to wait while she made some sort of defense.

"Drop the boxes," the man with the gun said.

Mg. Praff lowered his box to the ground.

"But—" Alvie started.

"Drop them!"

She let go of her box. It crashed onto the road. Mg. Praff, having stooped to lower his box, stood back up and raised his hands. Alvie followed suit. Her heart flipped back and forth in her chest. Was this really happening?

God help her, was she going to *die?* The air around her bit with a sudden chill. She searched behind the robbers for any help—

The man with the gun came forward. Alvie stumbled back into the stone wall of some building she didn't dare look at, for doing so would mean taking her eyes off the gun. The pistol looked right at her with its hollow black eye. The other robber bent down and, with the knife and a shaky grip, opened the box. He sorted through it, occasionally glancing at Mg. Praff. Bandages and syringes and even a bedpan went flying onto the cobbles. With a scowl, he moved on to the second box. His accomplice pointed the gun at Mg. Praff now. More supplies spilled onto the road.

The crouching thief shook his head. The one with the gun cursed. "All worthless," he muttered.

The sound of a second cocking hammer made Alvie's breath hitch. She turned, only to see a well-dressed man coming up the same path she had just taken. No mask. He had graying hair and a nearly white half beard. He, too, carried a firearm.

The thieves froze.

"Put it down, son," the man warned. He nodded toward her mentor. "Marion."

"Alfred." Mg. Praff said his name in greeting almost as if there weren't two armed robbers right in front of them. Alvie didn't know who Alfred was, but his firearm was pointed at the thief with the gun, so she instantly liked him.

The thief set the gun down and slowly stood. Alvie's eyes darted between the two thieves. She focused on the shorter one, on the way his clothes fit. He reached into his pocket.

She jumped. "Look out, he's—"

The robber's hand shot down. An explosion of . . . confetti? . . . engulfed both criminals. When the paper bits settled, the crooks were gone.

Alfred lowered his revolver and pulled what looked like a compact mirror from his pocket. "I need all hands down on Thompson. Two escaped robbers. One, one hundred seventy-eight centimeters. The other, one sixty-five. Both wearing brown coats and tan slacks." He closed the mirror and ran down the narrow lane to where it connected with the main road—Thompson, Alvie thought. He looked around, shook his head, and returned.

In the distance, police whistles screeched.

Mg. Praff let out a long breath. "You're a godsend, Alfred."

"I have a habit of being in the wrong place at the right time." He smiled.

"Pardon me." Mg. Praff ran a hand down his face, blinked, and seemed to reset himself. "Alvie, this is Magician Alfred Hughes. Alfred, this is my apprentice, Alvie Brechenmacher."

Mg. Hughes nodded to her. "I'll walk with you in case they return, or there's a third accomplice."

Alvie hugged herself against the cold December air. Her heart hadn't slowed yet, and her arms shook with anxiety. "F-Folders?"

Mg. Hughes shook his head. "I doubt it. Concealing confetti is a transferable magic. Likely purchased it somewhere. But the spell doesn't let you travel far."

Alvie nodded. Stepped on a bandage. Coming to herself, she crouched down and began reboxing all the supplies, even the wet ones.

Mg. Praff sighed. "We're just on our way to deliver supplies. My apologies again." He shook his head. He seemed anxious as well. "I'm slipping with my introductions. Alvie, Magician Alfred Hughes is the head of Criminal Affairs for England. I suppose that's important enough to include, isn't it?"

Mg. Hughes chuckled.

Alvie paused her boxing and looked at Mg. Hughes with wide eyes. "Truly? I, uh." She stood and wiped her hands on her slacks, then extended the right. "It's a pleasure to meet you, sir."

He shook her hand. His grip was firm. Oddly, it helped her relax. "And you, too. New to the place, I take it?"

"Yes, since September."

"Always nice to see a young lady keep her head in trying situations." He released her hand.

Mg. Praff bent down and picked up supplies. Mg. Hughes helped him. "What brings you here?" Mg. Praff asked.

"On my way to the Parliament building, what else? Hmm." He picked up a roll of bandages and turned it over in his hands. "What were they after, do you think?"

Alvie's mind flashed to the polymery. Could these robbers from the street be connected to the burglaries? Mg. Praff clearly thought it possible, because as soon as everything was repacked and they started for the hospital again, he shared the story about the break-in. Mg. Hughes hadn't heard, though Alvie wasn't too surprised. The man in charge of Criminal Affairs—one of the departments of the Magicians' Cabinet— likely had more important things to worry about than failed burglaries.

Another siren wailed as they crossed Thompson and came up to the delivery entrance.

"I see." Mg. Hughes nodded. "Keep me informed, Marion. I'll do the same." He turned to Alvie and nodded. "Good to meet you."

Alvie nodded in return. Mg. Hughes hurried back the way he'd come. Did he have a buggy parked back there somewhere, or had he merely been within walking distance of the Parliament building?

Mg. Praff knocked on the delivery entrance door.

Mg. Praff sighed. "I'm sorry about all of this, Alvie. Despite all the good we try to do, there are some terrible men in the world."

Alvie glanced at him, then back the way they'd come. "Not just men, Magician Praff."

"Hm?"

She shifted her box in her hands. "I'm fairly certain the shorter one was a woman." She wore men's clothes, yes, but they fit wrong. And she wore a hat as if to cover her hair.

"I . . . I didn't notice."

Alvie tipped her head in the direction Mg. Hughes had gone. "What is he a magician of?"

"Magician Hughes is a Siper."

"Really?" Siping was the magic closest to Polymaking. It was a Siper who had discovered plastic as a material in the first place. She wondered if Bennet would want to hear about that since his father owned a Siping factory. The same factory where Ethel had lost her arm.

Ethel.

Alvie looked down at the supplies in her arms.

Surely the person who'd attempted to burglarize the polymery, and—if her theory was correct—the robbers who'd assaulted them tonight, had been after Ethel's prosthetic arm. It was the only thing of true value inside the lab besides the Imagidome, but the latter could be easily traced back to Mg. Praff, making it impossible to sell. Yet Mg.

Praff's polymery was the *fourth* to be hit, and surely the other victims didn't have prosthetic arms in their labs! What was the thief after?

Something to present at the convention, Magician Ezzell? she thought. Granted, he had been burglarized as well, but . . . it didn't sit right with Alvie. It was like trying to solve a math equation with two variables, and there weren't enough real numbers to figure out the second.

Unfortunately for the thief, she was *very* good at math.

CHAPTER 14

ALVIE CAREFULLY PLACED HER wrapped presents in the center of her suitcase, surrounding them with clothes to cushion any bumps she was sure to encounter on her way home. An English pocket watch for her father—she'd removed the gold-colored faceplate and replaced it with a sturdy plastic one enchanted to be transparent, so that all the watch's gears were visible. For her mother, she'd made a plastic rolling pin with an Image Memory spell on it so that it would roll out dough on its own. She hoped they would be pleased. It would be wonderful to see them in person and not through the garbled interference of layers of mirrors. She had yet to mention the run-in with the thieves or the questioning from the police the following day. She hadn't wanted them to worry or, worse, insist she transfer somewhere closer to home. Besides, she didn't really care to remember the events herself; focusing on family and holidays was much more pleasant. She'd tell them after Christmas. Maybe.

Her gift for Bennet was tucked into the bag strung over her shoulder. She'd already mailed a box of chocolates and a copy of *Heart of Darkness* to Ethel earlier that week.

Mrs. Praff held nothing back for the holidays. The manor was strewn with evergreen boughs and holly. She'd even hired a Folder to install small snowflakes that hovered about the ceiling, swirling in various patterns. The Gaffer and Pyre lamps in the hallways glowed green and red at night, and not a single dinner had gone by in the last two weeks where she hadn't talked of the Christmas Day menu, or about having all three of her children visit in addition to her sister.

"Preston is quite handsome," Mrs. Praff had said to Alvie last night, referring to her eldest nephew. "He likes academic girls. Are you sure you won't stay an extra two days, just to meet him?"

Alvie smiled and closed her suitcase. No, she wouldn't. She itched to be home, and besides, there was only one Englishman she cared to see before she departed for Hamburg.

Emma's soft, familiar knock sounded at her door. She cracked it open. "Mr. Cooper for you, Alvie. Have him waiting in the main hall."

"Thank you. I'll be right down."

Emma smiled and left, and Alvie faced the mirror. She'd been tempted to have Emma do her hair for the trip—something extra for Bennet, whom she hadn't seen in person for weeks. But then, it wasn't sensible to be dressed up for travel, especially since part of her journey would be on a boat. Instead, Alvie had calmed her locks with a little serum and a comb and pulled them into a thick French braid falling down her back. She thought it made her glasses look a little larger, but nothing could be done about that.

She had, however, made one special exception to her usual wardrobe.

Grabbing her suitcases, Alvie stepped into the hallway. One of the footmen waited by the stairs and kindly took her luggage for her. Taking a deep breath, Alvie followed a few steps behind him, her maroon skirt swooshing about her black stockings on the way down.

She did like the swooshing. One plus to forgoing slacks.

She saw his sunshine hair first. He seemed to be studying the vase near the vestibule. The bright locks had been recently cut, which was a shame, for they reflected the light better when they were longer. He had on a long black coat, and when he turned at the sound of footsteps on the stairs, she saw his pressed gray slacks and cream-colored vest over a white shirt. He didn't wear a tie or anything similar, and the first button of the shirt was undone. Though it was silly, that trace of unkemptness made Alvie think, *Oh.*

His eyes found hers, and he smiled a bright smile that made Alvie feel like a magician already, or perhaps something even better. Alvie wasn't a great blusher, but her cheeks certainly warmed in the radiance of that smile, more so once she reached the floor and was level with it.

The footman addressed Bennet, who pointed out the front entrance. Alvie could see the fender of the Benz through the windows. The footman hurried on his way, letting in a snap of cold air when he opened the doors.

Bennet's gaze dropped down to Alvie's skirt. "You look lovely."

She shrugged. "Today I like the swooshing."

He laughed. "The swooshing?"

She nodded. "If you like, when I return, I'll let you try one of them on, and you can see the swooshing for yourself. Your hips can't be too different from mine." She measured him with her eyes.

Bennet chuckled, and Alvie beamed when she saw his cheeks redden. That was good, wasn't it?

"I might pass on that one. I'll admit to trying on one of Ethel's skirts in my boyhood, but I've sworn them off ever since." He held out his elbow. "I'd hate to make you late."

"One request before we go. Since it's Christmas and all."

His elbow lowered. "Hm?"

"Um." She dug her toe into the floor. "Can I touch your hair?"

Bennet blinked for a second before laughing. "You want to touch my hair?"

"Please?"

Pursing his mouth around a smile, he bent his head slightly and made a showy gesture with his hand.

Biting her lip, Alvie reached forward and combed her fingers through the sunshine. It was soft, lightly oiled. She wanted a blanket made out of it.

She did not tell him that, of course.

"Thank you," she said, and he straightened. Reaching up, Alvie fixed a tuft she'd swept out of place.

"You are one of a kind, Alvie. But this exchange must be reciprocal."

She blinked. "How so?"

He folded his arms and tilted his head to one side, his cheeks tight like he was hiding a smile. "In exchange for touching my hair, I insist on trying on your glasses."

Alvie snorted. "You're teasing."

Bennet waited.

Rolling her eyes, Alvie took off her glasses, squinting against the blurry world they exposed. She handed them over. The blur of Bennet tried on her glasses, and she wished she had a second pair so she could see how silly he looked in them.

"Whoa." He took them off just as quickly. "Alvie, you're blind."

"More or less."

He handed them back to her, and she slipped the arms over her ears. Everything snapped into focus. Bennet rubbed his eyes with the palms of his hand. Then he laughed. "No wonder you were so lost when I first met you. I've never met anyone with such bad vision."

Alvie smiled. "My papa said God gave me bad eyes so I wouldn't be too perfect." She laughed at the notion.

Bennet proffered his elbow again. "Maybe he was on to something. Here, a storm is coming in."

Alvie might have blushed, but she distracted herself by glancing out the window. "Is it safe to drive in bad weather?"

"I promise I'll be attentive."

She took his arm, shivering at the warmth of it, if that even made sense, and let him lead her out to the Benz. It was a bit blustery. Bennet helped her into her seat—*darn this skirt, making everything difficult*—and climbed into the driver's side. Alvie asked him about Christmas, and he talked a little about his family and Mg. Bailey as they made their way to the train station. Alvie watched his profile as he talked. He had such a nice profile. She hoped he would one day do a great feat so someone would make a copper bust of him, carving that profile for future generations to admire.

They arrived at the station, which was much busier than when Alvie had been there in September. Bennet insisted on carrying her suitcases, and she held on to his elbow, letting him guide her through the monstrous place. She bumped her knees into the suitcase on the right a few times and hoped Bennet didn't mind.

They found the platform and a dozen other people waiting for the same train. Alvie checked to make sure she had her ticket and all her documentation.

"I . . . well, I made you something," Bennet said.

She perked up. He'd set her luggage down, and he had a thin, rectangular package in his hands. It must have been tucked away in that coat of his. It was wrapped in brown paper and blue ribbon, and her heart managed to soften and pitter-patter at the same time.

She grabbed the tiny package out of her bag. It was wrapped with the shimmering silver paper Mrs. Praff had purchased for the season and was small enough to fit in her palm. "I made you something, too."

Bennet smiled. They both hesitated, then awkwardly exchanged gifts.

"You first," he said.

Taking a seat on the empty bench near them, Alvie slid her pinky under the ribbon, then carefully picked apart the paper. No tape or glue held it together, which surprised her only for a moment. It must have all been done via some sort of adhering spell.

Bennet chuckled. "You're supposed to tear it."

She shook her head. "I want to save it."

Inside she found a book—a neat little book with a dark leather cover. Inside was a newly sharpened pencil and pages of clean lined paper.

"For your notes," Bennet explained. "I've noticed you take a lot of them, in the polymery, and . . . in the back"—Alvie flipped to the back, where there were several sheets of unlined paper with rough edges— "those are Mimic spells. I have the other half. If, that is . . . if you wanted to stay in communication while you were gone."

The grin that spread across Alvie's face was so wide she didn't think her face could contain it. The notebook was very nice, especially if he'd assembled it himself . . . but the Mimic spell meant he wanted to keep talking to her while she was across the ocean. A happy giggle stirred like a giant butterfly inside her chest.

"I absolutely love it." She closed the book and jumped to her feet, then threw her arms around his neck. "Oh, Bennet, thank you."

His arms, hesitant at first, encircled her waist. It was a blissful, wonderful feeling, even better than the spell and the book. Alvie pulled back and looked at his face.

His eyes dropped to her lips, and his face reddened.

Thinking she'd embarrassed him, she let go and took a step back. "Now you."

Bennet cleared his throat and turned his attention to the tiny gift in his hand. It weighed almost nothing. He picked apart the wrapping. Inside was a hexagon-shaped piece of translucent plastic. He turned it over, confused.

"I saw your telescope in your room," she said, and his eyes shot up to hers. She rushed to explain. "Ethel showed me, and I was very proper about all of it, so don't think me strange."

He smiled.

She took his hand, the one palming the hexagon, in hers. Pressing her thumbs to the plastic, she said, "Image Memory: Orion."

The plastic darkened to a deep blue, and white dots depicting stars appeared on it. The constellation of Orion—Alvie's personal favorite.

"Look at that," he said, the words airy. He held the hexagon up to his face, studying it.

"You can't turn it off . . . I don't know how to transfer the spell. So it'll stay starry like that."

His gaze moved from the hexagon to her. "Why would I ever want to turn it off?"

Alvie smiled and pressed a hand to the light, balloonlike feeling in her stomach. The whistle of the train sounded, and the people around them collected on the center of the platform.

"I'll write to you, on the spell," she promised. "And I'll write very small so I can write a lot. And I'll draw a picture of something, too, if you want."

"I would like that. Very much. And I'll write to you, of course."

"And Ethel?"

He raised a brow. "I'm afraid I won't grant Ethel any space on those pages. She'll have to wait until you get back to chat."

The train stopped behind her. Doors opened, and people came out and went in. Alvie got her ticket in hand and grabbed her suitcases.

"If you insist." Then, in a burst of courage, she leaned forward and kissed Bennet's cheek. Though she was the instigator, her pulse raced, and she felt like her blood was carbonated, the bubbles pushing out against her skin. She smudged her glasses and hoped he didn't notice.

"Thank you, and good-bye," she said.

Touching his cheek, Bennet nodded. "Happy Christmas, Alvie."

———

Alvie greatly enjoyed the holidays at home with her parents, though for a few days, the house got snowed in, leaving her trapped in her room with no polymery and only a single textbook to occupy her mind.

And yet she wasn't bored at all—she spent the hours chatting with her parents, playing games with friends, and writing in very small penmanship on her portions of Bennet's Mimic spell to conserve space. Bennet was often quick to reply to her comments and inquiries, much to her delight. He wrote that Ethel was doing a little better every day, though she still didn't like to travel out of doors. His mother had knit a sock for her arm, and she was getting fitted for a temporary prosthesis that looked almost like a real hand but, of course, one that had no functionality. Hearing that, Alvie wanted more than ever to return to the polymery and finely tune the creation she and Mg. Praff were building.

Their messages weren't all business, of course. Bennet talked of his Christmas and his upcoming exam, of his family and the weather. At one point they were discussing English dog breeds when a few drops of water from Alvie's hair pattered against the page. They must have shown up on Bennet's end, since he asked, *Alvie, are you crying?*

Oh no, she'd replied. *Just got out of the bath.*

To which he was silent for several minutes until Alvie asked, *Isn't there a town called Bath over there?* And he went on to describe it.

Her papa invited some family friends over for the New Year, and they stayed up late eating Wiener schnitzel and bratwursts, springerle cookies, and fruitcake. Alvie went shopping with her mama on New Year's Day. Then, on the second of January, wearing a new pair of slacks she'd gotten for Christmas, Alvie made the long journey across the States and the Atlantic, back to the land of puddings and pounds and Polymaking.

Alvie had sent word ahead to Mg. Praff that she would not need his chauffeur, and when she stepped off at the *correct* train station, a young man with sunshine hair and his mentor's Benz was waiting to escort her to her second home.

Alvie beamed when she saw him. "Good evening!" And awkwardly dropped her suitcases to embrace him. This time, she noticed, he didn't hesitate to hug her back.

Bennet picked up her suitcases. "Dear Alvie, you sound more American than I remember."

"Do I really?"

He offered his elbow despite the suitcases in his hands, which made Alvie think he must not mind her knees bumping into them after all.

It was raining in London, as it often was. Bennet ran out to the Benz with her luggage first before opening the door for her. She hurried inside, listening to the cold drops pelt the retractable roof. When Bennet got into the driver's seat, she brushed raindrops off his hair and said, "At least it's not snow. Terrible to drive in the snow."

"Agreed." He hesitated, his hands not reaching for the steering wheel. "Alvie, I think you should read something before we head out."

She studied his suddenly serious expression and frowned. "What?"

He pulled out a newspaper shoved between their seats. "This is from three days ago. I didn't want to ruin your holiday, and I don't know how Magician Praff will feel about telling you."

Alvie blanched. What could it be? The prosthesis stolen? The Discovery Convention canceled? Or had Mg. Ezzell discovered the Compress spell?

He handed her the paper, pointing to a story on the front page. The headline of the second largest article read: "Scandal Storms Briar Hall When Servant Confesses Adultery."

Her mouth parted as she read the article. She was no great writer, but it seemed to be rather roundabout. They never named either the servant or the mistress, but "Marion Praff" was plastered in nearly every paragraph.

"This is libel," she said, reading the last sentences. "Magician Praff would never have an affair. He loves his wife. And he hardly has time to pick a mistress, let alone spend time with one!"

"I thought it sounded suspicious," Bennet agreed. "But it's even reached the telegrammed news, and two other papers."

She lowered the paper. "Who wrote the story? They usually list an author, don't they?"

Bennet frowned and took the paper, scanning the article. "Hmm. You're right, but I don't see anyone."

"Because no one wants to be held accountable when it's proved false." She folded her arms, then blanched. "Oh no."

"What?"

"The Discovery Convention is known for high academics and standards. Only the best of the best. This attack on Magician Praff's reputation might hurt his opportunity to present there."

Bennet paled, too. "I see."

She took a deep breath, trying to unwind all the gears inside of her that were rusting up. Her eyes felt hot, but they didn't threaten tears. The muscles in her back were taut as stretched leather. "Would you take me there, please?"

He nodded, shoved the paper between their seats, and drove the Benz onto the road. Alvie had a hard time thinking of anything else to say on the way to the manor, which meant poor conversation for Bennet. Which servant had gone to the press? Surely they were lying, for Alvie knew Mg. Praff, and she knew his wife, and it was simply nonsensical that an affair could happen. Even if their marriage were going poorly, the man simply *didn't have time* to keep up another relationship. For heaven's sake, Alvie had once needed to remind him to bathe!

Could a report like this, even an unfounded one, really hurt Mg. Praff's career?

Could it hurt hers?

No. No, stop it. She forced her thoughts to order themselves and march into a sturdy box for later examination. She was getting ahead of herself.

Bennet didn't seem put out by her mulling, at least. When they arrived at the estate, he even carried her luggage inside until Emma ran for a footman, who took the suitcases from him and carried them to Alvie's room.

Alvie grasped Bennet's hand. "Thank you. I'll . . . let you know what happens."

Bennet nodded and bid her good-bye.

———————

"Yes, it's been quite the mess." Mg. Praff pressed one hand into his eyes, as if to alleviate the pressure in his head, while he held Mrs. Praff's hand with the other. They sat in the salon on a couch printed with clusters of flowers; Alvie sat on a cushioned chair across from them. Mrs. Praff seemed only sympathetic, which was a relief—both because Alvie cared about the Praffs and because she couldn't imagine living in the midst of marital discord. If things got bad, she might be reassigned to a different Polymaker, and that would break her heart.

She tried to imagine being schooled under Mg. Ezzell and shuddered.

Mrs. Praff leaned forward. "You needn't worry about it, dear. We're taking whatever action we can."

"But of course I'll worry about it!" Alvie bunched the fabric of her slacks in her fists. "It's not right, publishing nonsense like that."

"No, it isn't." Mg. Praff lowered his hand. "We cannot find the source, of course. There have been no journalists on house grounds since the polymery break-in, and the newspaper that first published the report won't give up the author's name, nor the man who gave them the story. We've interviewed all the servants, and they all swear innocence. I'm inclined to believe them. Needless to say, we are pressing charges. A solicitor was here just yesterday." He sighed. "And I should mention that I received word from Magician Hughes while you were away. Those blasted muggers by the hospital were never found."

Alvie frowned. One piece of bad news after another. Was the universe so against them?

Maybe not the universe, but a jealous Polymaker. If only she could trace it back to him . . .

"Best thing to do now is to keep our heads low," he continued. "Let the solicitors do their business, and finish our work. We have lots of work, Alvie. Lots of testing to get done before the convention, if we want to make our mark."

"But what if the convention—"

"I only hope that my past reputation and this legal action are enough to prevent any action from being taken against me," he said.

She stood up. "I'm ready and willing to work, sir. Where should I start?"

Mrs. Praff chuckled. "Surely you want to rest first."

Alvie frowned.

A small smile pulled at Mg. Praff's lips. "Now, Lottie, surely you know Alvie well enough by now to know that rest waits when there's work to do." He stood. "Come, let me show you the patterns I compiled over the holidays."

Mrs. Praff clucked her tongue but made no objection as Mg. Praff released her hand and led the way to the polymery.

CHAPTER 15

ALVIE DEDICATED HERSELF ANEW to the prosthesis project. She wanted so badly for Mg. Praff to succeed—if things went poorly with the press and the solicitor, surely he could silence his naysayers with pure success. And Alvie's name was on that abstract, too. She wanted to ensure her first appearance at the Discovery Convention was a memorable one, and for the right reasons.

A few days after her return to London, a mail bird arrived with an invitation for skating from a certain Mr. Cooper. Unfortunately, it came on the same afternoon Alvie was helping her mentor make wrist models by allowing him to vacuum-form her wrist in every position possible, even if they differed in angle by a mere millimeter. And so a smaller bird went back with an apology and the statement that Alvie was absolutely the worst at skating, which was putting it generously. She could not so much as stand on ice without falling over, let alone do it with bladed soles.

She was surprised when Mr. Hemsley, looking irritated from his exercise to and from the polymery, returned with another mail bird. He stood, seething in irritation, while Mg. Praff draped Alvie's fore-arm in soft plastic and suctioned it against her wrist. Her skin was growing sore, and she was fairly certain there wasn't a single hair follicle left between her knuckles and elbow, but she didn't complain. In fact, despite the excitement of the bird, she held very still so they wouldn't have to repeat the process.

When Mg. Praff finished, Alvie took the bird. It read simply, *Don't worry, I'll hold your hand.*

And suddenly Alvie didn't care if she broke a leg on that pond, so long as she could go.

"Go on, Alvie," Mg. Praff said as he adjusted and hardened the plastic casting. "You've been out here long enough."

"But the Discovery Convention—"

He gave her a pointed look. "If you do not go, I will refuse to assign you any more homework."

She gaped. "That's hardly fair, sir."

He smiled, and she found herself smiling back. She took the Folded butterfly Bennet had sent with his bird and wrote back her confirmation.

The sun had set by the time Alvie returned from her first-ever second date, her ankles and legs sore but her heart light. She rubbed warmth back into her ears as she entered Briar Hall. Even her lips were chilly—Bennet had looked at them more than once, but he had not warmed them with his own.

Mg. Praff was at the base of the great staircase, talking in a low voice to Mr. Hemsley.

Alvie paused outside the vestibule, waiting for them to finish. It only took a moment. Mr. Hemsley nodded once; shot a quick, disapproving glance at Alvie's clothing; and strode off in the direction of the gallery.

Alvie watched him go before asking her mentor, "Everything all right?"

Mg. Praff sighed. "I suppose that depends on how you look at it. I've just told Mr. Hemsley to let Brandon go."

Brandon. Brandon. She worked to place the name, then recalled it belonging to one of the servants. "The footman?"

He nodded, the corners of his mouth drooping low, making him look much older than his years. "Emma came forward while you were away this evening. Near tears, the poor girl. Apparently she saw Brandon with a reporter just before that blasted article was published, but she's rather fond of the lad and didn't want to say anything. Seems the guilt finally got to her."

Alvie blanched. "Oh no, you're not going to terminate Emma, too—"

"Oh no, Alvie. She's a good worker, and I think she's tormented herself enough about the situation." Another sigh. He squeezed the banister of the staircase. "But I fear Mrs. Praff gave her a stern scolding."

Alvie relaxed. She had just gotten used to having someone else about her room, asking to dress her and do her hair. And she liked Emma.

"Why did he do it?"

"Hm?"

"Why would Brandon say such things about you?" Alvie clarified.

Mg. Praff shrugged. "I'm not sure. He did ask about being made first footman a while back, but I hired a new man for the job. Perhaps that. How was skating?"

She grinned. "It was wonderful. I mean, it hurt. I'm not very good at it. But Bennet was very patient with me, and it's astounding the sort of angles some people can get on their jumps and still land near perpendicular to the ice . . ."

The following week, after Alvie's multitude of bruises were mostly healed, she invited Ethel to come to the polymery. She gave her a tour of every single room, ending with the lab, where Mg. Praff awaited them.

"This is all very exciting," Ethel murmured, looking at the shelves of hands and arms. The footmen had set up the new shelves three days ago, since Mg. Praff was running out of storage space for his experiments.

"Indeed, it is," Mg. Praff said. He offered her a shallow bow. "It's good to have you here, Miss Cooper. Your cooperation has been critical to these experiments."

Ethel smiled. She wore the false arm Bennet had mentioned in his Mimic spell. The hand looked too large for her slim frame, the material too heavy. Alvie didn't like it one bit.

Ethel seemed nervous about taking it off, for whatever reason, but neither Alvie nor Mg. Praff looked at her stump with anything short of calculated study and a bit of fascination, so she relaxed quickly enough. Alvie handed Mg. Praff different models and sculpting tools as he fitted Ethel—apparently the stump could shrink and swell, so not all of Alvie's previous measurements were accurate. Once fitted, they tested the various amenities of the arm. At one point Ethel shifted, and the thumb and forefinger of the model hand she was testing closed.

"Oh my!" she exclaimed, lifting the prosthesis to her face. Tears filled her eyes.

Alvie hurried forward and grabbed the false arm. "Oh no, Ethel. Did it hurt?"

Ethel shook her head, her blond hair bobbing. "No, not at all. It's just . . . I know you're not done, but that's already so much more than I could do with the other prosthesis." She moved her arm one way, then another, until she managed to repeat the movement that had closed the pressurized thumb and finger. She laughed, tears running down her cheeks.

Mg. Praff leaned against the lab island and sighed. "Even without the convention, I think this moment has been worth every second of work, and every pence on top of that."

Ethel wiped her eyes with her flesh-and-blood hand. "Thank you. And I promise not to tell a soul until after the convention. Oh, thank you."

———

A few weeks later, after passing a test on the animation of plastic joints, Alvie found herself experimenting.

Not on a prosthetic arm, but on what she called "quick cuffs"—a plastic strip that could snap around a man's wrists to debilitate him. The fact of the matter was that Alvie had studied as much as even her brain could handle for one day, and her thoughts were stuck on the two incidents from the fall—the crooks outside the hospital and the failed polymery break-in.

She was not fond of feeling helpless, and a long, blurry mirror-communication with her papa back in Ohio had given her an idea of what to do about it. Why not create a protection device that could fit in a woman's purse or pocket and change shape on command to apprehend, say, a groper? No one liked gropers. The idea of such an invention excited her, and so she had set to work with equipment, spells, and her own hands. The difficulties of determining how to get the plastic cuffs to lock, let alone how to convince a nefarious person to put his hands together for cuffing, would come later.

Alvie picked up the piece she'd been working on. It looked like an overlarge tongue depressor and was slightly translucent. Beige. Stiff, but its body was full of unseen hinges locked into place. She slapped the thing on the corner of the island in the lab and watched the two ends curl up on themselves, forming a sort of simplified binocular. She hmm-ed to herself and straightened it out again.

163

The turn of a key in the polymery door drew her attention away from the project, and she glanced up and across the foyer to see Mr. Hemsley's frowning face as he opened the door and let Bennet in. Alvie's heart doubled the timing of its beats, making her a bit light-headed.

"Bennet!" she called.

Bennet caught her eye and crossed the foyer to the lab, which was the cleanest it had been in six weeks. He smiled. "Are you ready?"

She blinked. "For what?"

He sighed, though the smile stayed. "Dinner?"

She watched his face for a moment more before her heart froze in her chest like a stuck gear. "Oh! Uh, yes. I just need to change." Bennet had arranged the dinner a week ago when he'd convinced Mg. Bailey to give him time off for Valentine's Day. She looked down at her almost invention. She'd have to come back to it later.

"What is it?" Bennet asked.

She grinned. "Can I test it on you?"

He eyed her, wary. "That depends on what it does."

She stood quickly enough to knock over her stool, but Bennet's quick reflexes caught and righted it. "It apprehends wrongdoers! Or it will. Here." She grabbed both of his upper arms, quietly enjoying the feel of them, as she moved him away from the island. She drew her hands down his arms and set his wrists together, almost touching.

"I'm intrigued," he said, watching her face. The expression radiated warm swirls through her chest. For a moment she almost forgot what she was doing.

Oh yes. That.

She picked up the quick cuffs and stood about four feet from Bennet. "Hold still," she instructed. Aiming the plastic carefully, she threw it at him.

It bounced off his forearm and landed on the ground.

He stooped to get it, but she said, "No, no, I can—" and smacked her skull against his. She winced and righted herself, hand rushing up to the injured spot just behind her hairline. Bennet rubbed the side of his forehead.

"I'm so sorry!" she said.

"My fault." He pulled his hand back, revealing a pink circle on his skin. "I didn't hold still."

"Oh bother." She scooped down and grabbed the quick cuffs. "I don't think it's ready for testing. I can go change. I'm sorry."

Bennet's lips formed a small smile. He took her hand. "We'll just have matching bruises. Sort of like . . . a friendship bracelet."

"Except you can't see mine."

"I know it's there."

Their eyes met, and for a moment the lab was very quiet, enough so that Alvie could hear her pulse moving through the bruise on her head. She bit her lip, and found herself looking at Bennet's lips. Wondering if he would finally kiss her. Even though she'd gone and whacked him on the head.

It was quiet a little too long. Alvie inwardly groaned. She was so terrible at . . . this.

"Um," he broke the silence first. "I took a Polymaking class at Tagis Praff . . . maybe it would help if you made the plastic, I don't know, extend or something? It could thin out and extend before it hit the target, and then shrink back and stiffen . . ."

Alvie grinned. "That is a most excellent idea. I'll ask Magician Praff about it . . . I'm not entirely sure how to do it yet. You would have made a great Polymaker, Bennet—not that you're not an amazing Folder. Um."

Silence began to settle again, and Alvie broke it by clearing her throat. "I have something for you." She hurried to her workroom and set the quick cuffs on the desk—she wouldn't have much time to test

Bennet's theory until after the convention—then opened a drawer to reveal the four different valentines she'd handcrafted over the last week. She hadn't yet settled on which one to give him. She picked the rectangular one made of dark-maroon paper, with a ribbon woven through holes punched around the border. There was an inked message down the center that she'd practiced writing on three separate sheets of paper, front and back, before putting the pen to this.

> With separate "I" and "thou" free love has done,
> For one is both and both are one in love:
> Rich love knows nought of "thine that is not mine";
> Both have the strength and both the length thereof,
> Both of us, of the love which makes us one.

The words were not original; they were copied from the poet Christina Rossetti. Alvie wasn't good with . . . poems and fancy words. She'd tried—heaven knew she'd tried—but it always sounded wrong or foolish or too revealing. If she quoted someone else, she could sound elegant and assured; she could even be so daring as to use the word *love*. If Bennet thought it strange, she could merely claim it was a nice-sounding poem and this was Valentine's Day, after all—don't take it so seriously.

She sighed. Pinched the card between her fingers. There went her pulse again.

Swallowing, she hurried from the room and thrust the card at Bennet as if it were on fire.

Bennet took the card, his eyes softening at the ribbon. At least, Alvie thought that was what he was looking at. Then his eyes shifted to read the message, and only a few seconds passed before he began to laugh.

He was *laughing*.

Alvie felt the halves of her heart pulling apart as if stretching stitches held them together. She balled her hands into fists behind her back and weakly asked, "Wh-What?"

He stopped laughing, only smiled. Reached into his jacket to hand Alvie a card of his own. It was so beautifully made that Alvie could almost forget the throbbing beneath her breast. She took it delicately between her fingers. Red paper had been cut and trimmed around the edges to look like lace, folded like a heart without the slightest wrinkle or flaw. But, of course, what else could one expect from a Folder?

She turned it over, and there, written in less than perfect script, was the very poem she had quoted on the valentine she'd given to him.

Her heart sighed in relief as its halves sucked back together.

She smiled. "I suppose we have similar taste."

"I suppose we do."

She looked up at him, and the teasing glint that lit his eyes. Trying to match it, she said, "No flowers?"

His grin split his face. "Oh, Alvie, you would never be happy with flowers. I have something better. I'm going to let you drive the Benz."

Alvie almost dropped the valentine. "Really? *Really?*"

Bennet took a deep breath. "Yes. Just . . . don't tell Magician Bailey."

CHAPTER 16

LONDON WARMED UP SLOWLY, but the promise of spring only brought more rain. Alvie was no outdoorsman, but even she had begun to ache for some sun.

Fortunately, two weeks before the Discovery Convention, sunshine came to her.

She was studying a new homework assignment on the properties of glue in her workroom when Mr. Hemsley arrived. He stood outside her open door, his nose slightly pointed upward, and announced, "Mr. Cooper to see you. Again."

He departed without further ado. Alvie sat up straighter as Bennet slipped into the room.

He grabbed the back of the other chair and pulled it over to her desk. When he sat, his knees touched hers, and a tingle traveled up her thighs and clear into her jaw. He held up a piece of paper.

She read, *#1. Something to open a door*, before Bennet lowered the paper again.

"It's for my test." He grinned.

Alvie jumped in her chair. "You're doing it, then? Officially?"

He nodded. "I've been thinking about what you said, and I decided to go for it. April sixteenth is the day." He let out a shaky breath. "I'm nervous. But I think I can do it. There's a whole list of things I need to Fold and then present to my mentor and the other magicians who will be on my board. I might make two for each one. There's no rule that says I can't."

She grabbed his hands, careful not to wrinkle the test. His hands had become incredibly familiar to her over the last few months. He wasn't shy about holding her hand, touching her shoulder . . . but Alvie still dreamed about the eventual kiss . . . and hoped it was indeed *eventual* and not *impossible*. "Oh, Bennet, I'm so happy for you. You'll pass, I know it."

He smiled and ran his thumbs over her knuckles. She released him so he could fold the paper and tuck it inside his jacket. "I hope so. This means I'll be busy, though. Again." He sighed. "I brought you this."

He pulled a little booklet out of the same jacket pocket. Alvie instantly recognized it as a collection of Mimic spells. She and Bennet had filled the pages of the last one to every edge and corner.

"Since I won't be able to come by—"

"Perfect!" Alvie seized the book and flipped through its torn blank pages. "I'll write in it every day."

Bennet seemed relieved. Fiddling with a button on his jacket, he said, "You leave for the conference on the nineteenth?"

"Eighteenth, so we have time to travel and set up. Magician Praff said he wants to head out by noon."

"Do you need any help? Loading anything?"

An idea sparked in Alvie's head, one that made her smile, though she tried to hide the expression, as if Bennet might see the secret spelled out on her teeth. "Yes, I think that would be wonderful, if you can get away."

"I'll make sure." His expression softened. He took her hand again, which only made her grin expand. It seemed too good to be true—not only to know a man as kind and wonderful as Bennet, but to have him treat her this way . . . like she was important to him.

She found her gaze traveling up his arm to his mouth. Despite her disposition not to, Alvie flushed. Ethel had said Bennet was shy with girls, but one would think he'd have developed the courage to kiss her by now. Then again, the prospect made her insides squirm as though readying for a race.

"Are you all right?" he asked.

She cleared her throat. "Nine o'clock, then." She'd need him to arrive early for the surprise to work. "Just come back here. I'm sure Mr. Hemsley will be busy with other things, and Magician Praff knows you're trustworthy."

He nodded. "I'll be there. Promise."

———

Alvie could barely sleep the night before they left for the convention, in part because she stayed up until midnight making final preparations for the prosthesis display and then for another two hours putting the final touches on Bennet's surprise, with Mg. Praff's direction.

She'd asked Emma to wake her early, but Alvie was up before the maid could fulfill the duty. She took a bath and picked out a reasonable skirt to wear. There was a good chance she'd meet the convention chairman and other magicians upon arriving in Oxford, and she wanted to make a good impression. She tied her red apprentice's apron over that, then let Emma tame and pin her locks, which the maid then wrapped in a maroon headband with fabric flowers on it. It looked a little fancy, but Alvie found she didn't mind at all.

She cleaned her glasses thoroughly, which was a tricky feat for one who couldn't see the smudges on the lenses unless she was wearing them, and headed down to the polymery.

Though Mg. Praff had stayed up even later than she had the night before, he was already in the lab when she arrived. They'd pieced together an ankle joint in February, and he was testing it against the floor.

"Is it working?" Alvie asked.

"Yes, quite well." Mg. Praff straightened, his back popping several times as he did. He rolled his neck. "Ah. What an exciting time to be alive. Fred will be hooking up the trailer soon. You'd best set up before Mr. Cooper comes by."

Alvie nodded. Mg. Praff was bringing the Imagidome to the convention again, so its panels sat collected in a box in the foyer. She'd spent a lot of time with the dome pieces lately, programming new images to stun convention attendees. She pulled them out, sorting them by the tiny numbers etched on their sides. Then she began to build the dome, starting at the base. She'd be constructing it at the convention as well, and it never hurt to get a little more practice, especially when encumbered by a skirt.

An automobile horn honked nearby. Mg. Praff set the ankle model on the island counter and hurried out, likely to see how Fred and the trailer were faring. Alvie settled the last pieces of the Imagidome into place and slipped out of it to examine her work. She smiled. The next couple of days were going to be the best in her life; she could feel it.

The sun shined brightly through the plastic dome windows overhead, promising a warm spring. Alvie stretched as she stared up at them. She should get a ladder and make them transparent. This place could use a little more sky.

Though the door was cracked open, she heard a knock against it before Bennet appeared. She hadn't seen him at all these last two weeks, even in a mirror, but she'd written him every day. She smiled at him, at his warm brown eyes and bright hair and the nice button-up shirt he wore despite the fact that he was here for physical labor.

"Morning," she said.

"Morning." His eyes moved from Alvie to the Imagidome and back. "Goodness, is this it? I don't know how we'll get it onto that trailer."

She laughed. "It breaks apart, don't worry."

He circled around it, studying the pattern of hexagons. He tapped his finger on one of them. "This is what you gave me."

"Mm-hm."

He came to her side and took her hand. She wove her fingers through his. He ran his other hand across the scalelike texture of the Imagidome.

"It's strange to think I'd be able to understand this if I'd become a Polymaker. Ah, there are the seams."

"You don't regret it, do you?"

He looked at her. "Oh no. I was a little sour about being a Folder at first, but in the end I'm glad for it. I think I'd struggle more with something like this. If nothing else, the shortage of Folders promises job security."

He moved around the rest of the igloo, bringing Alvie with him. "Think you could build a replica?"

"Uh. Maybe." She adjusted her glasses. "It would take a long time." She pulled him toward the short door. "Here, go inside. I want to show you something."

His eyes lit up with curiosity. He crouched, opened the door, and crawled inside the dome. Alvie followed after him, tripping over her skirt and nearly banging her chin on the floor as she went. Once she straightened inside, she brushed the skirt off and closed the door.

The interior was nearly dark, but not so dark that she couldn't see Bennet or the shapes of the hexagonal tiles. "Okay. Close your eyes. Are they closed? I can't tell."

He chuckled. "Yes."

She pressed her hand against the panel right above the door and said, "Image Memory: October Picnic."

The enchanted scene bloomed to life, swallowing the tiles. She'd gone to Green Park to get a visual, though its trees were currently leafless and everything was dreary in the last weeks of winter. She'd improvised quite a bit.

"Open your eyes."

The picture gave off plenty of light to see Bennet's reaction. His mouth parted, and he turned slowly, taking in the scene.

It looked like they were standing in the middle of a park, on a flat space near a rolling green hill. A large black poplar tree grew near them, its triangular leaves sparkling with sunlight. The Imagidome didn't have a floor, but around its border one could see the edges of a checkered picnic blanket, and a large woven basket sat to one side, grapes spilling out of it. In the distance, a little boy flew a red kite near a white gazebo. The sky shined a brilliant azure, but if one looked all the way up, it darkened to a rich indigo studded with stars, including the constellation Orion.

Alvie dropped her hand from the wall and took it in, walking to Bennet's side. "Do you like it?"

"It's amazing," he whispered, craning to see the stars. He reached his hand up, trying to touch them. "October picnic?"

"Since I sort of snubbed it before."

His hand dropped, and his wide-eyed gaze fell on her. "You created this, not Magician Praff?"

She nodded.

He grinned and took her hand again. "It's wonderful. And there will be another chance for an October picnic."

Her heart beat a little quicker. "Really?" Would he still be holding her hand and visiting her and writing her notes all the way to next October?

He studied her face. Lifted a hand and traced her hairline. "I would very much like that."

They stood together, staring at each other for a moment. Alvie knew the look in his eyes—knew it even though no one else had ever looked at her that way. Knew it even though her thoughts wouldn't quite process it, though her heart did, because it pounded against her breast with so much vigor that she was certain Bennet could hear it.

He let go of her hand and took the arms of her glasses in his fingers, lifting them from her nose and sliding them up to the headband in her hair. It blurred him and the colors of the picnic, but it didn't really matter, because she closed her eyes. Lifted her chin. Bennet's hands cupped either side of her head, and his lips pressed against hers, warm and sweet and *oh*.

Kissing was much better than Alvie had thought it would be, or maybe that was just true of kissing him. Bennet was close enough to her height that she didn't need to strain. He smelled like tea and anise and some sort of aftershave that Alvie greatly enjoyed. She breathed it in and smiled against his lips. One of his hands shifted to the back of her head. Hers found his waist.

They were probably running long for a first kiss, but Alvie didn't much care. She tilted her head to kiss him better, and he captured her bottom lip between his. She sighed in the bliss of it. Not just in the touch and the smell, but in being wanted and loved, and being very certain in what *she* wanted and loved.

She leaned in to him, needing to be closer. He broke from her for just long enough to take a breath before meeting her again, and Alvie took the opportunity to slide her fingers into his soft sunshine hair. *Oh.*

She could kiss him forever. She was a terrible dancer, but this sort of dance was blissful and easy. Bennet's mouth moved against hers, and she parted her lips—

"Alvie?" Mg. Praff called from the foyer. "Are you in there?"

Bennet snapped back, and Alvie nearly fell into him. She clasped his shoulders for balance. Swallowed. "Um, yes!"

"All right. Be sure to box these panels up soon!"

"Yes, sir!"

She clung to Bennet, listening to her mentor's footsteps move away.

Bennet laughed. "Probably for the better."

"I disagree." She reached for her glasses and positioned the large frames back over her eyes. Bennet was smiling in a soft sort of way that made her want to curl up against him with a good book. Maybe even *Heart of Darkness*.

He put a knuckle under her chin and kissed her carefully so as not to smudge her lenses. "You are one of a kind, Alvie."

"I think you have nefarious purposes, Mr. Cooper. I certainly won't be able to concentrate on my display now."

He chuckled. "I wish I could see it." He kissed her forehead. "You'll do great."

Alvie beamed at him, then looked up at Orion. "Bother. I should probably take this apart."

"I'll help you. And show you the real constellation when you return."

She grinned at him. This time, when she exited the Imagidome, she bunched her skirt up between her knees and, miraculously, did not trip.

The trailer was a small white contraption that Fred had hooked up to the back of the automobile. It had Smelting spells etched into the bottom of it, but Alvie wasn't clear on their purpose—whether they were intended to guarantee a smooth ride or to make the trailer easier to pull. It seemed every servant in Mg. Praff's household bustled around that automobile and trailer, carrying this, adjusting that. Emma even polished the driver's mirror. Bennet carried the deconstructed Imagidome up from the polymery, and Alvie had a plastic container full of various tuning tools. Fred jogged up to the trailer from the direction of the garage.

"Everything is as it should be," he said to Mg. Praff, who wore his green Polymaker uniform.

Mg. Praff nodded as Bennet set his box in the trailer. "No harm done, then."

Alvie asked, "What happened?"

The chauffeur shrugged. "Apparently I failed to lock the garage last night. Could swear I did, but I mustn't have turned the key all the way."

Mg. Praff said, "Why don't you make sure the engine is warm for the trip? And, Mr. Cooper, thank you for the help."

"It's no trouble," Bennet said. One of the footmen came up to the trailer next, carrying the display stands for the prostheses. Alvie climbed into the trailer—she really should have changed into that skirt at the last possible moment—and began organizing everything as several footmen, Bennet, and Mg. Praff brought the supplies up from the polymery. She opened each bag and box to ensure everything they needed was inside, despite having checked the inventory yesterday. She didn't want to end up in Oxford with something critical missing.

The Imagidome took up the most space, and the prostheses themselves were wrapped in sponged plastic for cushioning, making them bulky. By the time everything was loaded, however, the trailer was still a third empty. Alvie pulled some straps across the boxes and bags to keep them all in place during the trip.

Emma appeared outside the trailer, her eyes scanning everything in it. "How exciting, Alvie! Can I help you?"

Alvie turned and nearly smacked her head on the trailer wall. "Oh no, we're all good!" She jumped out of the trailer, her skirt billowing as she did. She brushed her hands off. "I'll tell you all about it. What do you . . . oh, Emma. What happened to your hand?"

Emma glanced down at her right hand, which had an angry red cut across the back of it—a crescent that hugged the base of her thumb. She frowned at it. "Usual wear and tear of service, I'm afraid. It doesn't hurt." She glanced toward the polymery. Mr. Hemsley locked the door and began the trek up to the automobile.

Alvie gave Emma a quick hug. "I'll bring you something from the convention."

Mg. Praff took a deep breath. Checked his pockets. Looked about. Spied Mrs. Praff at the back door of the house. He ran up to her to give her a kiss good-bye. Mrs. Praff had continued to be wholeheartedly trusting during the newspaper scandal, and Alvie admired her for it. Fortunately, thanks to lack of further story and Mg. Praff's very expensive lawyers, nothing more had come of the issue besides that initial publication. The Discovery Convention hadn't banned him, either.

When Mg. Praff returned, he was breathless. "I've never been so nervous for a show! You're bringing out my youth, Alvie."

She smiled as her tutor checked the luggage straps.

Bennet, whose shirtsleeves were rolled up about his elbows in a way Alvie quite liked, put his hands on his hips. "I had best be going, then. You have the notebook?"

Alvie patted the bag hanging from her shoulder. "I'll tell you everything that happens, and then you'll have to make another one."

"I hope you do." He eyed Fred, who pointedly turned around and got into the driver's seat.

Alvie kissed Bennet on the cheek. Then, after glancing about to make sure no one was watching, she kissed his mouth. "Study hard," she whispered.

He took her hand and squeezed it. "I will. Be safe."

"Yes, sir."

He smiled and departed for the Benz just as Mg. Praff announced everything was set. Alvie climbed into the automobile. This one had glass windows and was a little wider than the other. Alvie briefly wondered how much Mg. Praff made to be able to afford two automobiles *and* a mansion. Would she have her own garage, once she became a Polymaker? Her own Benz? Perhaps Ford would have a new model by then, and she'd have one of those as well. Maybe she could rig something plastic in the engine . . . something that could make the vehicle run smoother but wouldn't get too hot. She'd present it at a future Discovery Convention. What a splash she'd make if she drove the automobile right into the main hall and—

"Alvie?"

Alvie blinked, noting that Mg. Praff had climbed onto the seat beside her.

"Oh, sorry. Did you ask me something?"

He chuckled. "Just making sure you have everything you need."

"Yes. Rechecked the trailer, too. We're set."

Mg. Praff slapped the back of Fred's seat. "And we're off!"

Butterflies filled Alvie's stomach as the automobile started and pulled around the manor. She looked for Bennet's Benz, but he had already departed. She pulled the new notebook out of her bag and wrote on its first page, *We're off! I've never been to Oxford. What an adventure!*

She tucked it away. Bennet wouldn't be able to respond while he was driving, anyway. They drove through London, past one train station, then another. Alvie marveled at how very old the buildings and bridges looked. Homes and shops grew smaller and more spaced apart as the automobile chugged west, until large stretches of green surrounded them on all sides.

Fred gripped the wheel and jerked it to the left. "Bad road," he commented.

Mg. Praff began talking about last year's Discovery Convention. He told Alvie what she should expect, when she would have free time, and whom she might be meeting. There was a slew of names she couldn't remember, and the convention sounded even larger than she had imagined. Each material—plastic, paper, rubber, metal alloys, glass, and fire—had its own section, though rubber and plastic took up the most space, being newer disciplines than the others.

They talked long enough for Alvie's backside to get sore on the seat. She glanced out at the green hills surrounding them, wishing she had some sort of camera to capture the shot. Had Bennet ever seen these hills?

She was about to pull out her notebook to see if he'd responded when the automobile jerked sharply to the left. Alvie hit the wall hard, pain lancing her shoulder. Mg. Praff grabbed the seat in front of him. The entire machine shook and jerked. Fred gripped the steering wheel, cursing, but managed to lead the vehicle to the side of the road, where it stopped.

"Good heavens, Fred!" exclaimed Mg. Praff. "What happened?"

"Don't know. Thing just went wild." He turned in his seat, and Alvie gasped at the blood trailing down his face from a gash near his hairline.

Mg. Praff yanked a handkerchief from his pocket and folded it. "Blast, Fred! Hold this to your forehead!" He pushed the cloth against the wound.

Fred obediently did so. Mg. Praff got out of the automobile. Alvie followed.

Nothing looked amiss on the vehicle—the tires were all intact. The engine sounded fine, and no smoke came off it. Even the trailer looked whole, though it must have gotten quite the shake.

"Turn it off, Fred." Mg. Praff waved a hand.

The engine cut.

Mg. Praff lifted the hood. Heat wafted from it and stuck to Alvie's face, but not an unusual amount. She said, "I wouldn't touch it yet—"

Mg. Praff touched the radius rod and jerked his hand back.

"It's still hot," Alvie finished.

Mg. Praff sighed. "Good thing we left early. You're familiar with this?"

"Yes, sir. Though nothing looks wrong on the surface. I'll have to get under it when it cools down . . . if it's even an engine problem."

Hands on hips, Mg. Praff walked out into the road and back a ways, likely looking for potholes. He shook his head upon his return.

In the cab, Fred groaned.

"Probably hit the steering wheel," Mg. Praff murmured, looking sidelong at the chauffeur. His gaze shifted, taking in their surroundings. They were between towns; greening land stretched out to either side of them.

Alvie's stomach twisted.

Mg. Praff moved to the driver's seat. "Fred, are you all right?"

"Just a little dizzy, sir."

"Do you know where we are?"

He looked up, one of his eyelids stiff with drying blood. "I think we're close to Maidenhead." He pointed weakly toward a hill.

That was a strange name for a town, though Alvie didn't voice her opinion.

Mg. Praff nodded. "I'll see if I can find help. Rest, Fred. Alvie, stay with the auto, and keep an eye on him."

"Yes, sir."

He nodded. "I'll try to be quick." He sprinted off the road, over one of the hills.

Worrying her lip, Alvie found a handkerchief in her bag and offered it to Fred; he was bleeding through the one he had. She stood near him as he leaned his head back on the driver's seat, eyes closed. She could see his pulse in an artery on his neck.

After a few minutes of being extremely unuseful, Alvie stepped into the road, peering up and down its length, praying for another automobile to come by. There weren't very many automobile owners, but she could hope. Even a man on horseback would do. She knit and wrung her fingers together, searching, waiting, but no savior came to their aid.

A sigh escaped her. She glanced back at the automobile. The engine. She walked over to it and peered down at it again. It was still hot, but not burning hot. Still, she was careful where she put her hands as she leaned over the thing. Her eyes ran over the pipes, valves, and casings. Her lip twisted into a frown. Whatever could have—

Her gaze caught on something near the cylinder head outlet hose, toward the front of the engine. Something sort of roundish, like someone had made a giant pig's nose out of very thick, opaque plastic. She racked her brain but couldn't determine what part of the engine it could possibly be. Did Mg. Praff put any spells in his automobiles to make them run better? Pressing her lips into a firm line, Alvie carefully reached down to touch it.

The automobile protested, one of its many parts biting her just as her fingers grazed the object. She hissed and pulled her hand back out. Black grease smeared her first two knuckles, and a long red line oozed angrily around her thumb. She shook her hand and blew on the cut before backing away from the vehicle. Her gut told her that wasn't supposed to be there. Hadn't Fred said something about the garage being unlocked—

Fred. She needed to check on him. Cradling her hand, she called his name. He didn't reply. Nearing his door, she said again, "Fred?"

"I'm here," he answered tiredly.

Knotting her fingers together, Alvie continued on to the trailer. There might be a bandage in there, and if nothing else, she should make sure their equipment had survived the jerking and jarring of the automobile. She opened the door.

Several items lay strewn on the trailer floor. Grimacing, she knelt down and examined each piece before returning it to its place, ensuring nothing had been broken. The repetitive work was almost calming enough to make her forget the sting from the shallow cut on her right hand. She checked until her knees ached. Everything put away, she stood and moved on to the Imagidome. She wanted to make sure it hadn't been damaged before she checked on Fred again.

Just as her fingers brushed the box, however, the trailer door slammed shut behind her, leaving her in darkness.

She spun around, heart in her throat. "Fred?"

The engine started.

"Fred!" she cried. She ran to the door—ran *into* the door—and pounded her fists against it. Fumbled for a handle or knob, but the door didn't open from the inside.

"Fred! Magician Praff! I'm *in* here! Help!"

The trailer jerked back onto the road, sending Alvie crashing onto her hip. She hammered against that metal door in the darkness and yelled until her throat was raw and her fists throbbed. Despite the cool March weather, the air within the trailer was sweltering. Already, loose pieces of Alvie's hair stuck to her forehead, and her glasses struggled to stay atop her sweat-slick nose.

She sat down as the trailer took a turn. Blinked a few times to clear her head. It wasn't entirely dark in the thing—a little bit of light seeped in around the doors. Her mind started calculating the interior space by cubic feet, but with a groan, she silenced it. That would do her no good, would it?

She struggled to breathe the thick air. Stood on shaky legs and felt around, but the trailer was solid Smelted metal, and the only exit was locked. Maybe with enough leverage and leaning, she could topple it and force the automobile to stop, but she'd risk damaging the trailer, its contents, and herself.

Gritting her teeth, she did the only thing she could. She banged both fists on those doors, trying to shout over the noise of the engine and passing road. By the time the trailer stopped, Alvie was hoarse and heat sick, albeit relieved.

She heard footsteps outside the trailer. The door opened. The light was blinding.

But it wasn't Mg. Praff or Fred who had come to her rescue.

It was Mg. Ezzell.

CHAPTER 17

H<small>E LOOKED JUST AS</small> surprised to see her as she was to see him.

"Bloody hell," he spat at the same time Alvie cried, "You!"

He moved forward. Alvie skittered back against the Imagidome, tangling up in her skirt in the process. "You! You thief!" She looked past him. There were trees. How far had they gone? They must have driven for an hour—

Mg. Ezzell put a knee up on the rim of the trailer and reached for Alvie's legs. She kicked at him, but he snatched her ankle and dragged her out of the trailer. In her flailing, her glasses slid to the very tip of her nose, and chunks of hair slipped free of Emma's handiwork and fell into her face.

"Hold still!" Mg. Ezzell grunted, wrestling with her. She peeked between locks of hair, trying to figure out where she was. A dirt road, trees. The automobile and trailer were parked outside some sort of old log house. A retreat home? An abandoned cabin? Something far away from witnesses, that was certain.

"Help!" she cried, and Mg. Ezzell's hand slapped over her mouth. His other arm wrapped around her arms and across her chest, and he hauled her away from the road, kicking open a door on the side of the house and dragging her inside.

"No one will . . . hear you," he said with effort. He cursed again, hesitated, then pulled her around the corner and down a flight of stairs. Alvie grabbed the rail and screamed for help. In his efforts to loosen her grip, Mg. Ezzell nearly fell down the stairwell. He took one hand off her to grab the rail himself. With an arm free, Alvie dove into her bag to find her plastic quick cuffs. When Mg. Ezzell moved to grab her again, she dropped her weight and turned to bring his wrists together, then slapped the cuffs down on them.

He growled and ripped them off with ease. Alvie watched as the only defense she had toppled to the stairs beneath her.

Mg. Ezzell grabbed her arm and yanked it behind her, sending a sawlike pain across her shoulder. She cried out, then screamed again.

"Shut *up!*" he shouted. He threw his weight against her and shoved her into the wall. Her forehead hit the painted wood, and for a moment the stairwell spun. She fumbled for the rail and found only air. Mg. Ezzell got her down the rest of the stairs and into a room that was empty except for a simple desk and a white boxy set of shelves scattered with a few pamphlets. Only one window let light into the place, and it was little more than a narrow slit peeking above ground.

Mg. Ezzell released her. Alvie tumbled to the floor, hair and skirt flying everywhere. Her forehead pounded. She flipped her hair back and pushed up her glasses, heart distending. "What are you *doing?* Fred! Fred's hurt, and you . . . you're the one who broke into the polymery!"

Mg. Ezzell scoffed. "Please. I seldom do dirty work." He frowned. "Seems I should have kept my hands clean a little longer. You are . . . unexpected."

He pushed his knuckles against his mouth, blocking the door, thinking as he stared at her.

"Unexpected?" she repeated. She looked out the window. It faced away from the road. At least, she couldn't see the road or the trailer through it.

What was *expected*, then? The theft of the trailer, but without an apprentice inside. And yet . . . how would he have known the vehicle would break down just then?

Her blood ran cold, remembering the plastic *something* in the engine. "You did something to the automobile."

"'You did something to the automobile,'" Mg. Ezzell repeated in a childish, singsongy voice. "Of course I did something to the automobile, idiot. Just my luck that it took out your driver and Praff went for help. I didn't think *you* would be there. What kind of fool brings a fledgling apprentice to the Discovery Convention? Blast." He grabbed his thinning hair with his hands.

She understood then. Mg. Ezzell must have gotten into Mg. Praff's garage last night. Put something in the automobile to make it crash—a spell, something he could control so the vehicle would crash away from city limits, or something that would activate after so many miles. That plastic thing in the engine, probably. Fred was incapacitated; Mg. Praff was missing. No witnesses, except for her.

And not only could she testify to his thievery, but he'd unknowingly abducted her as well. A twofold setback. A long jail sentence, for sure.

Her hands rushed to her mouth. Gooseflesh prickled her skin like the pricks of a thousand cold needles. "You killed Fred."

"He was breathing when I hauled him out of the cab." He growled. "None of this is your business."

His beady eyes darted around the room. He snarled and unbuckled his belt, then whipped it off. He came for Alvie. She backed up, not stopping until she had almost reached the wall. "Help!" she screamed, then tried to duck around him. His hand came out and seized her hair, yanking her back with a pop of her neck.

"Hold still!" he muttered, wrestling with her. Alvie kicked and screamed, but Mg. Ezzell was too strong for her to physically best. He scooted her toward the desk and looped the belt around her wrists, sitting on her to minimize her flailing. He secured the belt around the desk leg, tying her down.

He jumped off her swiftly, before Alvie could kick him. "I'll figure out what to do with you later." He smirked. "I have a convention to attend."

"It won't work!" Alvie shouted, twisting and trying to get a better look at him despite the awkward position of her arms. "You can't take credit for Magician Praff's work. He already submitted the abstract!"

The Polymaker barked a laugh. "What do you take me for? Praff never submitted an abstract."

Alvie stopped squirming. "But he . . . he showed me the confirmation."

Mg. Ezzell rolled his eyes. "I intercepted it. *I* sent the confirmation. The convention doesn't even know Praff is coming. This time *he* will understand what it feels like to be made a fool."

Her body grew heavy as she stared at him. If he got away with this . . .

Mg. Ezzell fished around in his pocket until he retrieved a pocket-knife. Pulling out the knife, he walked toward Alvie.

"Help! Help!"

"Idiot girl. No one will hear you." He steered clear of her legs and grabbed her bag, then slid the knife under the strap, cutting it. Bennet's Mimic spell was in that bag—her one chance to get out of this mess.

"Please, let me keep it," she squeaked.

"You read too many bad books. You imagine yourself the hero of the piece, no doubt, but do you really think I'm some overzealous villain ready to slip up so you can gain your freedom?" He snorted. He tossed the bag toward the door and pocketed the knife, then crouched by Alvie's side to check her skirt pockets. He pulled a few pounds from the left, a pen from the right. There was nothing in the apron. She squirmed under his clammy hands. He patted down her waistband, then checked her stockings for anything else. His hand rested on her knee for half a second before dipping beneath her skirt and up her thigh.

She twisted away from Mg. Ezzell, the leather of the belt digging into her wrists, and kicked his shoulder. He cursed and jumped back. Eyed her shoes. Wrestled those off, as well.

"Like I said." He retreated to the door, his breathing heavy. "I'll figure out what to do with you later."

He gathered her things and slammed the door shut. The sound of the lock clicking echoed through the vacant space.

———————

"Help!" Alvie screamed. "Help!"

She heard another door shut upstairs. Curling her legs up, she turned and balanced on her knees as best she could, though the position cut off the blood supply to her hands. She jerked hard, gritting her teeth as the belt dug into her flesh. She moved the desk a centimeter. The desk might have been simple, but it was heavy, despite its two drawers being empty.

She attacked the belt with her teeth, trying to loosen its knots.

She heard a motor start outside.

A tear ran down her cheek. She blinked it away and steeled herself. She needed to stay calm. She needed to *get out of here*.

She focused on her breathing—keeping it even, pushing the excitement from it. She needed to focus. She couldn't be here when Mg. Ezzell got back. She had to help Fred. She had to warn Mg. Praff. She had to do *something*.

She bit and pulled, jerking like a dog. The belt loosened a little, then stuck.

Alvie turned on her hip to let blood seep back into her strangled fingers. She looked around, searching for anything to help her, but the room was truly empty. She squeezed her eyes shut for a moment, focusing on her breaths, forcing them to go long and deep. Then she rolled onto her side and tugged, tugged, *tugged* until her thumb threatened to break from the strain.

So she rolled onto her other side, putting pressure on a different hand, and pulled. When that failed to work, she shoved her shoulder into the desk.

It hurt. A lot more than it should have. It took Alvie a moment to remember she was using the same shoulder she'd hurt in the near crash in the automobile. "You can do this," she told herself, blinking to keep her eyes dry. "You're a Brechenmacher, damn it."

She shoved the desk again, swallowing a whimper as the bruise on her shoulder deepened. Then again, digging her feet into the matted off-white carpet. They slipped. With some effort, Alvie swung around and brought her knees close enough to her throbbing fingers to unhook her stockings. She shimmied out of them, kicking and rubbing her legs together. Feet bare, she had a little more grip.

She shoved, pushed, groaned.

The desk tipped back, hitting the floor with a loud crash.

Laughing, she tugged the knotted belt off the desk leg, loosening it enough to pull her hands free. She rubbed them together, flexing wrists and fingers. The cut on her right thumb bled from the struggle. She blew on it a moment, then dabbed it on her apron.

She hurried to the door. Turned the knob. It turned and stuck, of course. The door—and it looked like a well-built, heavy door—was held to its frame by some sort of chamber lock. Or so she guessed, pressing her finger against the keyhole.

Turning around, she went to the window. It didn't open, and her head would never fit through it, let alone her chest and hips. She climbed atop the toppled desk and stood on the very corner of it, grabbing the window's sill to peek out. Her eyes were level with the ground, though overgrown grass obscured her view. Trees and grass. That was all she could see.

If only she were a Gaffer, maybe she could do something.

Gaffer. Magic.

"Plastic," she whispered, jumping off the desk. She spun slowly, scanning the room twice. Plastic. Anything plastic. She saw nothing.

She opened every drawer of the desk, finding only a nub of charcoal. She checked the shelves, hoping to feel something tingle under her fingertips, but there was only paper—a pamphlet on Rome, another with detailed instructions on how to use a telephone. A few scraps of paper without anything written on them.

The shelves were wood. The desk was wood and metal. The window was glass.

She checked Mg. Ezzell's belt. Leather and metal. She checked her pockets. Empty.

Dropping on her hands and knees, Alvie scoured the carpet, running her hands over its matted pile, searching for something lost in it. She found a staple, a bit of hardened food. Nothing else. Even her blouse had no buttons on it, and her skirt fastened with a metal snap.

She jumped on the desk again and pounded her fist against the window. "Help!" she cried. "Help!"

After several minutes, she stopped. Mg. Ezzell had been utterly confident that no one would hear her. She'd only gotten a glance at the exterior of the house, but she'd seen no other houses, no buildings, not even a shed. How far was his nearest neighbor? What were the chances of someone coming by here, and close enough to hear her through this little window?

She plopped down atop the desk, her stomach rumbling as if it, too, wanted to commiserate. A tear spilled over her eyelashes. She wiped it off, smearing her glasses.

Her glasses.

Her *glasses.*

"Oh, Magician Praff, I could kiss you." She pulled the spectacles off her face. The black frames instantly blurred in her hands. Everything blurred, but such was the ailment of Alvie Brechenmacher. She pushed her thumbs against the right lens; the tingling from the plastic filling her with hope. The lens came free with a satisfying *pop.*

She put the glasses back on. It disoriented her, having one eye blind and one eye with sight, and her glasses tilted a little to the left with the uneven weight. Still, it was better than no lenses at all. Better than no plastic.

She stared at the half-blurred lens in her hand. Plastic. Excellent. *Now what?*

Her mind ran through all the spells she knew. Image Memory. Harden, Soften. Melt. Adhere, Conform, Encompass. Clarify, Haze. Flex and Unyielding. Compress, Propel, Heed: Pattern. How were any of those to help?

She stared at the door, tilting her head so she saw it more with her corrected left eye than her blind right. What she needed was a key. Could she make one?

She hurried to the lock and studied the keyhole. It was a narrow opening, and not one that could be looked through, either. If only Alvie were a Smelter. Smelters could unlock anything made of a mixed metal, unless the lock was specifically enchanted to resist it, like the locks Mg. Praff had installed on the polymery.

"Soften," she commanded the plastic. It softened in her hand, and she flattened the lens before saying, "Harden." She stuck the plastic into the crevice between the door and the doorjamb, but the bolt was true and couldn't be pushed away. Alvie's pulse quickened. Fear pricked the back of her neck. She had to do this. She had to succeed. There was no food or water in this room. If Mg. Ezzell took his time returning, she might be dead before he figured out what to "do" with her. Maybe that's exactly what he intended . . . though murder would certainly be a poor thing to add to theft and abduction.

She knelt, turning the ruined lens over in her hands. *Think.* Maybe she could break the glass in the window. It would make her cries for help louder, but it didn't solve the problem of the house's seclusion. Someone still had to be nearby for that to do her any good.

She stared at the lock. The difference in her eyes made her forehead throb.

"Soften," she said, and she pulled the lens in half, hardening one half and setting it aside. The remaining portion she lengthened and narrowed, working it like clay. "Harden," she said, and shoved the plastic into the lock.

A key. She needed a key.

She snatched a pamphlet off the bookshelf and held up the end of the plastic stick with it. If it didn't touch her hands, it might ignore her next command, but she didn't want to risk losing even a particle of her material. Touching her finger to the plastic at the lock, she said, "Melt." She only wanted to shape the edge of the plastic, where the key's teeth would be.

The tip of the stick melted, filling in the lock, and the other bit more or less kept its shape, thanks to the pamphlet. After a couple of seconds, Alvie said, "Harden," and turned the stick.

It didn't budge. Of course it didn't. It had just filled the entire contraption. What was she thinking?

She let go of the plastic and paper and rubbed her head. She *wasn't* thinking. She was panicking. A quiet, dignified panic, so she thought, but panic all the same. Perhaps she should try breaking the window after all. She had evidence of being a very good screamer.

So Alvie took the other half of the lens in hand, ordered it to harden until it couldn't harden any more, wrapped it in her fist, and banged it against the window until the glass cracked and broke. She beat away the remaining fragments, earning a few nicks in the process, and screamed until her throat threatened to bleed.

No one answered her. She heard no vehicles or horses coming up the unseen road.

She collapsed atop the desk, catching her breath. Returned to the door and reached her fingers under it, hoping to find something, anything, within reach. She touched only more matted carpet. So she reeled back and slammed her heels into the door, hoping she could break the lock, or maybe break through the wood itself. It didn't even dent. And her efforts bruised her bare feet.

The sound of a motor wafted down to her. Alvie jumped to her feet and ran to the window, climbing atop the desk one more time. She strained to listen over her heavy breaths. "Hello?" she called, but no one answered. She gritted her teeth, listening for the sound of human life, but all was quiet. Her imagination was as desperate as she was.

Sighing, Alvie hopped off the desk and sat again by the door, staring at that plastic-stuffed lock. Mg. Praff would have returned to the road only to discover the automobile and trailer gone. Had he come with help? Had he reached Fred in time? He would report the theft to the police.

She couldn't help but wonder how long it would take Mg. Ezzell to arrive at the convention with his ill-gotten goods.

Even if Mg. Praff hadn't *seen* Mg. Ezzell steal his inventions, Mg. Ezzell had them. The man could lie and fib all he wanted, but even if he'd figured out the spell that powered the prosthetic hand, he'd made a crucial mistake. He'd hired someone to steal the prototype from the polymery. The London police had seen the prostheses in Mg. Praff's possession first. Had the man been driven so mad by competition that he'd failed to piece that together? Or did he have another plan? Something to do with the feigned break-in at his own polymery?

Could he accuse Praff of stealing *his* prostheses?

She chewed on her lip. The police had seen the prostheses in the Praff polymery, hadn't they? What if they had been stowed away and, for the sake of surprise, Mg. Praff hadn't told the police just what the burglar had been after?

A breath whooshed out of her. The mugging at the hospital. The crooks had been more interested in the boxes of supplies than money. *"Worthless,"* the man had said. Had he been looking for the prostheses? Was he one of Ezzell's lackeys? *"Please. I seldom do dirty work."*

Alvie gritted her teeth and pushed herself onto her knees. She grabbed the plastic and twisted it until the handle broke off. With a couple of spells, she melted it back into place. Ethel and Bennet were witnesses, of course. But perhaps Mg. Ezzell had "witnesses" of his own. Fortunately, Alvie had kept all her notes and diagrams of the arm as well, though proving the date of their creation might be tricky. Perhaps Bennet would know a spell to reveal the age of writing on paper. She could only hope.

"Retract," she said, hoping to pull the plastic back. It stayed nestled in the lock. "Soften. Retract." It didn't heed her. She hardened it again and pressed her lips together. Polymaking had all sorts of undiscovered spells. Could she find one to help her?

"Soften. Compress." The plastic shot forward and bounced back, seeping out of the lock on her end. She stopped it with a Harden command.

The house creaked. She stiffened, holding her breath. Listened. Just the house settling, but it brought a new possibility to mind.

What if Mg. Ezzell wasn't the only person with access to this place? What if one of his . . . *dirty* workers . . . did, too?

And what if this "worker" showed up while Alvie was still trapped in the basement? She thought of Mg. Ezzell's hand running up her leg. What if . . . ?

When she grasped the plastic stick this time, it was with trembling fingers.

She had to get out. She had to get out *now*.

"Break. Open. Unlock. Twist. Soften. Break. Open. Unlock. Twist. Harden. Melt. Break? Open. Pull. Please!"

She wiggled the stick forward and backward, side to side. Broke it again, fixed it. Her fingers grew slick on the plastic. She pressed her bruised forehead against the door.

"Soften. Pick. Open. Release. Un . . . bolt. Unlock. Undo. Unlatch."

The bolt was sucked into the plastic-filled chamber with a muffled *click*.

Alvie released the stick. Stared.

She touched the doorknob. Gripped it, pulled.

The door opened.

She jumped to her feet, breathing quickly. But . . . Unlatch was a Smelting command, wasn't it? She distinctly recalled Mg. Praff saying it wasn't in the Polymaking repertoire. Had he been wrong?

Did it *matter*?

Well, yes, it did. But not right at that moment.

Grabbing her skirt in one hand, Alvie launched up the stairs. She'd get to the door, find the road Mg. Ezzell had taken to get here, and—

A meaty hand clamped around her arm.

"Oh no, you don't," said a short but wide man, his fingers squeezing until Alvie's skin bruised beneath them. Her throat constricted too tightly to let the scream in her belly pass through. He was huge everywhere but his legs—large head, wide chin, arms the width of barrels and a chest like two Benz tires pressed together. Dark circles rimmed his eyes, and stubble speckled his cheeks.

She *had* heard an engine turning off on the other side of the house. This man, this *lackey*, arriving.

The one who does dirty work. Alvie's body lost its strength at the thought. Her knees buckled, and her arms went slack.

The lackey had not been expecting to hold up all 130 pounds of her with a single hand, and he jerked forward, nearly tumbling down the stairwell. He grabbed the rail to catch himself. His moment of weakness revitalized Alvie, and she found the energy to jerk her arm from his grip.

But she couldn't go back downstairs. The only way out of the house was up the stairs.

So she darted past her large assailant, sprinting up those last steps. If she could just make it to the door—

He grabbed her calf. Alvie fell forward and hit her chin on the floor. Her jaw snapped shut on the impact, sending teeth into her tongue. The iron taste of blood filled her mouth, and she gagged, spitting it out.

The lackey grabbed her leg with his other hand, reeling her in like she was a fish on the line. Alvie dug her nails into the crevices between floorboards, snapping one off in the process. Away. She had to get away. Before . . . before he . . .

She kicked at him with her free foot, a blow that might have affected him had her foot been shod. Instead, the man simply grabbed her ankle and hauled her back. Each of his fingers left a bruise.

"Help!" Alvie screamed, searching for anything within reach—a heavy object, something to hold on to, even a dust bunny would do! There was nothing save the other lens of her glasses. Being blind was better than whatever alternative this man had in store for her, surely . . . but if she failed, she'd never make it out of these hills. She'd be lost in their murky blur for the rest of her life.

Suddenly Alvie was weightless as the lackey threw her up into the air. She landed on one of his wide shoulders. Air rushed out of her like a crushed bagpipe.

The lackey muttered something foul and trudged down the steps. Alvie clawed at his back, strained for the rail—

Saw her quick cuffs lying on the edge of a stair.

The prototype might have been a failure, but it was still plastic.

She scrambled, her toe finding the lackey's belt buckle. She pushed off it as hard as she could, propelling herself forward just enough to upset the man's balance. They both tumbled down a few steps, he on his back, she on her belly. Lunging with her right hand outstretched, she snatched the edge of the curled cuffs.

The lackey spat a foul name and spun around, grasping her by her waist. "I'm going to make you regret that!"

He hauled her up, and when he did so, Alvie kicked off the stairs. He pulled back too hard and crashed into the doorjamb at the base of the stairs. His grip went slack for only a second, but a second was all Alvie needed. She jumped from his grip, freeing herself. He pushed to his feet and reached for her. When he did, Alvie grabbed his wrist and slammed it against the rail. With the quick cuffs in hand, she shouted, "Melt!" and the cuffs melted into a blob of plastic, which Alvie slathered across the lackey's wrist and around the rail. "Harden!" she said. "Harden, Harden!"

The plastic obeyed, solidifying as hard as it would go.

The lackey growled and pulled back, but the plastic held firm. He swiped at her with his muscled paw, but she danced back up the stairs, out of his reach.

She didn't know how long the plastic would hold, and she was hardly going to experiment with it. The urge to run propelled her forward. She leapt up the stairs, bolted around the corner, twisted the lock on the front door, and threw it open, all while the lackey yelled and cursed after her. Ignoring a sudden stitch in her side, she sprinted down the road, away from the hills, toward what she could only hope would be civilization.

CHAPTER 18

THE BIGGEST MISTAKE MG. Ezzell had made was leaving Alvie with her glasses.

The smartest thing he'd done was taking her shoes.

Alvie ran down the middle of the road, where there was more grass and softer earth to cushion her feet, but her bruised soles still felt every rock, grain of dirt, thorn, and barb. She stopped once to try to rip bandages for her feet from her skirt, but she couldn't tear the well-executed hem, and then decided the venture was taking too much precious time. So she moved on, stumbling frequently—in part because of the uneven ground and in part because her depth perception was hindered by the absence of her right lens.

But she couldn't stop. She couldn't risk being somewhere indefensible when Mg. Ezzell or any of his lackeys returned. She couldn't let the Discovery Convention celebrate the wrong man for Mg. Praff's work. She couldn't wait around for a rescue.

Alvie was no athlete; it didn't take long for her lungs to start burning, even if the road was mostly downhill. She pushed herself forward, jogging when she couldn't sprint, moving up grassy hills when she came to some, in the hopes of orienting herself at their crests. She'd felt several turns from inside that trailer after Mg. Ezzell unknowingly abducted her, but not at the beginning. He'd driven the automobile straight for some time, which meant he'd gone farther west than Maidenhead. That didn't tell her a lot, but it was something.

Alvie kept going, tearing up the soles of her feet, until she was a sweaty mess and the stubborn edge of her skirt was ruined with dust and mud. But as the sun neared the western horizon, she saw another road. A *paved* road.

She thanked God and ran toward it with renewed energy. Saw a sign pointing toward Reading. And then, most blissful of all, she heard the familiar rumble of an automobile engine.

A Ford had never looked more beautiful to her in all her life.

It was an open cab, without a roof or windows. A lone man drove it, dressed in finery, the wind blowing through his gray hair. He certainly didn't look like an accomplice, so Alvie hedged her bets.

She ran out into the middle of the road and waved her hands. Jumped, though it sent pangs through her feet and ankles. "Stop! Please stop!"

The vehicle's brakes squealed, and the driver pulled off the side of the road to avoid hitting her. Once the automobile came to a stop, the man looked at her and angrily sputtered, "What are you *doing*?"

He spoke in a heavy German accent.

Her heart filled her entire chest. Surely angels were looking out for her. "Please!" she replied in German, earning a shocked look from the driver. *"Ich brauche Hilfe! Sie müssen mir helfen!" I need help! You have to help me!* She ran to him and gripped the driver's-side door. Still speaking German, she rushed, "My name is Alvie Brechenmacher. I've been abducted."

The man's eyes widened even further. He looked her up and down, taking in her unshod and bloody feet, her disheveled hair and clothes, her lopsided glasses. The astonished look on his face told her that he believed her.

"I'm the apprentice of Magician Marion Praff. We were on our way to the Discovery Convention in Oxford when our vehicle was sabotaged. My driver was injured. I don't know where I am. Please. Where am I?"

He cleared his throat and spoke in soft German. "My dear girl, I'm so sorry. We're near New Hinksey. Get in. I'll take you to the nearest police station."

"No, I need to go to Oxford!"

He leaned back from the force of her plea.

"There are police in Oxford. I *must* get to the convention, good sir. I must stop Magician Ezzell."

"Magician Ezzell?"

"He's the one who abducted me."

The man's expression slackened. "I certainly didn't expect this on my evening ride."

"I'm terribly sorry. I know it's far—"

"Not too far, my dear. Not too far. I'll take you. Get in."

Tears stung her eyes. "Thank you, thank you." She winced as she climbed over the rough pavement to the other side of the vehicle. The dratted skirt got caught in the door, but she didn't much care.

The man put the Ford in gear and pulled out onto the road, changing directions several times to turn the automobile around. Once it was going the correct direction, he asked, "Are you sure? There's a station in New Hinksey. Some food there, too."

"You're too kind. But I must get to Oxford. I must find Magician Praff."

He nodded. "Very well." A pause. "That isn't the one who founded the school, is it?"

It wasn't hard to find a police officer once Alvie reached the Bodleian Library, where the Discovery Convention was to be held. Two of them were guarding the front entrance.

The lovely man who'd driven her clear to the University of Oxford helped her toward the door. The sight of a distraught woman leaning heavily on a well-kempt man's shoulder alerted the officers at once, and the words "I've been abducted" had them moving quickly—opening enchanted compact mirrors to alert fellow officers. They ushered her inside. She did not see where her chauffeur savior went, much to her dismay.

The officers took her to a small room in the library, a study room of sorts, with barely any books or furniture, and sat her in a chair. She propped her throbbing feet on another chair and pushed her uneven glasses up on her nose.

She related the story in as much detail as she could remember, from leaving Briar Hall to her tussle with the lackey to finding the German Ford driver on the road—a man whose name she'd forgotten to ask, but whom the police were also questioning. The young officer she talked to wrote down her words with an incredulous expression, then stepped out into the hall to converse with others. She saw two more men in uniform outside. She had caused a stir. Good.

Alvie was examining her aching feet, carefully picking tiny pebbles and thorns from them, when the officer returned.

"We've got Magician Ezzell in for questioning, Miss Brechenmacher, but Magician Praff isn't here. He's not on the roster for the convention."

"Because Magician Ezzell intercepted our abstract. We have a telegram stating our acceptance . . . but it's in London." She sighed. Her body was giving out on her, sore and weary and aching for rest, but her mind buzzed with desperation. "You have to find him. And our driver. He . . . he must have been left on the side of the road near Maidenhead. Oh, Fred . . ."

She wrung her hands together. Mg. Ezzell had implied he hadn't killed Fred, but she didn't trust him at his word. Who knew how many hired men he had? Perhaps the one whom Alvie had left chained up in the stairwell had done the deed. What if Fred was dead and lying in a ditch, or almost dead and lying in a ditch? Her stomach tightened and pulsed at the thought. Weariness pulled at her limbs, as if great, hulking chains were dragging her down.

The officer nodded and left. He closed the door behind him—a door that had at least one other officer guarding it. Like she would run away. Like she *could*. The door muffled their voices, but she heard "find Marion Praff" among them. She sat, waiting, trying not to think of her burning and raw feet. To her relief, half an hour later, a female officer came in with a medical kit, water, and some fancy-cut vegetables that looked like they'd been prepared for the convention's opening day tomorrow. Alvie thanked her and munched on the carrots. Her nails dug into the armrests of the chair when the officer cleaned out the multiple lacerations on her feet and wrapped them in gauze and bandages. What a bother, but Alvie was grateful. The officer left as soon as the work was done.

Even with food, water, and medical treatment, Alvie began to grow antsy. It was thoroughly dark outside, probably at least ten o'clock. She squirmed in her chair. The police officers would only let her out of the room to go to the lavatory, and she needed help just to walk there. At least she looked victimized. That helped her story, didn't it?

Sighing, she leaned her neck against the backrest and stared at the ceiling. Started measuring it with her eyes. Eight feet by twelve, perhaps, give or take a few inches. Her pulse throbbed in her feet, and she started timing it. Her heartbeat was about seventy-nine beats per minute. Not quite restful.

She sat up straight again, if only to take pressure off her tailbone. She used her thumbnail to pick her other nails clean. It had to be nearing midnight now. She was exhausted, but not sleepy. Eager. Anxious. A little hungry.

She closed her eyes, trying to alleviate the headache that had set in as a result of her mismatched vision. When she opened them again, her gaze fell onto her hands. With the pad of her index finger, she traced the scabbed-over cut along the base of her thumb—the crescent-shaped mark the automobile's engine had bestowed upon her.

"Usual wear and tear of service, I'm afraid. It doesn't hurt."

Alvie paused, remembering Emma's words before Alvie, Fred, and Mg. Praff left Briar Hall. Remembered the cut on the maid's hand—a crescent-shaped slice that curved around the base of her thumb.

The exact same cut that now traced Alvie's skin.

Gooseflesh sprouted across her arms and legs. Surely it was a coincidence—

"Apparently I failed to lock the garage last night. Could swear I did, but I mustn't have turned the key all the way."

Alvie leaned forward in her chair. Would Emma have access to the key to the garage?

Her mind flew from the broken automobile to the newspaper in Bennet's Benz. "Scandal Storms Briar Hall When Servant Confesses Adultery."

She chewed on her lip. For that piece of libel, Mg. Praff had let Brandon, the footman, go. Yet hadn't Emma been the one to reveal him? To claim she'd seen him speaking with a reporter?

Her mind worked like kneaded dough. Emma had told her not to go to the polymery the night it was broken into. She'd been very willing to get inside to help clean up the mess, though maids never cleaned the polymery. Only Mr. Hemsley did, for he was the only servant who was allowed a key.

One of the robbers near the hospital had been a woman of Emma's size . . .

Alvie's eyes glanced back to the cut on her hand. All the while, she felt herself growing smaller and smaller in her chair.

Chatter sounded outside her door, though Alvie's mind was sluggish in processing it. ". . . him . . . filed missing person report . . . Maidenhead . . ."

The door swung open hard enough to slam into the wall behind it. There stood Mg. Praff, his own hair disheveled, his shirt half untucked, his eyes rolling back with relief.

"Thank God," he said, hurrying to Alvie's side. He saw her bandaged feet, her broken glasses. "Are you all right?"

"Well enough." She tried to smile, but found her mouth too heavy to do the job. "Where were you? Fred?"

"Fred is in a hospital in Maidenhead. He was unconscious on the road when I returned with help. The auto and the trailer were gone, along with you. I've been searching high and low for hours." He ran a hand back through his hair. "I'm so glad you're well."

Behind him, an officer said, "Can you tell us where this cabin is?"

The request pushed through the molasses of Alvie's thoughts. "Um. Is the driver still here?"

"We took his information and testimony and let him go."

"Where he found me," she said, "there's an intersection with a dirt road that winds up through some hills. The cabin is a ways up there. Maybe . . ." She tried to calculate the length of her stride walking, jogging, and sprinting, then estimated how much time she'd spent doing each, taking into account her stop to attempt to make bandages for her feet and the variations in her speed—how she'd slowed at the crests of hills and sped up going downhill. She tried to remember where the sun had been at the beginning of her escape versus at the end.

"Miss Brechenmacher?" asked the officer.

"She's thinking," Mg. Praff snapped.

"It's about 3.4 to 3.8 miles north of that intersection," she guessed.

The police officer hesitated for a moment, then wrote down the numbers. "We'll send someone to investigate."

"That man might still be there. I don't know how well the plastic will hold . . . and there will be plastic in the lock," she added, stalling him. "The lock to the room in the basement. From my glasses. And the window will be broken. And . . . can I have that lock?"

"Pardon?" the officer asked.

She glanced to Mg. Praff, who also looked inquisitive. "When you're done collecting evidence, or looking . . . can I have the lock with my lens in it?"

"Alvie," Mg. Praff began, "I'll make you a new lens."

"It's not that. I just . . . I need to look at that lock, if I can."

The police officer raised an eyebrow, but he wrote on his paper again, nodded, and left the room.

"Why the lock?" Mg. Praff asked.

While that was a conversation of great interest to her, Alvie switched to a more pressing subject. Lowering her voice, she said, "Emma, sir."

"What does Emma have to do with a clogged lock?"

She shook her head and showed him the cut on her hand. "Nothing. I mean, *Emma* . . . I think she's been . . ."

She could hardly bring herself to say it. It felt wrong to accuse a woman who had been nothing but friendly to her since her arrival. So she didn't. Instead, she recounted all the evidence she herself had just collected, bit by bit, to Mg. Praff. From the way the Polymaker's face paled and slacked as she continued to speak, she knew he was coming to the same conclusion.

"Blast," he swore, shaking his head. "Emma . . . I'll have to send a telegram straightaway. Have her apprehended. And Brandon . . ." He rubbed his eyes, then swiped his palm over his face.

"About the lock, sir."

He glanced up.

Alvie swallowed. "It's how I got out. I melted the plastic in the lock, but I swear I used a Smelting spell to open it, and—"

The door opened. The police officer who'd bandaged Alvie, again. "I apologize, Magician Praff, but I need to record your story before you speak any further with Miss Brechenmacher."

The Polymaker stood. "Yes. Yes, of course. Immediately. Whatever you need."

The officer nodded, and Mg. Praff followed her out, leaving Alvie alone once more.

———————

"That's preposterous!" Alvie shouted across the desk.

She'd spent some time sleeping in that chair in the library before the police officers had escorted her to the Oxford police station and given her a cot. She had shoes now, sized large to accommodate her bandages, and a tie for her hair, though she still wore the same dirty clothes as the day before, and her glasses were a sorry mess. She had taken to winking often to favor her left eye. Beside her, Mg. Praff sat stiff as if all his insides were full of knots. She knew the police had contacted the locals in London concerning Emma, but her knowledge of the situation ended there.

The two of them sat across from the chief of police, a desk between them. He had just finished relating Mg. Ezzell's side of the story, which was what had elicited Alvie's outburst.

"I'm merely regurgitating what was told to me," the older thick man said patiently. He was broad shouldered and shaped like a rectangle, with a thick gray mustache and thicker gray eyebrows. "You must understand that Magician Ezzell did have an abstract submitted to the Discovery Convention for the items you claim he stole. We're working to get a copy of it now. He has witnesses to testify to his locations yesterday. His own polymery was broken into five months ago, and he claims plans for this prosthesis were among the items stolen."

"Sly dog," Mg. Praff muttered.

"Every single plan? I would very much like to read that abstract," Alvie insisted. Had Mg. Ezzell submitted the exact same abstract he'd intercepted from Mg. Praff? Had he somehow lost it, and thus Emma's attempt to get another copy? So many questions assaulted her, and Alvie suffocated trying to answer them.

The chief of police sighed. "*I* will read the abstract, Miss Brechenmacher. We will get to the bottom of this."

Mg. Praff asked, "The cabin?"

"Yes, we found the cabin, and everything was as Miss Brechenmacher said it would be. There was no man chained up at the bottom of the stairwell, but there was melted plastic looped around the rail. Torn fabric was embedded in it. Scuffs on the wall indicated a struggle." He looked down at a paper in his hand. "The deed for the property is in the name of a Mr. Garrett, whom we are also trying to locate, but we've found no other records with his name."

"I see," said Mg. Praff.

The chief of police took a deep breath. "I should also inform you that Magician Ezzell is very put out by these accusations. He's hired a solicitor and has begun the process of having Miss Brechenmacher deported. He'll have a good case if he can link you to the burglaries."

Alvie felt her body temperature drop at least 0.7 degrees. "You're joking."

The man looked at her with his stern, aging face. No, he was not joking.

"I assure you," he went on, "that nothing will go forward until we determine the truth of this incident. But I also cannot allow either of you to leave."

Alvie hugged herself. "But the convention—"

"Neither you nor Magician Ezzell will be allowed into the convention until we sort this out."

Mg. Praff nodded, ever pragmatic. "Very well."

A few hours later, another officer arrived with a change of clothing for Alvie, straight from her closet—meaning he'd gone to Briar Hall. He'd probably questioned the family and servants while there. Maybe he'd even apprehended Emma, but he wouldn't answer when Alvie asked. Everything inside Alvie was tightly wound, but she felt some relief when she discovered a pair of glass lenses sandwiched between the blouse and skirt. Mg. Praff must have told the officer where to find them. With some effort, she popped the right one into her frames. Her headache almost immediately subsided. It felt wonderful to be able to see again, even if she might not be seeing England for much longer.

Deep breaths, Alvie. She needed to stay calm. She needed to trust the system. Mg. Ezzell couldn't keep his ruse up forever. He couldn't pin the burglaries on her—she hadn't even been in the country for the first two!

It wasn't until late afternoon—the first day of the convention was nearly over—that Alvie and Mg. Praff were called into a conference room. Several police officers filled it. At the far end of a long table, Mg. Ezzell sat with a man Alvie presumed to be his lawyer.

"You!" He stood up, but the heat of his gaze fell on Alvie first, not Mg. Praff. "How dare you—"

The lawyer placed a hand on his shoulder, and the chief of police said, "Sit down, Magician Ezzell, or this will take longer than I have the patience for."

Mg. Ezzell sat down. Alvie scowled at him. He was a terrific actor.

The chief sat down on a chair equidistant from both ends of the table. Alvie and Mg. Praff sat at the end closest to the door, opposite Ezzell. The other police officers remained standing.

The chief gestured to a young, balding man in uniform. "This is Officer Caldus, of the North London Police Department. He is one of the officers dealing with the string of polymery burglaries, most recently Magician Praff's."

The lawyer said, "A burglary in which the culprit was never caught . . . to which only Miss Brechenmacher was witness. Obviously a staged cry for attention, or means to cover up greater crimes."

Alvie bristled. The chief ignored the lawyer and said, "Officer Caldus?"

"We have written documentation of Magician Praff's testimony, which includes his concern over the possible theft of a prosthesis. We also have a testimony from Magician Ezzell detailing what was taken from his property last October, though nothing specifying prosthetic limbs."

Mg. Ezzell's shoulders straightened into razors. "Do you think I'd give away the secrets for my greatest work? So they could be printed in the paper later for all to see?"

The lawyer said, "My client can provide records."

Mg. Ezzell leaned over to the man and whispered something to him. The man nodded. Neither of them said anything more.

Alvie's heart tried to grow legs and climb right out her throat, but she settled it down with a cough.

The chief reached under the table and set Ethel's prototype before him.

"You went through my room?" Mg. Ezzell asked.

The chief raised a brow. "You think I wouldn't get a warrant to do so?"

Mg. Ezzell remained quiet. His lawyer whispered something to him.

"We've obtained a copy of the paper submitted by Magician Roscoe Ezzell to the board for the Discovery in Material Mechanics Convention on November 14 of last year. However, while the paper discusses a project promising to change an 'entire facet of medicine,' it does not specifically mention a prosthesis."

The lawyer said, "It's common with this convention for such submissions to remain vague."

"It is." The chief nodded.

Alvie worked the words over and over in her brain as her fingers smoothed the wrinkles from her skirt. Wasn't that something similar to what she'd said to Mg. Praff at the polymer depository?

She dug her nails into the table. "Maybe you should ask him about Emma," she mumbled.

"Excuse me?" the chief of police asked.

Alvie cleared her throat. "I said, maybe you should ask him how much he's paying my maid, Emma."

Mg. Ezzell blanched, though his expression remained neutral. "I'm not familiar with your employees, Miss Brechenmacher."

The chief continued on about the arm, not Emma, but Alvie couldn't hear him above the buzzing in her mind. Ezzell was in possession of the prosthesis. He knew all about it. Perhaps had already drawn out sketches to look like early plans for the thing to use as later evidence against Mg. Praff and herself. No doubt he'd dumped the Imagidome and any other materials that might be incriminating. And yet . . . if Alvie and Mg. Praff had been detained this entire time, then Mg. Ezzell must have been, too. He wouldn't have had much time to study the prosthesis, to learn more about it. To experiment with it, just as Alvie had experimented with that door in his basement.

Mg. Ezzell had asked Alvie if she really thought he was some overzealous villain ready to slip up. But he was, and he had. He'd set up everything so perfectly—the break-ins at the other polymeries, making himself a victim, using thugs so he'd never be found at a crime scene. But the appearance of Alvie had thrown a wrench in that. She was not only a witness, but her unexpected presence had eaten up Mg. Ezzell's precious time. His crime was behind schedule.

"Excuse me."

All eyes turned to her, and she realized she'd interrupted the chief midsentence.

"Alvie," Mg. Praff warned.

She ignored him. "Sorry, but . . . if Magician Ezzell is the true creator of this work, why not ask him how the prosthesis works?"

The rogue Polymaker's expression finally slipped.

"Excuse me?" asked the chief.

"This woman is in contempt of—" started the lawyer.

"This isn't a bloody courtroom," snapped Mg. Praff.

Alvie stood up. "If this is truly Magician Ezzell's creation, then have him demonstrate how it works."

Mg. Ezzell snorted. "Please, it's only a prototype."

She didn't even look at him; she kept her eyes locked with the chief's. "The abstract Magician Praff tried to submit to the convention discusses a previously undiscovered spell in Polymaking. Obviously the true creator of this prosthesis would know the spell. So have Magician Ezzell tell us what it is."

The lawyer said, "This is harassment."

Mg. Ezzell added, "This is to be the highlight of my display! I can't possibly—"

The chief turned his steely gaze onto Mg. Ezzell. "We're hardly a large audience. Do as she says."

The lawyer said, "This is unfair treatment of my client. As Mg. Praff said, this is not a courtroom, and you do not have the right to demand anything from my client."

The chief of police glowered. "I have the right to throw him in a jail cell until the system affords the time to appoint a trial."

Mg. Ezzell's white fingers gripped the edge of the table, yet his jaw was set in what looked like confidence . . . or maybe determination. He stood swiftly, knocking his chair back, and came around the table, moving toward the chief of police. He stared at the prosthesis for several seconds before reaching forward to grasp it.

The Polymaker held the prosthesis in both hands. Turned it this way and that, subtly, but his behavior screamed that he had yet to discover the spell. Alvie sat back down as she waited for him to speak. Everyone did. The room was silent as a morgue.

Mg. Ezzell held the arm out like it was an extension of his own and said, "Heed: Direction."

Alvie's thoughts rushed through her mind in a blur. *That* was what he'd decided to try? An already-discovered spell, and one a first-year apprentice would know?

He'd lost it.

The arm didn't move. He knew he had lost, and now everyone in the room knew, too. Mg. Ezzell's eyes glistened, and Alvie almost felt bad for him.

Almost.

The chief of police stood, but before he could utter a word, Mg. Praff rose from his seat and reached forward, taking the prosthesis from Mg. Ezzell's hand. He didn't even clear his throat before saying, "Compress."

The liquid plastic inside the plastic tubes of the arm pressurized and straightened out all five of the prosthesis's fingers.

Alvie grinned.

The chief groaned. "Arthur, place Magician Ezzell under arrest for the theft of property and abduction. We'll add to the list later."

Mg. Ezzell jerked back as though struck. "He's tinkered with it somehow! This is hardly conclusive evidence! This is outrageous!"

"Do quiet yourself, *Mister* Ezzell," the chief of police said in an almost bored tone. "Or you'll give me even more fodder for charges."

Mg. Ezzell's mouth snapped closed just before the policeman named Arthur came behind him with a pair of handcuffs.

Giddy relief surged through Alvie like a geyser. Jumping from her chair, she threw her hands up in a cheer, then landed on her sore feet and promptly fell over.

CHAPTER 19

THE DISCOVERY CONVENTION WAS to last three days. On the morning of the second day, Emma confessed to collaborating with Mg. Ezzell in exchange for a lighter sentence, sealing the rogue Polymaker's fate of prison time and a permanently revoked magician's license. In the evening, the police found the rest of Mg. Praff and Alvie's equipment in a nearby storage shed and their automobile and trailer in a ditch just outside Oxford. One of the officers assigned to the case found a lead on the thug who had attacked Alvie at the cabin and expected to make an arrest soon. The owner of the cabin had not been found, causing the chief to believe either Ezzell or one of his colleagues had used a false name to purchase the property. On the third day, Alvie and her mentor were finally allowed to attend the festivities.

The enormous Imagidome drew in a swarm of attendees, new and veteran, and for hours Alvie managed the line for it, passing out tickets and fulfilling requests for the three visuals provided—Starry Night, Arabian Sand Sea, and His Majesty's Courtyard. While the Imagidome and its otherworldly delights garnered oohs and aahs, it was the prostheses that had magicians, scientists, and inventors alike engaged, asking questions and studying the prototype. The captive audience gasped when Mg. Praff put a sock over his fist and moved it around in the socket made to fit over Ethel's stump, the various movements causing the fingers to jump and flex. Every time Alvie heard a "Remarkable," or an "Incredible," she beamed. Polymakers came by the dozen to investigate and learn the new spell. So many of them clustered together, discussing other potential applications for compressed polymers, that Alvie got multiple complaints from Imagidome attendees about the noise disrupting the "theatre."

At two o'clock, four hours before the convention was to end, Mg. Praff set a hand on her shoulder and said, "Your turn."

Alvie adjusted her glasses, which Mg. Praff had thankfully fixed so that she was no longer bug-eyed on one side. "Pardon?"

He gestured to the prosthetic ankle and arm. Newcomers were already approaching the display.

She swallowed. "But it's yours—"

"Ours," he corrected.

Taking a deep breath, Alvie nodded and tightened the strings of her apprentice's apron. She slipped between bystanders, most of whom were men, and said, "Welcome. These prototypes are of a prosthetic ankle, arm, and hand, which Magician Marion Praff and myself designed."

"Yourself?" repeated a young man.

"Yes, sir. I'm his apprentice."

He looked doubtful. "Your name?"

"Alvie Brechenmacher, sir."

Another man asked, "You're not related to Edison's Brechenmacher, are you?"

"Yes, sir. He's my father."

"The light bulb?" another spoke up.

"Forget the light bulb," a fourth shouted. "Show us the *fingers*!"

Alvie smiled and took up the white sock, pulling it over her hand and making a fist. "The socket is sensitive to pressure. I'm sure you've heard of the discovery of the new Polymaking spell, Compress. You see, these tendons are hollow and filled with liquid polyethylene . . ."

Alvie discussed the prototypes for two and a half hours—the time went by quickly, and she enjoyed every minute of it, but she was still thrilled when Mg. Praff returned and excused her to see the convention for herself. She certainly couldn't experience everything in only ninety minutes, of course, and the inability to explore and learn to her heart's content hurt worse than her still-sore feet. But it wouldn't do to waste what time she did have by sulking.

She started off in the Polymaking section, browsing the aisles of booths backdropped by shelves and shelves of library books. One magician had created a new material for parachutes, and another had invented a thinner, clearer kind of tape. She would have loved to describe it to Bennet, but her bag containing his Mimic spell had yet to be found. It hadn't been with the other items from the trailer—she imagined Mg. Ezzell had thrown it away with her shoes and luggage long before arriving in Oxford. She sighed. At least there hadn't been anything *too* sentimental in there.

She explored the very small section for Folders, looking at textbooks with moving images and giant suspended displays full of flapping birds or swimming fishes, where even the strings were made out of curls of parchment. The Pyres had a self-lighting fireplace that featured color-changing flames, as well as self-lighting cigars. There was quite an extensive jewelry display with the Gaffers. Mg. Ezzell had taken her money, but Mg. Praff had kindly reimbursed her, so she bought a long necklace of clear beads for Ethel and a hair clip shaped like a pond lily for herself. She found bouncing balls that never stilled unless commanded in the Sipers' section and got two, one for her papa and one for Bennet.

There were oddball displays between sections by other scientists and innovators, including demonstrations for the nonmagical on how enchanting materials worked, as well as machines designed to do simple tasks in an extraordinarily complicated fashion. Alvie watched as ball bearings were dropped into the "start" bucket of one of the contraptions. This first action moved a string that tumbled over a stack of cards that shifted a pencil that tapped a weight that came down over a candle to press a weighted wax seal into a letter. As she passed another booth, she overheard someone explaining to a group of adolescents the differences between man-made and nature-made glass. Part of the presentation was a beautiful, warped piece of glass that had apparently been formed after lightning struck out in a desert. Such glass could not be enchanted by man, just as naturally started fires couldn't be tamed by Pyres, and pure metals couldn't be worked by Smelters.

The Smelter section was last on her route. Alvie ogled displays of enchanted train tracks and skeleton keys among the Smelters. She wished the latter were for sale. She certainly could have used a metamorphing key in that basement.

She shuddered at the thought as a bell rang out through the halls, signaling the end of the convention. There was a dinner being held afterward. Alvie wondered if she could skip it and snoop around the exhibits some more. Ah well, there was always next year. The Discovery Convention was to be held in New York City for 1907. A good excuse for a trip home.

Alvie and Mg. Praff returned to their hotel late—it was a small one down the street, since the closest ones had already been filled. Alvie had her own room, and she wrote a letter home before turning in so she could remember everything she'd seen. She would break the news of her cabin adventure through Mg. Praff's enchanted mirror when she returned to Briar Hall. She woke early the next morning, got dressed—unfortunately, in a skirt—and headed home in a hired buggy. Fred had been discharged from the hospital, Mg. Praff told her, but he was resting at home. He wouldn't be back to work until the following Monday.

The buggy pulled into the drive of Briar Hall close to noon. Alvie was eager to get out. Her feet only ached a little bit, but her backside was tired of the cushioned seat in the back of the buggy. She'd only been stretching for a moment when she noticed a Benz parked ahead of them.

"Bennet!" She rushed into the house, startling the housekeeper. She didn't need to go far to find Bennet Cooper—he was in the gallery with Ethel and Mrs. Praff, who was giving them a tour of the various portraits there.

"Bennet! Ethel!" she exclaimed, startling the lot of them. Upon seeing Alvie, Mrs. Praff ran out of the gallery, likely to find her husband. Bennet and Ethel stayed, and Alvie lost her air when Bennet threw his arms around her.

"Are you all right?" Her hair muffled his voice.

Ethel said, "Oh, Alvie, we were so worried about you!"

Bennet drew back, and Alvie said, "You heard?"

He nodded. "We had Oxford policemen showing up on our doorsteps, asking us questions about Magician Praff's work."

Alvie's mouth formed a small O. It made sense—she wondered if the Oxford chief of police had determined Mg. Ezzell was guilty *before* Alvie had requested a demonstration with the prosthesis. Whatever witnesses Mg. Ezzell was able to provide, they had Ethel—the woman who'd inspired the project in the first place—and her brother, who had visited the polymery several times, on their side.

"You're all right?" Bennet asked again, his hands on her shoulders.

She nodded. "My feet are a little sore, and I'm in a skirt, but other than that, I'm fine."

Ethel laughed at the same time as Bennet asked, "What happened to your feet?"

Alvie related the story then, about the automobile problems and the trailer and the basement. Ethel covered her mouth with her hand the entire time, leaning forward as though Alvie were reciting some great play. Bennet, on the other hand, paled a little more with each detail. She didn't mention Mg. Ezzell's hand on her leg.

"But the convention was great!" she hastily added at the end. "It really was. I'm sorry I couldn't write to you, Bennet—"

"You hardly owe me an apology." His voice was a little weak. "Oh, Alvie, I'm so sorry that happened to you. I wish I could have done something."

Ethel elbowed her brother with her good arm—her left still wore that heavy, false-looking hand. "You helped acquit them. That's enough."

Still, Bennet's eyes were downcast with guilt. Alvie stepped closer to him and took his hand, earning a small quirk of his lips in response.

"Ethel!" Mg. Praff's voice echoed through the gallery. Alvie turned to see the Praffs standing arm in arm, both smiling. "Just the young lady I want to see. I believe I have something for you."

Ethel lit up like a light bulb. "Really? Right now?"

Mg. Praff grinned. "Come, I'll have the footmen bring it around to the polymery."

Ethel's grin shined brighter than an enchanted lamp.

Alvie slipped her hand in Bennet's. "Come on. It will be perfect."

A package arrived from Oxford three weeks later. Alvie took it to her workroom without even opening it. She cleared off all her desk and counter space, putting away new spells and the books detailing them. She opened the package with her pocketknife and pulled out the lock.

Grabbing a set of tools, she carefully pried the lock apart, which was tricky to do since the plastic had melted and reformed inside it.

She didn't dare soften it up to quicken her work—that would botch the integrity of the discovery.

And discover she did. When she finally got to the guts of the lock, her suspicions were confirmed.

The plastic had melted with delicate metal parts.

Not melted *against* them, but *with* them. The metal of the inside cylinder had merged with the plastic, as though Alvie had melted that, too.

But she couldn't have. She wasn't a Smelter, and the Melt spell shouldn't have been nearly hot enough to affect the metal.

She marveled at the lock, turning it this way and that, then began to diagram it. Later, in the lab, she began building a lock of her own—a simple design, with all the components made of plastic. The task took her a day and a half to complete. She missed a homework deadline but couldn't bring herself to care as she molded and formed and shaped.

She installed the new lock in her workroom door, about a foot above the handle, to test it. Sure enough, it locked. She commanded it, "Unlatch," but the plastic did not respond.

So she made another lock, taking care with each component to ensure its integrity. Missed another deadline. Installed it above the first and commanded it, "Unlatch."

The plastic didn't heed her.

It was when Alvie collected her monthly stipend and asked Fred to take her to a hardware shop that Mg. Praff finally asked, "Alvie, what are you up to? We're supposed to be discussing thermodynamics in thirty minutes."

"I'll be right back. It's very important," she promised.

Mg. Praff sighed, but nodded his consent. He, of all people, understood the draw of discovery.

So Alvie went out and bought eight locks, all of the same make, all with a dead bolt. She studied them in her workroom—took them apart, replicated them. Took notes, built theories. Stared at the lock from the basement in the cabin.

By the end of it, her door had over a dozen locks installed in it. Most of the metal ones were useless, their keyholes pumped full of plastic.

Eleven days after the first lock had arrived from Oxford, Alvie began writing a paper. On the twelfth day, Mg. Praff came into her workroom near ten o'clock at night.

"I'm going to have to get you a new door," he said, eyeing the locks.

Alvie was taking notes.

"Alvie?"

"I think I figured it out," she said, lifting her head and setting down her pencil. She rubbed a cramp from her hand. "I have a theory, Magician Praff."

He folded his arms and leaned against the counter. "Oh? And what is this theory that's kept you here all hours of the night, barely stopping to eat, putting off your assignments, and ruining a perfectly fine door?"

She handed him the lock from the basement. "Look at this."

He studied it. He must have noticed the way the metal and the plastic had melted together, for his brow furrowed and his lips formed a small frown.

"This is how I got out of that room. I'm calling it Bending, for lack of a better word." She opened a drawer and fished through the mess of papers within it, including several used-up Mimic spells from Bennet, and pulled out a smudged diagram—a circle of all seven magics, including Excision. "Imagine this. A magician who can *Bend* into an adjacent material, according to that diagram—it's not a perfect diagram—and manipulate it."

Mg. Praff lowered the picture. "I'm not following you."

Alvie plucked the diagram from his hands and laid it on her desk. "I think that's what I did. I think I somehow Bent into Smelting when

I was in the basement. That's why the plastic merged with the metal. Why the Unlatch command worked."

"Alvie—"

"It worked with metal because they're both from the ground, see?" She pointed to her diagram. Plastic and metal were wedged next to each other. "And I think it would work with Siping as well, since the disciplines are so closely related and share a lot of raw materials. Think of it! Maybe a Smelter could perform a Gaffing spell, since their materials are both, fundamentally, made of stone. I think a Folder could even do something with Excision, given that their raw materials are both organic, or that, well, all magicians are flesh and blood, and—"

"Wait, Alvie. Stop there," her mentor urged. "This is getting . . . large."

Alvie chewed on her lip a moment. "It makes sense, I think."

Mg. Praff set the malformed lock on the counter. "And have you been able to replicate this?"

Her shoulders drooped. "No, sir." She'd tried over and over again, doing exactly what she'd done in that basement, uttering the same spells, even the ones that had proved fruitless. She wondered if she was forgetting something, or if it had to be a special sort of metal or an old lock, or if she just hadn't been able to enter the same frame of mind.

"But nothing else explains it," she added.

Mg. Praff sighed. "Maybe this is a fluke. Or maybe the door wasn't locked all the way—"

"It was locked all the way."

"—or perhaps you got the plastic hot enough to do this." He gestured to the lock. "We might never know what outside force helped you with this, but until you can repeat the incident, the theory won't hold. Neither in the scientific world nor the magical one."

Alvie frowned. She knew this, of course. Hence all the locks on her door.

After a moment of silence, Mg. Praff said, "We should return to your studies."

Alvie nodded. "Yes, we should." She rubbed her eyes under her glasses. This would require a lot more study on her part, and a lot more experimentation. A lot more time than she could dedicate at the present moment. And maybe, once she'd mastered Polymaking, all of this would make more sense to her.

"In the morning." He clapped a hand on her shoulder. "Let's get some rest tonight. And I'll have Hemsley look into fitting you with a new door."

She nodded, glancing down at the messy drawer, at the torn papers scribbled with both her and Bennet's handwriting. Before Mg. Praff departed, however, she said, "Mg. Praff?"

"Hm?"

"Are apprentices allowed to marry?"

His brow raised enough to thoroughly wrinkle his forehead. "Well, yes. There's no rule against it."

Alvie nodded.

Mg. Praff lingered a moment more, perhaps waiting for Alvie to say something else, but when she didn't, he slipped away, closing the many-locks door behind him.

Alvie sat in her chair a long moment, not thinking of anything in particular or looking at anything specific. After that moment, however, she opened another drawer, which contained a short typed paper titled "The Merging of Materials: A Theory of Bending." It would never be published or taken seriously unless she could repeat whatever it was she did in that cabin. As she moved to return it to its drawer, however, she hesitated. Considered. Glanced at the locks. Then, tucking her diagram inside the papers, she folded them into thirds and tucked them into an envelope, on which she wrote her home address beneath the name Gunter Brechenmacher.

The rest she'd worry about later.

Alvie sat in the fourth row of the enormous Royal Albert Hall in London, her hands clasped tightly together, her back erect to help her better see the stage. The Gaffer lights hanging from the ornate chandeliers above had been dimmed, while the ones illuminating the stage burned bright. Her chair was upholstered in scarlet to match the carpeted aisles. Large balconies filled with seating loomed behind her, but no one occupied those. This was a grand occasion, but not the sort a person bought tickets to attend. Alvie had asked her new maid, Jane, to do her hair so its waves were tamed and partially held back by the water-lily barrette she'd purchased in Oxford. It matched the slightly green tint of her pants. She had intended to wear a dress, as this was a formal occasion, but Bennet had asked her not to. *"It isn't you, Alvie,"* he'd said in their most recent Mimic spell book, which was tucked securely into her new purse.

Mg. Pritwin Bailey sat beside her. He didn't talk much. Or look at much. He had a pale complexion made all the paler by his dark hair. He wore thin, silver-rimmed glasses—Alvie wished, not for the first time, that she could wear glasses so small. She'd mentioned plastic lenses to him earlier, a topic that had appeared to utterly bore him. He did, however, become a little more animated when she mentioned the textbooks at the Discovery Convention. They'd also discussed the amount of wattage that would be required to keep the Royal Albert Hall alight should the Gaffer lights be replaced by electric ones.

She tried to imagine having Mg. Bailey as a mentor and decided she was much better off with Mg. Praff, who was off in Romford all week attending various meetings. Fred was well again and back to work, fortunately. He'd dropped her off at the hall about an hour ago.

Mg. Bailey suddenly straightened. Alvie's gaze flew back to the stage. Two rows of chairs occupied its left side—her left—and she smiled at the man next in line.

From a podium on the right, an aging man—Mg. Tagis Praff, Mg. Praff's uncle—said, "Magician Bennet John Cooper, District Six."

Alvie clapped as loudly as she could as Bennet, looking smart in his white Folder's uniform, stood and crossed the stage. He smiled as he shook Mg. Tagis Praff's hand and accepted his magician's certificate.

He'd done it, just like Alvie had known he would. She continued clapping until he exited the stage and sat in the front row with the other new magicians, two of whom wore green Polymaker's uniforms. That would be her, soon enough. She'd estimated completing her apprenticeship in two years, seven months, one week, and two-point-six days that morning. That would put her own graduation ceremony in December or January.

But today wasn't about her. Her eyes watched Bennet, his hair bright even beneath the dimmed lights. The rest of the graduates passed by in a blur. Beside her, Mg. Bailey had also lost interest.

Once the last person exited the stage, Mg. Tagis Praff addressed the audience: "Ladies and gentlemen, let us give these new magicians another round of applause."

Alvie clapped until her hands hurt.

"It has been a long road for these men and women, but they have prevailed. They have overcome difficulties of all kinds to be sitting here today, representing their disciplines. I give them the highest praise." He turned and cleared his throat. "To you magicians, I give you the admonition to continue to persevere. Make your mark on this world. Expand your gifts. Reach out to those in need, and reach high to your Maker. Treat your magic with respect and loyalty, and it will do likewise. Leave this world a better place than it was when you entered it. The future calls to you. Now is the time to answer."

The audience clapped again. Mg. Tagis Praff bowed once and exited the stage. Mg. Aviosky, the Gaffer who had been present at Alvie's bonding, stepped onto the stage and congratulated the magicians, announced the location of a reception hall should anyone wish to attend and speak to the new graduates, and closed the meeting. The Gaffer lights overhead brightened to their full power, stinging Alvie's eyes.

She grabbed her purse and jumped to her feet, waiting for her row to clear so she could make it to the aisle. Mg. Bailey seemed more interested in something behind him than in escaping his chair. Alvie followed his gaze, and for a moment, she thought she saw the magician from the post office. But the flash of orange hair disappeared out one of the hall's many doors, out of sight.

Finally freed, Alvie hurried down the aisle and toward the stage, where Bennet stood with his family. She paused behind his mother for a moment, waiting for a gap in the conversation between Bennet and his father, when she caught Bennet's eye.

He grinned and stepped forward, taking her hand and pulling her up next to him. "This is Alvie," he said to his father.

His father was a broad man with a thick brown mustache and thicker brown hair. He also had brown eyes—that was where Bennet and Ethel had gotten theirs from. "Well, I'll be. The woman I've always heard of but never seen. It's a pleasure, lass."

Alvie smiled and offered her hand—Mr. Cooper shook it vigorously. He had quite the grip. "It's nice to meet you."

Bennet introduced her to his two other sisters—Elizabeth, who was married and sat between Bennet and Ethel in age, and Hattie, the youngest at nineteen. She was the only one who shared her father's dark hair. All of them had his dark eyes. Alvie had already met Mrs. Cooper, but she let Bennet make the introduction all the same. Mrs. Cooper seemed much more amiable this time around than when Alvie had popped up on her doorstep in the rain.

She turned to him when the introductions were finished. "You did it!" She beamed. "You're a Folder now. Oh, Bennet, there's so much you can do! Are you going to specialize?"

He laughed. "Probably, but I haven't decided on a focus yet. I'm sure you're full of ideas."

She nodded but, glancing at the family, figured now was not the time to blather about how excellent he would be in ancient text restoration or banquet décor.

The group chatted a little more before Mr. Cooper directed them to the reception hall, after which they'd go out to dinner to celebrate. Alvie laced her fingers with Bennet's, and as they shuffled from the grand chamber, Ethel weaved her arm through Alvie's. Plastic fingers closed softly around her forearm.

Alvie nearly jumped at the touch. "Ethel! You're getting so good at it!" In the first weeks with her prosthesis, Ethel's grip had been hard and painful.

She grinned. "I know! And watch!" She stared hard at the false hand and lifted her index finger, middle finger, and ring finger, each one separate from the others. She frowned. "That little finger is still giving me trouble."

"No one needs pinkies," Alvie offered.

Ethel rolled her eyes. "You can't properly drink tea without a little finger!"

Bennet said, "You drink tea with your right hand."

She shrugged. "I want to have the option."

Alvie laughed. It thrilled her to no end that Ethel was doing so well with the prosthesis and that she was getting out of the house more because of it. The plastic hand wasn't quick or weighted enough to let her play the piano, not yet, but there was always the option for a second model, and a third, and a fourth. Perhaps that would be Alvie's specialty, once she became a Polymaker. And after that, she'd create something new, something unheard of. Something to present at conventions all over the world. Something to sign her name to.

After all, it wasn't about the magic. It was about the discovery.

ABOUT THE AUTHOR

Born in Salt Lake City, Charlie N. Holmberg was raised a Trekkie alongside three sisters who also have boy names. She is a proud BYU alumna, plays the ukulele, owns too many pairs of glasses, and finally adopted a dog. Her fantasy Paper Magician Series, which includes *The Paper Magician*, *The Glass Magician*, and *The Master Magician*, has been optioned by the Walt Disney Company. Her stand-alone novel, *Followed by Frost*, was nominated for a 2016 RITA Award for Best Young Adult Romance. She currently lives with her family in Utah. Visit her at www.charlienholmberg.com.